Brushed Between Cultures

Samarra St. Hilaire

Crafting the words of this book has been a profound journey, an odyssey fueled by passion and dedication. I'm eternally grateful for the genuine love, support, and encouragement you've given me, Joseph. Every day, I thank God for such a wonderful husband and friend. To my children Josephine, Aaron, Charlisse, and Faith, you're my most significant accomplishment. I love you more than words can express. Manman, mèsi anpil pou tout sa ou fè pou mwen. Lè mwen te timoun, mwen te wè jan w te travay di chak jou pou asire w ke nou te gen yon kote pou dòmi ak manje pou manje. Menm lè tan yo te difisil, mwen pa t janm tande w k ap plenyen.

To my friends, your unwavering support, encouragement, and prayers have been a beacon. With you, I've found a safe space to be my most authentic self without judgment.

As you delve into these pages, remember one thing: There is an untapped well of greatness within you, waiting to be discovered!

Love,
Samarra St. Hilaire

Part I

Chapter 1

Sometimes, I think my parents forget they live in America. Like when my mother suggests I wear a Sunday dress and fancy shoes to the dentist to make a good impression. Or take a tin container filled with a hearty serving of tassot and rice to school instead of a cutesy sandwich wrapped in foil or placed in a small plastic container. I had to get used to the curious stares from classmates unfamiliar with the aroma and look of Haitian cuisine.

Don't get me wrong; I absolutely love my culture, especially the food. Every Sunday, the scent of griot, pikliz, and fried plantains fills our home, reminding me of the richness of my Haitian heritage. I love the way the older generation tells stories in such an animated way—filled with gestures, voice intonations, jokes, and exaggerations.

See, the problem is that I can't do any of the fun stuff like other teenagers. For instance, every time I ask my parents if I can attend a sleepover, my mom's first question is, "Manushka, you don't have bed in your house?" which is immediately followed by a stern "No." What she doesn't understand is that a sleepover is not about sleeping. It's about movie marathons, food, face masks, endless conversations, and pranks—hanging out with your friends all night. Or so I've heard.

As much as I want to attend sleepovers, my mother is right. I do have a bed in my very own room, which I would describe as being aesthetic; kind of like something you'd see in a magazine. Between custom paintings, bursts of color, fluffy pillows, and a comfy beanbag chair, I can spend all day in my bedroom but being social is an essential part of my high school experience. Long phone conversations, texting, going to the movies, and hanging out with friends are all the things that I need, want, and have to do at this age.

Whenever I mention friends at school, my mom says, "I don't send you school for friends; I send you school to learn, to be a doctor or nurse." I wish someone would tell my parents, my mother especially, there are more than just two professions in this world. I'm scared to tell her I want to be an artist. I don't even know how to translate that; no matter how I say it in Haitian Creole, it will sound like failure. Anywho, it's time for me to get to school. Oh, and I forgot to tell you—actually, I didn't forget, I was trying to avoid it altogether—but since we're getting to know each other, I figured I'd be honest. My nickname is Manunu; yep, Manunu. Out of all the cute nicknames in the world, I get that one. Shh!!! Let that be our little secret. There is no way in this world I want anyone to know. I mean, I do have a reputation, kind of, I hope.

My full name is Manushka Marie Jean-Pierre. Both of my parents were born in Haiti, hence the name. I'm a first-generation American, Haitian American.

Before we go any further, I need to clear up some misconceptions about Haitians. For one, we do not eat cats! Secondly, we do not all practice Vodou. Religious beliefs are personal choices for us just as much as they are for people from other cultures. In my household, we're Christians—we go to church on Sundays, Wednesdays, and some Fridays if there's a special event; yep, seems like pretty much every day. My mom always says, "Legliz, lekòl, lakay," which means "church, school, home." In other words, no social life. My father only goes to church on holidays since he works a lot.

I attend Paul Millerson High School in Brooklyn. I weave through the bustling streets every morning, hop on the crowded bus, and then switch to the equally packed train. It's a thirty-minute journey filled with reggae, hip-hop, and R&B sounds. The chatter in multiple languages and the scent of food from people who decided to eat breakfast fill the train. I'm sixteen years old and in the 11th grade. I have two best friends, Janae and Widelene. They're sixteen, too. My crew is feeling kind of mature, especially since we'll all be seniors next year.

Despite being the shortest among us, Janae packs a punch with her spirited opinions. Her stature might be small, but her presence is mighty. She's quick to share her thoughts unapologetically, especially when it comes to defending others. I still remember the day we met. Some kid was pushing me on the playground. Out of nowhere, I heard a voice shout, "You better leave her alone or else.' That was Janae coming to my rescue in first grade. We've been best friends ever since.

My other friend, Widelene, we go to the same church, L'Église de Dieu, which means Church of God. We've known each other since third grade. Widelene didn't speak any English when she arrived at school. Luckily, our third-grade teacher relied on my superb translating skills, which gave us the chance to build a friendship. Widelene, like me, grapples with the unique struggles of finding the balance between two cultures. Her parents are much older than mine, and with their deep-rooted traditions and values from Haiti, they often find it challenging to navigate the cultural nuances of raising a child in America.

For the most part, Janae, Widelene, and I are pretty much inseparable, like most best friends.

I can trust them with everything, including my secret boyfriend, Devonte. Yes, that's right, my secret boyfriend. When I say secret, I mean super-duper top secret because my parents, specifically my mother, would totally flip out. I can already hear her screaming at the thought of me having a boyfriend. The screaming would be followed by threats of sending me to Haiti, you know, sort of like a scared straight program. Sometimes, I wish my mother would have conversations about dating and puberty instead of using scare tactics and pretending she never dated as a teenager. In my household, the puberty talk was pretty much, "You're a woman now; don't get pregnant and stay away from boys." Seriously, what kind of puberty talk was that? I hoped for guidance, understanding, and maybe even some stories from her youth—not just a cautionary warning.

Staying away from boys is practically impossible; it's not like I go to an all-girls school. And between subjects like algebra and language arts, there is Devonte—those dimples, that charisma. Devonte is so irresistibly good-looking; I mean, you'd have to see him to understand just how *fine* he really is. Every time he walks into a room, it feels as though the walls lean in, just a bit, to listen, to watch him. His tall frame and dark skin that contrasts with his light brown eyes have every girl's eyes on him. Yep, that's Devonte. That's my boyfriend, yeah, that's my boyfriend! Even though education is important to me, when he looks at me with those eyes, I find myself glossing over the fact that he failed seemingly effortless classes like P.E. and Art. It doesn't matter, right? Who needs P.E.? I see so much more in Devonte. Because of his height, everyone assumes he plays basketball, but Devonte isn't interested in playing any sport, at least not right now.

Every week, it's the same routine after school. I chat with Janae and Widelene, sharing stories and secrets, as we walk to the train station together to make our way home. We fill each other in on all the details of our day and any drama we've heard. I usually look forward to going home after a long day of school. My bedroom is my refuge.

I arrived home later than usual after a train and bus delay on that particular day. In case you're wondering, I live on the second floor of a two-family house. My parents plan to buy their own home one day, but they're renting for now. I took a deep breath, then unlocked the door. I stepped into what seemed like the entire congregation sitting in the living room. Why today of all days? My cheeks burned as I tried to navigate the room, avoiding too much attention. I was expected to greet all these people with a kiss on the cheek, even the creepy-looking old man in the corner. I'm not rude or anti-social; I just think being forced to greet people with a kiss is invasive and uncomfortable. I should have the choice to wave—that's a polite gesture and method of greeting a person. I had to think quick. *If I randomly start coughing, I may not have to kiss all these people.* Right after I said, *"Bonjour,* Mommy," I began coughing profusely. Of course, my mom pounded my back in hopes of helping me. Someone shouted, "Give her some cold water," "Make sure she drinks tea with lemon," and "Rub her chest with lwil maskriti tonight." Just so you know, lwil maskriti is Haitian castor oil, which we use for everything, I mean EVERYTHING. It's our magical oil for hair growth, a salve for aches and pains, a laxative, you name it. Shifting our focus back to the situation at hand: everyone stared as I continued to cough. And just like that, I made it through the living room without having to kiss anyone aside from my mother.

Yes! If you ask me, I could have won an award for "Best Avoidance of Awkward Cultural Norms." Once in my room, I grabbed a brush for the acceptance speech. "Ladies and gentlemen, I would like to thank the academy for granting me such a prestigious award. To my family and friends: I appreciate your prayers and countless hours of support. To all the young people out there: Always remember that if you can believe it, you can achieve it." I wiped the imaginary tears after concluding my speech. Sometimes, you just have to laugh at the world and hope it's as good for the heart as they say.

After a little chuckle, I decided to call Devonte while my mother was still talking to her friends; it was the perfect opportunity.

Before Devonte, having a boyfriend was more so a thought. I imagined what it would be like to have a boyfriend, to walk hand in hand throughout the halls in high school—you know, the kind of things you see in teen movies. Thankfully, I don't have an imaginary boyfriend anymore.

I dialed his number as fast as possible. He picked up by the second ring.

"Hey, Devonte. I missed you at school today. Why did you skip classes?"

"I just didn't feel like going today. I missed seeing your beautiful face, though."

Concerned, I said, "Really? You do understand how important it is to get an education, right? It's important to me that the people I hang out with take education seriously." My voice was stern.

"You're right. I'll try to do better, but the best part of school is seeing your face."

"Boy, you so crazy." And just like that, I was smiling from ear to ear and blushing. Devonte knew precisely what to say to make me feel special. I also knew he had dreams—dreams he rarely spoke of—but I saw glimpses during some of our conversations through the words he used and the way his eyes smiled.

"So, when are we goin' on a date?" he asked. "I been asking you for so long. How about we go see that new movie, *Super Charm*? You know it's gonna be mad dope."

"Well, you know my parents don't play. I have to find some kind of excuse to go to the movies. Let me work on it, then let you know," I said, immediately thinking of plans to make our first date happen.

"Aight, do what you gotta do. All I know is I wanna chill with my girl."

"Okay, Devonte. I gotta go, see you at school tomorrow."

OMG!!!!!! *Devonte wants to take me out on a date.* My first date with a boy ever! I couldn't stop silently screaming in my room, Ahhhhh! I had to scream into my pillow since there's no such thing as privacy in my house. My mom will burst into my room if she hears anything. Sometimes, she randomly opens my door and looks around the room for no reason without saying a word. Back to the exciting news, I needed a plan. I was sure Widelene and Janae would help me come up with something.

Chapter 2

I waited in my room until my mother's guests began to leave. One by one, they all said goodbye. When the door finally closed, I knew it was safe to leave the room. As I walked toward the kitchen, my mother immediately interrupted my thoughts. "Manunu, come clean the chicken."

Great, time to clean the meat. My mom insists on having me learn how to cook. She says I need to cook if I want to find a suitable husband in the future. Interestingly enough, we still haven't discussed the birds and the bees, yet she wants me to learn how to cook for my future husband. If you ask me, that makes no sense. But I digress. Time to go cook.

Our kitchen is a little small. Despite the size, it's still my mother's favorite place in the apartment. The walls are light beige, making the cherry wood cabinets stand out. The stove is next to the sink, directly across from the fridge. The width of the kitchen comfortably allows only two people at a time, so my mother makes sure to use the space wisely. Big pots, small pots, fancy bowls, plastic containers, and special dishes—she organized everything so well. My mother uses our time in the kitchen together for conversations about school. During talks, I often sit on the windowsill near the stove, which gives me some relief from the heat and a view of cars and people passing by.

"Manunu, you do your homework?" she asked, standing with a hand on her hip, facing me.

"Not yet, Mommy. I'll do it after I cook."

Cleaning chicken takes forever in a Haitian household. Lime, vinegar, boiled water, hot water from the faucet—then rinse. After that long cleaning process, we season the meat with epis, a blend of parsley, thyme, garlic, onions, pepper, cilantro, and scallion. Then, we finally cook the chicken. We can't forget the rice and beans. Rice on Sunday, Monday, Wednesday, Friday, and Saturday—you catch my drift. We eat rice almost every day. Haitians have a special recipe that some call black rice. It's really called diri djondjon in Creole and is made from black mushrooms that my mother usually gets sent to her from Haiti. I enjoy some aspects of cooking but didn't like how long it took that night, especially since a date with Devonte was all I could think of. What would I wear? Could this date happen? Was I crazy for even considering a date?

"Manunu, make sure you clean the chicken good." The sound of my mother's voice snapped me out of my thoughts.

"Don't worry. I remember everything you taught me. Mommy, can you help me make the rice? I have a lot of homework tonight."

"Okay, Manunu, when you finish cleaning the chicken, go do your homework."

Yes, she believed me! Now, I didn't have to make the rice, salad, or boil plantains. I actually didn't lie; I did have homework, just not a lot. I think the term is a little "white lie."

"Thank you, Mommy!" And off to my room to get some work started.

Briefly sitting on my beanbag chair, I began strategizing. All right, I'll start with science homework, then math, then French. Believe it or not, French is my most challenging class. I just can't seem to understand past participles. For some odd reason, I thought French would be easy because I speak Haitian Creole, but sadly, I was beyond wrong. I wish someone would tell Mr. Dupont that all Haitian people do not speak French fluently. He always expects me to know the answers. I try my best to avoid eye contact in hopes he doesn't ask me questions because I ran out of bathroom passes—no escaping for me.

I always save art for last. I love art so much that I don't even consider it homework. I can create, draw, and paint all day. Not school-related, but I also love upcycling. Turning old clothing into something new and trendy brings me joy. I must say my love for upcycling resulted from the back-to-school shopping tradition in my household. My mother thinks back-to-school shopping means going to the local bargain center and purchasing three shirts, three pants, socks, and a backpack. The most embarrassing part of back-to-school shopping is when she determines if a pair of pants will fit me by placing the waist portion of the pants around my neck. I know it sounds crazy, but somehow it works. To look somewhat fashionable, I learned how to upcycle.

As usual, I got a little distracted by thoughts of Devonte, so some of my homework wasn't done by dinner time.

"Manunu, time to eat. Your father is home."

"Okay, Mommy, I'm coming."

I have to serve my father dinner. I don't see the point of using so many different dishes: a bowl for the sauce, which some people may call gravy; a plate for the rice and meat; and a plate for the salad and plantains. Guess who has to wash all of the dishes? You guessed it, *moi*. *Moi* is French for me, and that's about all I can remember from class.

I placed the food on the table in front of my father. By the smile on his face, I could tell he was pleased by the display. We all sat down together and enjoyed the meal.

"Manunu, the chicken not bad." That's my dad's way of complimenting me.

"Thanks, Papi."

"Remember I tell you, you have a sister in Haiti?"

Oh yeah, the sister I never met. I've seen a few pictures, that's about it. We have the same father but different mothers. "Yes, I remember, Papi."

"Fabienne is coming to live with us in December," he said, waiting for my reaction.

My mother sat by and was surprisingly quiet as he spoke—a rare occurrence since she always takes over conversations.

Breathe, Manushka. Just breathe. I had to play it cool even though I was *not* happy about this news. September, October, November, December. Ahh!!! Four months until I have an older sister. Most people get cars, clothing, and money for Christmas, but I was getting an older sister. I hate to sound selfish, but I'd have to share my room. How in the world would I be able to sneak in nighttime calls to Devonte without getting caught?

My father stared directly at me with his hands clasped on the table. "She's a nice girl. I need you to help Fabienne learn English. Be nice. Okay, Manushka? She's your sister." My father wasn't asking; he was pretty much telling me what he expected when Fabienne arrived.

"Okay, Papi, don't worry. I'll be nice. Can I go finish my homework now?" Before he could respond, I rushed to my room to shed a few tears.

I love you, bed. I love you, wall. I love you, dresser. I love you, rug. I love you, pillow. I love you, closet. In just four short months, I'd have to share everything. While I still had privacy, it was time for the late-night call with Devonte.

"Hey, Devonte!" I whispered, feeling a little somber.

"Your voice sounds different. Are you okay?"

"Oh, I'm fine, I guess." I didn't want Devonte to think I didn't want to speak to him, but I couldn't help how I felt.

"There has to be a reason you sound so sad. Is there anything I can do to help?" he asked, awaiting a response.

"Well, I just found out my older sister will be living with us in a few months. The worst part is that I have to share my room." I couldn't help but sigh thinking about my soon-to-be new reality.

"You never mentioned having a sister. How old is she? Where does she live now?"

"Her name is Fabienne, and my father said she just turned eighteen. Fabienne lives in Haiti with her mother. I barely know her aside from seeing a few pictures."

"Wow, that's crazy, but give it some time. Think positive. You never know; she may be nice."

"I'll try to think positive, but it's not easy. Girls are so much more complicated than guys. We tend to take things more personally. Like if your best friend doesn't invite you to a party or something—for guys, it's no big deal. But for girls, it's the end of the world! We start wondering if our friends like us, did we say something offensive, and in some cases, we assume the friendship is ending."

"True, I've seen some serious girl drama at school."

"So, Devonte, what do you want to talk about?" I asked, wanting to change the subject. I desperately needed something else to think about.

"I'm going to Donald's birthday celebration this Friday," Devonte said nonchalantly.

"Oh, that's exciting. Where's the party?"

"Not sure, but he mentioned something about go-kart racing and bowling. When it comes to go-kart racing, no one can beat me; I got skills. For now, it's the closest I can get to driving alone. My parents promised me a car when I graduate high school." I could hear the excitement in Devonte's voice once he started talking about driving.

"You're brave because the thought of driving in New York City is intimidating. People drive so fast and are always quick to press the horn. I'll be taking the bus and train for a very long time."

"Listen, once I get my car, I got you. I'll be your private chauffeur as long as you're my girl."

"I know for a fact that I'll have the most handsome private chauffeur. I could talk to you for hours, but I still have homework. I should go." Ending conversations with Devonte was a little hard because we always had so much to talk about. "You can hang up first," I said.

"No, you hang up first. Ladies first, remember?"

To avoid going back and forth, I said, "How about we both hang up on the count of three?"

"Sounds like a great idea."

1. 2. 3. "Goodnight."

After speaking with Devonte, all I could do was think about him as I lay in bed. He always complimented me, which is a real confidence booster, especially since I battle with self-esteem sometimes. Most people don't know that I'm very self-conscious since I pretend to be confident most of the time. See, I'm really skinny, which some may perceive as unhealthy. The truth is, I eat a lot, probably more than the average teenage girl, but I never seem to gain weight. Everyone says the weight will kick in one day, so I'll just have to wait. As for my complexion, in elementary school, a couple of boys used to make fun of me; they thought I was too dark. I can still remember the names they called me to this day.

Some say words don't hurt, which is a complete lie if you ask me. Every word spoken by those boys used to hurt so much until I came across a book about affirmations when I was in middle school. An affirmation is pretty much something positive you say about yourself out loud. So, whenever I feel down about my size or complexion, I pick a couple of affirmations to give myself a pep talk. It's a journey, but I'm learning to love and appreciate myself a little more every day. Once I feel more confident about my body and complexion, I'll work on building some confidence in my art skills.

Chapter 3

Oh no, it's 7:35 a.m. I was supposed to leave at this time, not wake up! I took a deep breath and stretched before rolling out of bed. Between taking a quick shower and packing up, there wasn't enough time for breakfast. Thanks to late-night calls with Devonte, I fell asleep before finishing my homework again. I had no choice but to work on the train. Luckily, there was an empty seat, but it was a little tight, thanks to one of the guys. This whole manspreading thing never made sense to me. But seriously, why in the world does this tiny man feel the need to manspread? If he didn't wear those skintight pants, I'd have a whole seat to myself. Somehow, I have to find a way to get comfortable enough to complete this assignment.

Completing art homework on the train was easy; there's always so much inspiration. New York City train riders are unpredictable; I never know what to expect between the performances, fights, panhandling, singing, questionable fashion choices, and the couple who can't keep their hands off each other. Just when I thought I'd seen everything, a man wearing a horse costume, heels, and a disheveled wig galloped across the cart. Just like I expected, he decided to perform his dance and singing routine right before me. Of course, being the New Yorker I am, I thoroughly enjoyed his performance without any displays of emotion to avoid having to place any money in his hat. I'm far from cheap; it's just that my parents don't seem to understand the concept of allowance. I guess some things just aren't cultural. Pretty sad, huh! The bright side is I'll grow up one day.

After I left the train station, I found Widelene and Janae standing in front of the corner store. This was the perfect morning meet-up spot because the awning provided shelter from the rain and shade on sunny days. And that's where we bought candy, snacks, or bagels before school. The guy at the cash register knew us by name. As usual, I was the last one to arrive.

"Hey, Manushka!" Widelene waved to me. She's energetic every morning; I guess she would be considered a morning person. Widelene was wearing a bright yellow shirt that matched her happy mood. Widelene loves the natural look and often wears her hair in an afro, so she doesn't mind getting it wet. As I admired Widelene's hair and outfit, the look on Janae's face caught my attention.

I could tell Janae was upset by the downward angle of her eyebrows and the tightness of her lips. She stood in front of the store, clutching her umbrella with one hand and her breakfast with the other. Rain or snow can't stop Janae from looking fashionable. With her jacket, jeans, and latest high-top sneakers, Janae looked flawless. Her hair was swept to the side with each braid resting on her shoulder. As our eyes met, I knew it was only a matter of time before she said something.

"Hey, girls!" I said with a big smile as I hugged Janae.

She did not return my embrace. "Girl, why are you always late every day? You do realize it's raining, right? Why didn't you try getting here earlier?" Janae was clearly frustrated with me by the look on her face and how she emphasized every word.

The truth is, I'm late almost every day, so I ran out of excuses. Janae was extra annoyed because of the rain. Widelene looked on as she ate her toasted raisin bagel with cream cheese. She is used to Janae giving me a lecture about being late. Lectures come naturally to Janae since she is co-captain of the debate team, a role she takes very seriously.

"You know I'm Haitian." I chuckled, hoping Janae would find my joke funny.

"Girl, don't even try it. Widelene is Haitian, and she's always the first one to arrive. Just wake up a few minutes earlier. Use an alarm or something. Standing out here waiting for you in the rain today is not cool." Janae thinks quickly on her feet. She usually has a comeback within seconds.

"I'll try to do better tomorrow. Now, time to address a pressing matter. I need your help! Devonte asked me to go on a date to see that new movie *Super Charm*. You know my parents not tryna hear anything about goin' on no dates."

"Just tell them the truth," Janae said. She doesn't understand some aspects of Haitian culture. She has an open line of communication with her mother. Janae can tell her mother almost anything. Sometimes, they seem more like friends than mother and daughter.

"Janae, girl, I'm trying to live past seventeen," I said, shaking my head to dismiss her idea immediately.

"So, Widelene, what do you think Manushka should do?" Janae asked with a puzzled look.

"Tell them you're going to the library to do research about being a doctor so you can catch an early show, the matinee." Understanding Haitian parents, Widelene came up with the perfect plan.

"Great idea, Widelene. My parents would totally fall for that because they're convinced I'm going to be a doctor one day. Ahh!!!!!! My first date! What should I wear?"

Widelene placed a hand on my shoulder. "Wear that cute jacket you upcycled with a skirt and boots. But remember, you have to look like you're going to study."

"Good point. See you at lunch, girls," I said before walking to class.

The first four periods passed, and all I could think about was my soon-to-be first date. I even thought about the first time I met Devonte.

So, we met on the third day of school; it seems like yesterday. The math teacher made us work in groups of two to solve a few problems. You guessed right, Devonte was my partner. Our eyes met for a split second as we worked on solving equations. We both smiled, but I had to look away, you know, play it cool. Before I knew it, he touched my hand. Ahh!!!!! Even though he touched my hand accidentally, at that moment, I knew we were meant to be.

About five weeks passed before Devonte asked me to be his girl in the cutest way. He gave me a note unexpectedly. In the message, which I keep in my special box at home, he wrote the question, "Would you be my girlfriend?" Underneath the question were three boxes with the words *yes*, *no*, and *I need to think about it*. Of course, I wanted to play hard to get by checking the think-about-it box, but I was too eager about having a boyfriend. I checked yes and drew a smiley face. We've been dating for twenty-one days, seventeen hours, and fifteen seconds. I know this sounds weird, but I like keeping track of anything special.

The abrupt lunch bell interrupted my thoughts about Devonte. I quickly made my way to the cafeteria.

"Hey, Manushka, we're over here," Janae shouted in her usual loud voice while waving.

I walked toward my friends, eager to catch up.

"How was class?" Janae asked. She's been an "A" student since first grade, never missing a school day and always managing to make the honor roll. Janae never seems to have a bad school day.

"It was okay, but all I could think about was my date on Saturday. How do you think I should do my hair? Do you think I should wear makeup? " Despite being excited about the date, my self-consciousness was definitely kicking in.

Widelene is quick to set me straight whenever she notices my pattern of self-doubt. "Girl, your hair always looks amazing. A slick-back ponytail would look nice with your outfit. As for makeup, you truly don't need it. Your skin stays flawless. Just wear lip gloss." Widelene is not a fan of makeup. She is more so into natural beauty and natural hair. She rocks her natural hair in afros, ponytails, cornrows, beads, you name it. Her hairstyles stay versatile. I admire her confidence. I secretly hope some of her confidence will slowly rub off on me one day.

Before we knew it, lunch was over, and it was time for French. *I hope Mr. Dupont is absent. For real, because I hate that class.* I arrived there just before the late bell rang. As I slowly walked in, wishing a fire drill would take place, Mr. Dupont was nowhere to be found. Could it be? Yes! He was absent. Thank you, Lord, for answering my prayers. I sat down with the biggest smile then pulled out my sketchbook. Because the substitutes never spoke French, it was usually a free period.

As I began to draw, the alarm rang, yep, a fire drill. The entire school made their way outside and waited. What a waste of a free period. But really, nothing was getting in the way of my excitement. All I had to do was get through two more periods.

Finally, the day was over—time to go home and prepare for my first date.

"Hi, Mommy. I have to go to the library tomorrow morning. I want to do research about being a doctor. Can I go?"

"Yes, okay, Manunu, very good." My mother smiled from ear to ear when she heard me say the word doctor. A part of me felt bad about lying, but not for too long.

The evening went by fast. After dinner, I did a little homework before laying out the perfect outfit for a date with my boyfriend.

Chapter 4

I woke up extra early, thanks to my alarm. To be honest, it felt like I was waking up every hour to check the time. The combination of my first date excitement and lying to my parents made it difficult to sleep through the night.

"Good morning, Mommy. I'm going to the library soon."

"Library? You don't tell me about the library."

I told my mother last night. There was no way I was missing my first date.

"Mommy, remember, I told you after school yesterday. I'm going to do research at the library about becoming a doctor."

"I don't remember, but you can go. Manunu, please be careful outside."

"I will. Don't worry, Mommy."

I quickly got dressed, grabbed a bite, then went on my way to meet Devonte.

Arriving a few minutes early, I had enough time to put on lip gloss and adjust my clothing, hoping to impress him.

"Hey, Devonte!"

"What's up, Manushka?" Devonte hugged me so tight; in that moment, it felt as though I melted in his arms.

"I'm so excited about our first date," I blurted, excitement was getting the best of me.

Like the perfect gentleman, Devonte opened doors whenever he could. "I'm excited too. What time do you have to be home?"

"By five o'clock."

"That's enough time for us to watch the movie and grab a bite."

"Great!"

Devonte purchased the movie tickets along with the snacks.

Just like we expected, *Super Charm* was a hit. After the movie, we ate at a local restaurant, which was a special treat. My parents—or, should I say, my mother doesn't believe in going to restaurants. Whenever I ask my mom about going out to eat, her response is always, "We have good food at home." I must admit, she's right because we always have meals in the fridge since my mother enjoys cooking so much.

Refocusing on the matter at hand, I tried to relax and enjoy the moment, but I was a little nervous about someone seeing me. The last thing I needed was for my parents to hear about me hanging out with a boy.

Our conversation was natural as Devonte and I talked about school, family, friends, and goals. We then took a short walk along the Brooklyn Bridge. Being the artsy person I am, I couldn't help but take some time to admire the skyline. At that moment, I envisioned a successful career as an artist. Just when I turned around to ask Devonte a question, our lips met. *He kissed me!* My first kiss was so epic! Who else has their first kiss on the Brooklyn Bridge? Epic, I tell you!

After the kiss, we held hands and slowly walked across the bridge. My excitement caused me to lose track of time.

"Manushka, it's four o'clock; you need to head home. I don't want you to get in trouble."

"Yes, you're right, I have to leave now. I wish our date didn't have to end." I gazed into Devonte's eyes.

"Don't worry, we'll have time to go on more dates in the future," he said reassuringly.

I rushed to get home by five o'clock. Right before walking through the doors, I wiped off the lip gloss.

As usual, my mom was cooking something delicious. The aroma of the meal filled the entire apartment.

"Hi, Mommy." I kissed her on the cheek followed by some small talk instead of heading to my room. The guilt of lying to my mother bothered me more than I expected. To bring some degree of peace to my mind, I hung out with her in the kitchen. We laughed at a couple of jokes while cooking and cleaning, then watched a movie. As I hung out with my mother, thoughts of sharing details of my date with Janae and Widelene constantly crossed my mind. Telling them details about the date over the phone wasn't enough. I needed to tell them everything in person.

My mother interrupted my thoughts. "Manushka, don't forget we have church tomorrow."

"Yes, Mommy. I know."

We never miss church. Snow, rain, storm—nothing stops my mother from going.

I went to sleep early, knowing Sunday would be a long day.

Despite the rays of sunlight piercing my curtains, I was determined to rest for a few more minutes by any means necessary. Tossing and turning, I covered my head with a pillow and used my blanket as an added layer to block the light. Just when I'd found a comfortable position, I heard my mother's voice: "Manunu, Manunu, let's go!" After stretching, I dramatically rolled out of bed. All I needed was just five more minutes of sleep. Somehow, I found the energy to get ready.

The ten-minute walk to church felt longer on cold days. We still arrived at precisely 8:55 a.m., five minutes before service began. I immediately spotted Widelene walking into the sanctuary, but there was no way for us to talk about my date since the service was about to begin. I'd have to wait until Monday.

Our church wasn't too small. Wooden benches filled the main sanctuary, and red carpeting covered the floor. Large bouquets of artificial flowers adorned the pulpit, drawing everyone's eyes to the front of the church where the pastor preached his weekly sermons. The pastor was pretty animated, frequently moving around the pulpit while preaching. No matter where he moved, the large cross behind him was visible from every angle. Most of the adults at our church were affable, except for one woman. I tried to avoid her as much as possible: Sè Françoise, the church gossiper. Somehow-someway, she knew everyone's business while keeping her life a secret.

By noon, I could hear my stomach and feel the internal acrobatics. Seems like the sermon was good, based on the applause and multiple shouts of Hallelujah, but I was still on cloud nine as I thought about the date with Devonte. Part of me still feels terrible about being dishonest and sneaking around, but my parents just didn't understand the importance of communication; it's like I didn't have a choice. The truth is, I would have loved to talk to my mom about Devonte and all the drama that comes with being a high schooler, but she's so set in her ways. Until my parents see the value in honest communication, there are just some things I'll have to figure out on my own.

Chapter 5

At the sound of the alarm, I jumped out of bed, no time for the usual morning dramatics. I was ready at record speed. Determined to be on time, I left for school a few minutes early. As I approached our morning meet-up spot, I could see Janae looking in my direction.

"Could it be, Manushka is early, or am I seeing things? Please pinch me Widelene because I'm definitely hallucinating." Playing along with the joke, Widelene pinched Janae.

I knew Janae would be the first to crack a joke about me being early. She was right, though. "I see you got jokes, Janae." I laughed.

"You know she's right," Widelene said with a smile.

"Widelene, how you not gonna defend me? Just joking, I know I'm always late, but I'm trying to do better. Now let me fill you in about my date with Devonte."

"Yes, be sure to share all of the juicy details." Widelene rubbed her hands together in anticipation. "You know I'm nosy."

"Yes, you're nosy, Widelene." I laughed again. "So, we met in front of the movie theater. I arrived early enough to make sure I was looking good and to put on some lip gloss."

Janae interrupted me. "Wait up! Did you say early?"

After we all laughed, I continued, "*Super Charm* was a hit; you should see it. As we watched the movie, Devonte placed his arm around my shoulders and gently drew me closer to him. Lord knows I was happy because the theater was cold. I should've worn something warmer, but you know I was trying to be cute. So, after the movie, we went for a walk along the Brooklyn Bridge. I was admiring the skyline. When I turned around, Devonte was right behind me. Our lips met, and HE KISSED ME! AHH!!! MY FIRST KISS WAS ON THE BROOKLYN BRIDGE. THE BROOKLYN BRIDGE!"

"OMG! I'm so excited for you," Widelene said. Then she looked genuinely concerned. "You're brave, kissing in such a public place. You know someone from the church could have seen you. Be careful next time."

"I did take a risk and the thought of someone from the church seeing me crossed my mind. You know some people love to gossip about other people's children when their kids be out there doing the most ratchet things. Regardless, the risk was worth it. I would do it again and again. The entire date was absolutely perfect, kind of like something you would see in the movies, except there was no glass slipper, castle, and hopefully no evil witch. It's time to get to class already. See you all at lunch."

I got to class ready to get my work done. To my surprise, Devonte made it to class on time. He was focused and volunteered to answer questions while periodically looking at me.. I hope the discussion we had about our future had a positive impact on him.

As much as we enjoyed spending time together, Devonte and I didn't sit at the same table during lunch. We decided it was important to have time for our relationship *and* our friends, a healthy balance. Some girls be so lost when they have a boyfriend. They end up forgetting about their friends. I didn't want to be that girl fawning over her boyfriend every second of the day. The bell rang, and I headed straight to the cafeteria.

"Manushka, tell us more about your date," Widelene said. "My dating life is non-existent, so I'm going to live through you."

"I've talked about myself enough for the morning. I want to hear what's going on with you all." I didn't want to be that selfish friend who always talked about herself. Knowing how my friends were doing was important to me.

Widelene began. "I finally found the right mixture and measure of ingredients to create the perfect hair moisturizer since I last tried it on you guys. My mother has been using the moisturizer for two weeks and loves it."

Before Widelene could finish, Janae jumped in. "That is amazing. I can see you being a teenage mogul. Girl, when can I place my order?"

I was excited about Widelene's news. "Wow, you're so talented. You know I have a nonexistent allowance. So, I'll take any free samples you have. As soon as I have money, I'll place an order, like a real paying customer."

With teary eyes, Widelene said, "I love you, guys. Thanks for the support. Thanks for believing in me. You know, I've always been fascinated by hair. I guess spending time in the salon watching my mother work as a stylist impacted me. I remember trying to be just like her as I played with my dolls. My goal is to one day have the top-selling natural hair care product line. So, this is just the beginning."

Curious, Janae asked, "What will you call the product line? Did you finally make a decision?"

"YN-M, the acronym for Why Not Moisturize." Widelene touched her perfectly moisturized hair.

"Creative. I like it! How did you come up with the name?" Janae asked.

With a big smile, Widelene said, "Keeping natural hair moisturized is an important part of maintaining healthy hair and promoting growth. The name is pretty much asking people a question. The question is, 'Why not moisturize your hair?'"

"Wow, that was so well thought out. I can see it on a billboard: YN-M by Widelene Jean-Charles." Janae held a ten-dollar bill in her hand to place the first order.

Widelene pocketed the money before asking a question. "Janae, fill us in. What are you working on?"

Jane smiled confidently. "My goal is to be like RBG, you know, Ruth Bader Ginsburg. I'm determined to become a Supreme Court Justice. That's why I take my grades seriously, going above and beyond in all subjects. The idea of being a Supreme Court Justice is intimidating sometimes, but my mother keeps encouraging me to dream big. This Brooklyn girl is going places! I'm not letting anyone or anything deter me. Who knows? I might be the first female president."

After Janae shared her future goal, we all sat quietly, taking in her wisdom. Then I said, "Janae, that was so inspirational. You got me thinking I can fly if I work hard enough. But seriously, I believe you have everything it takes to be the president of the United States one day. Janae and Widelene, I'm proud to have you two as best friends."

I loved speaking to my friends, but unfortunately, lunch was over, and it was time for French. I knew Mr. Dupont wouldn't be absent again, but one could always hope. I walked through the halls, apprehensively approaching the classroom. Yep, he was standing right beside the door, ready to take attendance.

"*Bonjour, Manushka! Comment vas-tu aujourd'hui?*"

Why, oh why, did he feel the need to speak to me? I'd disappear if I had superpowers, anything to avoid answering his question but since I didn't, I had to respond. "*Bonjour, Monsieur Dupont!* I'm doing fine."

"Manushka, I'm happy you're doing fine, but you did not fully answer my question. This is a French class, so you must speak French when you enter the room. You said you're doing fine, so repeat after me, *Je vais bien aujourd'hui.*"

"*Je vais bien aujourd'hui,*" I repeated begrudgingly after Mr. Dupont as the entire class looked on. At least, it felt like the entire class was staring at me. I then quickly found a seat way in the back of the classroom, far enough to hide.

I headed straight to the train station when the final bell rang since Janae and Widelene stayed after school. I made my way down the street only to run into Devonte. Turns out he was waiting for me.

"Hey, Manushka!"

"Hey, Devonte!"

"I was wondering if you wanted to go on another date with me?" he asked with a smile.

"Yes!" I said without hesitation. Hopefully, I didn't sound too desperate.

"What do you think about going to the Botanic Garden?"

"Great choice, I love the Botanic Garden. The landscape is so beautiful. I can sit and draw for hours."

"So, it's a date. I can meet you at your house." Devonte seemed excited about picking me up, but there was no way I'd let that happen, at least not anytime soon.

"No, I'll meet you there. My parents aren't ready to entertain the idea of me having a boyfriend."

By the look on his face, I could tell Devonte was slightly bothered. "I understand. I hope you can tell your parents about me one day. So, would noon work for you?"

"That time is perfect! See you at noon."

I smiled from ear to ear the entire way home. Nothing would spoil my mood—not the crowded train, not the person having a loud phone conversation on the bus, nothing. I walked into my house on cloud nine.

"*Bonjour,* Mommy," I said, greeting my mother with a kiss.

"Hello, Manunu. You have a good day at school?"

"Yes, Mommy, I did. I have to go to the library tomorrow. Is that okay?"

"Yes, what time?" she asked.

The fact that she was busy made it a little easier to tell an untruth. I would much rather say *untruth* than use the word *lie*. *Untruth* feels more harmless. Containing my smile, I said, "I plan to leave at ten in the morning. I should be back home at 3:30."

This time, I set two hours aside to study for upcoming exams before meeting with Devonte. As much as I enjoyed spending time with him, my future and personal goals were far more important.

Bright and early Saturday morning, I hopped on the train to make my way to the library. Science and math were the first two subjects I tackled. Sticky notes, highlighters, graph paper, textbooks, and my phone were all laid out on a table. Finally, I spent some time studying for Mr. Dupont's quiz. As much as I disliked French, failure was not an option. Failure is never an option.

Two hours had passed, and it was time to meet Devonte after a productive time studying. I was proud of finding a healthy balance between my studies and my boyfriend. The library was just a short walk from the Botanic Garden. By the time I got there, Devonte was waiting for me.

"Hey, Manushka!"

"Hey, Devonte! I hope you weren't waiting too long."

"Nah, I just got here. Besides, you're worth waiting for." Smiling, I gave him a playful tap on the shoulder.

"You're worth waiting for too." That was the only thing I could think of to say. His words caught me by surprise.

We walked hand in hand into the botanical garden. The scenery was picturesque. After walking around for fifteen minutes, I showed him my favorite spot. Once seated, I immediately pulled out my art kit. Devonte was my subject. I drew him to include a beautiful background. In a moment of vulnerability, I showed him a sketchbook of some of my most personal drawings. As much as I want to pursue a career in the arts, out of fear, I often find myself apprehensive about sharing the work I have created. My fear probably stems from my parents being adamant about my becoming a doctor or nurse. As Devonte looked through the sketchbook, I turned away, making every effort to avoid eye contact. I desperately wanted feedback but also feared my art wouldn't measure up.

"Wow!"

Shocked by this unexpected outburst and not realizing the source of the sound, I clutched my bag and scanned the area; that's the New Yorker in me.

"Wow!" Devonte went again. He loved the finished product. "Manushka, this is amazing. I knew you were good at drawing, but I didn't know you were this talented. What do your parents think of your art?"

Pleased by his feedback and slightly saddened by the question, I said, "I'm happy you like it. My parents have seen some of my artwork but don't seem excited. They see it as more of a hobby than a career path."

"Don't worry; one day, they will see your talent, especially when those checks start rolling in."

With a deep sigh of relief, I hugged Devonte. Wanting to change the subject, I asked him, "What do you want to talk about?"

Devonte shrugged; he couldn't think of a topic. My question had caught him off guard.

I decided to be more specific. "How was the party you went to with your friends?"

He adjusted his shirt in a way to indicate confidence and victory. "It was cool. We went go-karting, and I came first in all three races. No one can touch me when it comes to go-kart racing, but bowling was a whole different story. I had so many gutter balls, I almost asked for those kiddie guardrails."

We both laughed before I said, "It couldn't have been that bad."

"Trust me, it was bad," Devonte said. "I had to redeem myself at the arcade with a couple of wins."

We joked around a little before it was time to leave. Since I was taking a risk by meeting Devonte on Saturdays, I made sure to be home early.. Didn't want to give my mother any reasons to be suspicious. My life was predictable—church, school, and home. Periodic dates with Devonte added some spice to my monotonous weekly schedule.

When I arrived home, a few people from the church were at my house again. I shouted, "Hello" to everyone as I rushed to the bathroom to think of a strategy to avoid the kissing round. But it was inevitable. I slowly walked out of the bathroom to greet everyone with a kiss on the cheek. The bright side is that the creepy old man wasn't there.

In my rush to the bathroom, I totally overlooked the fact that Widelene was sitting beside her mother. We went to my room to catch up. Most of our conversation took place in the form of a whisper. The last thing I wanted was for my mother to hear about my date with Devonte.

"So, Widelene, how long have you been here?"

"Not too long, about twenty minutes."

I was excited about having my friend over unexpectedly. "Great, that means we get to hang out for a good two hours. You know, when the old folks start talking, they never wanna stop."

We both giggled, reminiscing about the many times we waited for two or more hours after church as our parents talked.

"Manushka, I need you to make me a logo for my business. If anyone can create something amazing, I know it's you," Widelene said confidently.

"Of course, I can, but are you sure? I mean, I'm not sure how—"

Before I could finish the sentence, Widelene threw her hands in the air, bringing my words to an immediate halt. "Listen, girl, I can't understand why you continuously deny your God-given talent. YOU ARE AN ARTIST, not because of school but because God gave you this gift. Think about everyone's reaction to your drawings, paintings, and upcycled clothing. What do all the reactions have in common?" Widelene intently stared into my eyes waiting for a response.

I wasn't sure if I was supposed to be encouraged or hide. "Um, I guess they like it," I said shyly.

Widelene stood in front of me with both hands on her hips. "You guessed wrong! How do you not see people's reaction to your work? People don't like your art; they LOVE it! Get that through your thick head! I can understand some moments of insecurity, but you need to start believing in yourself more. Now, would you please draw my logo?"

We both laughed at the fact that Widelene went through two extremes in less than three minutes.

"How did you go from 0 to 100, back to 0? I'm scared of you, girl. Yes, I'll draw your logo. While I do it, do you mind fixing a few of my braids?"

As I drew Widelene's logo and she braided my hair, I secretly wished I had more confidence in my talents. I guessed she was right; I was good at this art thing. I could be one of the greats one day, I hope.

"Widelene, don't braid it too tight at the edges."

"I got you, girl, don't worry," Widelene said as she focused on my hair.

The moment I started drawing, I entered my happy place. Drawing and anything art-related brings me indescribable joy. Within thirty minutes, I created a logo for Widelene's business, YN-M.

"Okay, are you ready to see your logo?" As usual, right before handing her the finished product, I looked down, afraid she wouldn't like it.

"Listen, Manushka, I need you to stop turning away when people look at your artwork. Looking away is the reason you never see people's reactions. Now, look up!"

"I guess you're right." For the first time, I found the courage to look up while sharing my art. It felt good not to hide and deny my gift, even if only for a few minutes. I watched Widelene intently; her facial expressions would give me the answer I needed. Was my art good enough? Did I measure up? Did I really have a gift?

"Manushka, this is freakin' AMAZING!" Widelene shouted. "I love it! Girl, this logo is everything. How did you come up with this concept so quick? Between the silhouette of the woman with the afro, the colors, letters, and the throne, everything is perfect, just perfect."

"I'm happy you like it; I mean *love* it. I got the concept by listening to you. Between your strength, confidence, and goals, you know I had to add a throne." Watching Widelene's reaction to the logo was a much-needed confidence booster. Although she fully believed in my talent, I had to find a way to believe in myself.

Widelene was still staring at the logo. "One day, you, me, and Janae will be sitting on a yacht somewhere, celebrating our successes. I can feel it."

As Widelene spoke, I could imagine myself on an elegant yacht in the middle of the ocean, sailing to an exotic location. Dreams are possible, so at that moment, I decided to start dreaming big. Like Janae said, I needed to dream beyond my circumstances.

But my thoughts of dreaming big were interrupted by my mother summoning Widelene to the kitchen. It was time for her to leave.

"Widelene, thanks for being such an awesome friend," I said.

"Anytime, girl, I appreciate you too!" She walked out the door, waving.

Chapter 6

After my conversation with Widelene, I decided to believe in myself a little more. I walked into school with newfound confidence— not cocky or rude, just feeling better about myself. My art teacher had been encouraging me to enter a competition that required creating a painting about the impact of culture on identity. Out of fear, I ignored her constant nudging for weeks. But not today.

"Mrs. Franca, if it's not too late, I want to enter the art competition you've been telling me about." Thinking about the competition was one thing; uttering the words was different. I was making a commitment. At that moment, my armpits began to sweat. *Run, hide, tell her it was a mistake*—all these thoughts ran through my mind as I stood before Mrs. Franca. But it was too late.

"Manushka! I am so relieved you finally decided to go for it! Though you missed the deadline, I'll move mountains to get you into this competition. Your talent is undeniable. I'm blessed to get a glimpse of your greatness. When you get an award one day, don't forget to mention my name."

"Thank you, Mrs. Franca!" Her level of enthusiasm was overwhelming considering the fear and uncertainty I was feeling. But her show of support, in a sense, confirmed that entering this competition is the right decision.

Mrs. Franca handed me a sheet of paper. "Manushka, I need you to return this permission slip signed by your parents ASAP."

I couldn't wait to tell Janae and Widelene about it. I made a beeline to the cafeteria as soon as the bell rang. "Hey, girls!"

"Hey, Manushka!" they exclaimed.

I continued, "I decided to enter an art competition today. Mrs. Franca was so excited she had to stop herself from hugging me to death."

"I'm so proud of you!" Janae said with a huge smile. "It's about time you enter some of these art challenges."

"I'm proud of you too." Widelene hugged me.

"How's your day going, Janae?" I asked.

"So far, so good. I have to study for an upcoming algebra test. You know math isn't my thing, but I'm determined to get an A. I plan to study at the library on Saturday. Do you guys want to join me? "Janae asked.

Widelene nodded. "I'm down to meet at the library. Getting work done at home is hard because my little brother insists on hanging out in my room all day, every day."

"I use the library as an excuse to meet up with Devonte, but I also try to get a little work done before meeting him," I said. "I'll be there around ten o'clock. I can stay for about two hours."

I was getting used to meeting up with Devonte on Saturdays. I must say, I was becoming a little reckless, though, because I stopped worrying about one of my mother's friends seeing me with him.

"Great! Let's meet at ten o'clock in front of the library. I'm putting it on my calendar right now." Janae is one of the most organized people I've ever met. Her notes, backpack, locker, and bedroom are always neat. All appointments on her phone are color-coded with weekly and sometimes daily reminders.

The bell rang, and it was time to return to class. The latter part of the day went by surprisingly faster than usual. French class was a little less painful. Mr. Dupont asked me one question I could accurately respond to in French. *"Oui, oui,"* I answered. As soon as the day ended, I went straight home, excited about getting my mother to sign off on the permission slip.

`"*Bonjour,* Mommy," I said, kissing her on the cheek.

"*Bonjour, pitit mwen,*" she said.

"Mommy, there's an art competition I want to be a part of. Mrs. Franca, the art teacher, really believes I can win. The competition is free so you don't have to pay anything." Fumbling through my bag, I found a pink pen. "Here, just sign right next to the X, pretty please." She analyzed the paper before reaching for the pen. I often mark off where my mother needs to sign forms; sometimes, I even sign for her. I've been reading and translating documents for my parents and some of their friends since first or second grade. Can you imagine sounding out words way above your grade level, then trying to translate the information? It's a tough job but someone has to do it. I handed her the pen while eagerly waiting and watching as she finally signed the permission slip.

"Thank you, Mommy, you're the best." I quickly ran to my room to think of potential concepts. The impact of culture on identity is an interesting topic. There's no way I can deny my Haitian ancestry and how cultural norms shape decision-making, mannerisms, food choices, and more. I also can't deny the influence of being raised in New York City. Somehow-someway, I have to intertwine Haitian culture with some aspects of American influence on my identity.

In my excitement about the competition, the nighttime call with Devonte went from one hour to twenty minutes. I was happy he understood why I had to cut our conversation short. I loved the fact that he was so supportive. I fell asleep with my sketchbook and pencils on the bed, trying to think of an initial sketch.

My Saturday mornings became somewhat of a routine. I looked forward to studying just as much as I did meeting Devonte. One week, I insisted that we remain in the library rather than go to a restaurant or elsewhere. I wanted to win the art competition. For the first time, I believed in my talent or gift— as Widelene would call it. Being the supportive boyfriend he was, Devonte agreed. Since he'd been taking school more seriously, Devonte wanted to make time to study also.

I arrived at the library at nine o'clock, an hour before meeting my girls. I found a quiet place and began to jot down the many aspects of Haitian culture I had grown to love. I also wrote down the aspects of American culture and societal norms that positively influenced me. I dedicated an hour to generating the approach for the art competition. Before I knew it, Widelene and Janae arrived. I was lost in my thoughts as I considered various visual concepts.

"Are my eyes deceiving me? Manushka is early again?" Janae loves joking about my lateness as long as she isn't standing in the rain waiting for me. She's funny, funny enough to be a stand-up comedian. I guess Janae will be known as the joking Supreme Court justice.

"Yes, I'm early—in fact, an entire hour early. There are times in life when one must blossom. Some call it maturity; others may call it growth. I have turned what you would call a new leaf." I confidently made this declaration, my right hand firmly pressed firmly against my chest. I also had to include a serious look—you know, to be more convincing.

"Girl, please, I know you'll be late to school on Monday," Janae said.

Both Janae and Widelene began laughing uncontrollably. I couldn't help but join in the laughter until the librarian signaled for us to be quiet with the flick of a finger. The security guard was standing nearby, so we contained the laughter.

Wanting to understand the inspiration for Janae's outfit, I asked, "Girl, since when did you start wearing glasses and carrying a big pocketbook?" Janae wore stylish black-frame glasses that complemented her above-the-knee black dress, knee-high boots, and red pocketbook. She pulled back her hair, creating a nice sleek low ponytail look.

Janae sat down and repositioned her glasses by pushing them back with her pointer finger. "This is what I would call my professional look, considering my future goals. I figured I'd switch my style up a little, you know, considering we're in the library today. The pocketbook and glasses belong to my mom; you know I like to raid her closet."

Widelene was coincidentally wearing a dress, but instead of boots, she put on a pair of cute low-top sneakers. Her dress was burgundy, but more so on the bright side as she wasn't a fan of dark colors. She wore her hair in a high puff ponytail with a simple yet perfect pair of hoop earrings. "Janae, look at this amazing logo Manushka created for me. I absolutely love it! The next step is digitizing it to add to the labels for my products. I'm launching the product on March 5th, my birthday. Today, instead of studying, I plan to purchase a domain name, you know, the name for my website, www.yn-m.com. I also need to pick a company to host the website." With every word, Widelene spoke faster as her excitement grew. She did her research thoroughly.

"Go ahead, young CEO! Go Widelene, go Widelene!"

Janae joined as Widelene, and I started a little two-step dance with our hands in the air. Our celebration ended abruptly as the security guard cleared his throat. We quickly shifted focus and got to work.

It turned out Devonte couldn't meet me at the library because of a family emergency. I spent the entire time in the library with my friends, followed by a little retail therapy. We took the train to my favorite thrift store.

"Manushka, you need to hook me up," Widelene said. "I need all the help I can get. I always feel overwhelmed when we go to thrift stores. I never know where to start. After this, we have to stop by the beauty supply store. I need more ingredients to complete my first batch of moisturizers." She was easily overwhelmed when we went clothing shopping. But if you put that girl in a beauty supply store, she was undoubtedly in her element. Widelene knew the beauty supply store like the back of her hand.

I was in my element at the thrift store, any thrift store. I knew where to start, what to look for, and how to combine the oddest pieces to create something beautiful.

"Manushka, we need to go. I want to head to the mall before going to the beauty supply store. Widelene has some products to pick up," Janae said as she stood by the exit, waving at me. She loved going to the mall. This time, she needed to pick up a pair of sneakers that had just dropped. She also bought pretzels and Cinnabuns. Janae couldn't leave the mall without buying pretzels. The people at the pretzel shop knew her by name.

We strolled around the mall, having fun and minding our business until these guys made passes at us. "Aye, girl, let me get your number. You lookin' good over there!" They shouted louder and louder as we walked away.

We hated the cheesy and sometimes vulgar pickup lines; they were especially scary and uncomfortable when walking alone. Out of caution, I avoided having a funky attitude with these guys. Many of them appeared to be insecure while trying to impress their friends. You never knew which one would attack you if they felt disrespected and rejected. Finally, we were far enough to no longer hear their voices..

After about an hour, we left the mall and headed to the neighborhood beauty supply store.

Widelene immediately began loading her cart with products. As I browsed the store, I wondered how much money the owners made daily, monthly, or yearly. Between the hair extensions, wigs, lashes, and weaves, they always had customers in the store. Widelene took about twenty minutes to gather everything she needed; she was always decisive.

Unfortunately, our time together ended soon.

At home, I helped cook dinner, hung out with my parents, and cleaned. Since I told my mother I was hanging out with Janae and Widelene, no questions were asked. My mother liked Widelene, mainly because we attended the same church. She loved Janae because she was a fan of my mother's food. As I headed to my room, my parents reminded me about Fabienne again. I guess they wanted me to get used to the idea of a sister and shared space.. I figured I'd start the thirty-day countdown at the end of November. I hadn't even shared the news with Janae and Widelene yet but planned to do it soon, but for right now, I had way too much to think about.

Chapter 7

I worked on my submission for the art competition and finalized the concept. It was time to pick a color scheme, which was the best part. The power of colors is often overlooked by many. Colors can impact someone's mood, highlight facial features, and change the atmosphere of an entire room. I decided to choose a tetradic color scheme—bold and vibrant. It would make my concept stand out for sure. My thoughts were interrupted by a call from Devonte, which, of course, I didn't mind.

"Hey, Manushka!"

"Hey, Devonte," I quickly said. Did I tell you how much I absolutely love the way he says my name?

"So sorry I had to cancel on you today. I missed seeing your beautiful face." He sounded very apologetic.

"I missed you too, Devonte. What happened?"

"My mother has been on call at the hospital. You know she's an emergency room doctor. My dad stayed late at work, so I had to stay with my little brother."

"Oh, I forgot your mother is a doctor. That's okay; we can go out any time." I smiled so much whenever I spoke to Devonte that my cheeks hurt.

"I wanna make it up to you. How about I take you on a special surprise date?"

"A surprise? When and where? I need details to pick the right outfit. And how much money should I bring?" The thought of a surprise date was overwhelming. "Really, though, as much as I love surprises, you don't have to make it up to me. Life happens. I'm just happy everything worked out okay."

"Don't worry about money, I got you. I have some money saved up from working for my dad sometimes."

"That's so sweet, Devonte. Just wondering, since your mother is a doctor and your father is an architect, have you ever considered one of those professions?" I asked out of curiosity. I know many people follow in their parents' footsteps for career choices. In some cases, it's almost an expectation.

After a few seconds, Devonte said, "To be honest, I don't want to be a doctor or an architect. I never told anyone this before, so don't laugh." He paused as though taking a deep breath. "I want to be an astronomer because I've always been fascinated by planets, stars, the moon, you know, the entire galaxy. I tried to mention it to my dad a couple of times, but all he does is talk about work. He wants me to be an architect to help run the family business one day, but that's not what I wanna do at all." Devonte stopped speaking, but I could tell he wanted to say more.

"What's wrong? Why did you stop speaking?"

After some encouragement, Devonte began speaking again. "I love my family and all, but my parents are always busy. They work long hours. So we spend a lot of time alone. I skipped school a couple of times and since they were too busy to notice, I guess it became a habit. But to be honest, it was getting kind of boring, you know, just hanging out with the boys all the time or playing video games. After speaking to you about school and grades that day, I decided to stop skipping class as much and take my grades more seriously. The last thing I want to do is spend an extra year in high school. I'm not tryna be a super senior."

"Devonte, you want to be an astronomer! That's awesome! I think you should try speaking to your parents again; I'm sure they'll listen.

But I totally understand where you're coming from. Like I told you before, I want to be an artist, but my mom and dad want me to be a doctor or nurse. Both are great professions, but just not for me. The day will come when I tell them being a nurse or a doctor isn't for me, but I'm avoiding the topic altogether for now."

"You're right, Manushka. I'll try speaking to my parents this week. You should take your own advice too. Try speaking to your parents about becoming an artist."

"Trust me, that's not a good idea now. But let me know how it goes. Hey, I have to go now. Goodnight, Devonte!"

"Goodnight, Manushka!"

I loved ending the day with my nightly conversations with Devonte. He was right about taking my own advice but for now, I couldn't stop thinking about the special date. What did he have planned? Where did he want to take me? Most importantly, what in the world was I going to wear?

The week flew by faster than usual, possibly because I was so busy. I passed all my tests, including the pop quizzes. I made time to work on the first draft of my painting. Finally, it was Saturday and time for my secret rendezvous. As much as I enjoyed my dates with Devonte, I still couldn't get used to the fact that I was lying to my mother almost every week. If only we had an open line of communication, I would tell her everything. Since we didn't, I'd have to keep lying. I mean, telling untruths.

Chapter 8

B efore the surprise date, I had to mail a draft of my submission for the art competition. I hesitantly walked to the post office. Surprisingly, the line was shorter than expected.

"Next!"

I could hear the woman calling me to the register, but my legs wouldn't move. I finally made my way to her and provided the mailing address. As I handed over the envelope, my hand began trembling.

"Are you okay?" She looked at me with concern.

"I'm okay, just a little nervous about submitting my artwork for this competition," I said.

"Is this your first time entering a competition?" she asked.

"Yes," I replied.

"Okay, that makes sense. Starting something new always causes some degree of nervousness and fear. Just hope for the best. You should be proud of yourself for taking a chance. If you win—no, I mean *when* you win—please stop by and let me know." She smiled.

I made my payment and left the store.

It was a brisk day in mid-November as I walked to the train station to meet Devonte.

Our date started at the Metropolitan Museum of Art. I was in awe as we walked through the exhibit halls. The art, the concepts, the colors, the messages—you name it, I loved everything. The second part of the date was a pleasant stroll along Central Park, walking hand in hand. For the grand finale, Devonte took me to a restaurant for lunch. Not just any restaurant—this one was fancy. You know, the kind of restaurant with the lovely chandeliers and candles on the table. We couldn't pronounce half of the items on the menu, but we managed to order food and dessert.

As we sat at the table, Devonte's mother sent him a text instructing him to meet her at the hospital immediately. I didn't want him to go alone, and I wasn't ready for the date to end. We headed to the hospital together, which took about twenty-five minutes between the train ride and the walk. This was my first time meeting his mother.

Smiling from ear to ear, Devonte said, "Mom, this is Manushka, the girl I've been telling you about, my girlfriend."

Nervously, I said, "Hello, Mrs., um, Dr. Robinson, it's nice to meet you." I stuck my hand out to give her a firm handshake.

Devonte's mother approached me with open arms. "Manushka, come here, child, and give me a hug. I've heard so many great things about you. I would love to have you and your family over for dinner one day." She hugged me tightly like we had known each other for years. For an emergency room doctor, she had a cheerful attitude. I can't imagine how much stress she experiences daily.

Although I loved the invitation to dinner, there was absolutely no way in the world my mother would consider it, let alone accept the fact that I have a boyfriend. To be polite, I just smiled.

"Devonte, you forgot your keys at home. The expected delivery of the new appliances is between five and six o'clock, but I won't make it home in time. And your dad will be home later than usual since he has to work out the details for a new contract. I need you to be home for the delivery. You'll be home alone for a couple of hours. Don't worry about your brother. He has a playdate at William's house. I'll pick him up at 8 p.m." She pulled out her wallet. "Here, be sure to give the delivery guys this tip. I appreciate your help, son. I love you! You can have the leftovers in the fridge for dinner or order food if you like."

"I love you, too, Mom!" Devonte said. "See you later." After his mother left, he appeared to be sad.

"What's wrong?" I stroked the back of his hand.

"I told you, my parents are always so busy. I was hoping to talk to them tonight about becoming an astronomer and wanting to spend more time with them."

"I'm sorry you feel that way. The bright side is that both of your parents will be home tonight. Try talking to them then."

"I guess you're right."

He leaned in to kiss me on the lips, so naturally, I closed my eyes to enjoy the moment.

I opened my eyes, only to see *her* staring at me.

Our eyes met, and it indeed was *her*!

It was her.

I wanted to cry, but I also didn't want to ruin the final moments of my date. This was potentially my last date ever because of her.

Chapter 9

W ho is *her*, you might ask? It was Sè Françoise, a fellow church member. She's what I would call Nice-ty, pretending to be nice but really nasty. She isn't just any church member but the BIGGEST gossip at the church. She knows everyone's—and I mean everyone's—business. All she needs is 0.5 seconds to share the juiciest gossip with the entire congregation. I don't know the whole Bible, but I'm sure it says something about gossip being a sin. Somehow-someway, Sè Françoise conveniently either did not read or skipped this scripture. She knows everyone's business but can't keep track of her children. Her daughter Daphne is a complete garden tool; that's the nicest way to describe her. Her son barely attends school. He was supposed to graduate from high school last year; I think he needs another two years to get enough credits for a diploma. You would think she'd redirect some of her gossiping energy toward helping her children. Some people feel better about themselves by dragging others. Sè Françoise is definitely one of those people.

I contemplated saying hello to her based on cultural norms, even though "Hi" was the last word I wanted to utter to that woman. There was no need to greet Sè Françoise because she left with a sinister smile.

"Manushka, are you okay? Why are you shaking all of a sudden?" Devonte stared at me with a puzzled look, waiting for my response.

Trying to mask my fear and anger, I said, "I'm fine, just a little cold."

"Well, come closer so I can keep you warm." He reached to hug me.

As much as I wanted and needed a comforting hug from Devonte, there was no way I could let it happen now. "Hey, I need to go home; it's getting late."

I was a little paranoid as we walked to the train station together— no hand-holding or hugging for me. Instead, I searched for familiar faces. Devonte and I got off at the same stop. He wanted to walk me home, but I insisted on walking alone. The last thing I wanted was for my mother to see us together. I wasn't sure if I should run home or walk slowly. I was prepared to face the consequences; I lied, and now it was time for me to be accountable for my actions. It was only a matter of time before I got caught. Within seconds of opening the door, I heard my mother's voice. She didn't even give me a chance to walk through the door.

"Manushka Jean-Pierre, *vin jwenn mwen kounye a. Chita la!*"

My mother just called me by my first *and* last name. She just demanded I come to her and sit down. My heart rate rose with every step taken toward her. All I could do was breathe in deeply to maintain composure. Maybe she doesn't know. *No, she knows.* I don't think she'll kill me in front of a witness. My godmother Naomi, who happens to be twenty-one years old, was sitting on the couch observing the situation. I wasn't sure if my mother asked her to come over or if it was divine intervention. If anyone could reason with my mother, it would be Naomi. Thank God that she's here. Despite believing that Naomi would come to my rescue, my heart rate continued to increase. At this moment, it feels like my heart is about to leap out of my chest.

Although my mother is only five feet tall, she's a feisty little person. I tower above her at 5'7", but nothing can stop her from giving me a serious a** whooping. As I took extremely slow steps toward her, she shouted, *"Fè vit!"* Hurry up. I quickly sat on a chair to avoid getting her more upset. Lord, if you can hear me now, please save my life. I know I lied; I promise not to lie anymore and to pay attention at church if you save me from what my mother is about to do, please. There was no way of escaping this moment without divine intervention.

"Manushka, I no send you to school for boys; I send you to learn, to be a doctor, to be a nurse. Sè Françoise tell me she see you with a boy! Manushka, a boy, hmmm!" With both hands on her head, my mother paced back and forth while speaking to herself in Creole.

At this point, I'm sure people outside could hear her, but I didn't care. The look of disappointment on her face as she yelled broke my heart and hurt more than any belt could. She trusted me, and I took advantage of her trust. I started crying uncontrollably, but my mother maintained her stance and continued to yell. Naomi interrupted my mother mid-sentence, asking for a moment to speak to me in my room. My mother was so disgusted by my actions that she agreed, as she wanted me to be removed from her sight immediately.

As soon as we entered the room, Naomi and I sat on the bed. She gave me a tight and comforting hug.

"Manushka, I have to ask: what were you thinking? You know your mother don't play," Naomi said with a perplexed look.

"I wanted to tell her, but I knew what her answer would be. I wish we had better communication. I want to talk to her about so many things, but—" Embarrassed by my actions, I could only look down as I spoke to Naomi.

"Manushka, I totally get where you're coming from, but it is what it is. Even though you don't agree with some of your parents' rules, you need to follow them or face the consequences. It's simple."

I was in complete shock by Naomi's response. My mouth dropped and my eyes widened at the lack of support and understanding; I needed an ally for safety and emotional support.

Naomi continued to speak despite my reaction. She looked directly at me. "Look, I don't know what you expected me to say. You messed up."

What happened to my supportive godmother also affectionately known as "Nennenn"? Naomi always has the best advice, but not today. Aside from my friends, she's the one person I used to feel comfortable talking to on most days. Her mother, Rosaline, died when Naomi was ten, so my mother pretty much raised her; Mommy went above and beyond to provide for, support, and encourage Naomi. Naomi also has a special place in my mother's heart because she greatly resembles her mother. Aunt Roseline and my mother had been practically inseparable. And when she died, my mother went into a deep depression for about a year. I don't know much about counseling, but I'm sure my mother would have benefited from having a few sessions. The whole idea of counseling is taboo in the Haitian community. The misconception is that counseling is for crazy people.

Circling back to Naomi, she attends Hunter College in the city. Her goal is to become a pediatric occupational therapist. Naomi is tall, beautiful, creative, and soft spoken. People are naturally drawn to her, so I'm sure she will be a great occupational therapist. Just so you know, occupational therapy is a healthcare profession that works with people of all age ranges. Naomi says the goal of occupational therapists is to help clients become independent in everyday activities like dressing, shopping, driving, cooking, writing, coloring, and so much more. Occupational therapists can work in hospitals, schools, homes, community centers and a lot of other places. It sounds like a great profession, but that's about all I can remember her saying about it.

"You need to tell me about this boy you're so into," Naomi said. "Seriously, is he worth the risk?"

Finally, I had a reason to smile after being reprimanded by Naomi. "Well, his name is Devonte. I was planning to tell you about him one day, so I guess today is the day."

Naomi did not find my little dance amusing at all; she remained expressionless.

I continued. "He's so nice to me, and he's cute too. No, I mean fine! We can talk about almost anything. He's not like other guys—not that I have dated other guys before. What I mean is that he really respects me, you know. We talk about school and careers, and even went on a couple of dates." I leaned over to whisper in her ear. "We had our first kiss on the Brooklyn Bridge."

Shocked, Naomi moved back and stared at me. "Wait! You kissed a boy on the Brooklyn Bridge, where anyone and everyone could see you? I've heard enough. Let me go speak to your mother to calm this situation down." She walked toward the door. As she reached for the doorknob, Naomi took one last look at me and shook her head in pity.

Not even one ally in the house—the one person I expected to stand by my side was disappointed in me, too.

"Naomi, please—" I attempted to plead my case again, hoping to get her to understand. I wanted her to convince my mother that having a boyfriend now wouldn't ruin my future. "Naomi, my favoritest, bestest, and most amazing nennenn in the whole entire universe—" I got on my knees and clasped both hands.

She pulled the door, paused, and turned around. "And for the record, I'm your only godmother. Now, be quiet before you get into more trouble."

I kneeled silently for a few seconds as the door closed, then sprang into action. Once she left the room, I ran to the door, hoping to hear everything. My mother was yelling at first, but she became much calmer as time progressed. As I pressed my ears against the door, the phone rang. It was Devonte. I fumbled with the phone, trying to silence it quickly. Nerves got to me, and I dropped the phone before answering. Speaking to him even for a second was a risk, but I had to do it.

"Hey, Devonte!"

"What? Why are you whispering? I can barely hear you. Are you OK?" he asked.

"I'll have to fill you in on Monday. I have to go now," I said quickly.

"But Manushka—"

I had no choice but to hang up on Devonte. The last thing I needed was for my mother to hear me speaking to him. So, I turned off the phone and put it away. I was sure my mother was contemplating taking it from me at some point.

After about an hour of standing at the door, I was tired and wanted to go to the bathroom. But stepping into the hallway was not a good idea, at least not until my father got home. My dad is easygoing, a go-with-the-flow kind of guy. Everyone loves him. Nothing seems to bother him too much, although sometimes he's easily influenced by my mother. He works washing dishes at the Ritz-Carlton Hotel in Manhattan six days per week but never complains. My dad takes great pride in his work and ability to provide for his family.

My mother works as a home health aide only four days a week. My parents knew each other as teens in Haiti but lost contact for many years until fate brought them together one afternoon at a party. Determined never to lose touch again, they were married within seven months. They've been married for seventeen years. I honestly think they dated as teens, but my parents would never admit it.

I heard footsteps coming toward my room. Boom, boom, boom. It wasn't my imagination: the floor was literally shaking. Is this it? Is this the end of my teenage life? No, it can't end this way. I hopped on the bed, pretending to do homework. What a relief, it was Naomi.

"Manushka, I was able to calm your mother down. You have to regain her trust again. She wants to speak to you now."

"I'm scared but want to get the punishment over with. Let's go, Naomi." I waited for her to join me as I walked toward the door.

"Your mother wants to speak to you *alone*," she said with a serious look.

"ALONE? Are you crazy? I need you to go with me; no witnesses mean she can kill me out there. Papi, the only other person who can save me, isn't home. I beg of you, Naomi, please come with me." I kneeled on the floor again, hoping she would acknowledge my pain and fear.

"I never knew you were so dramatic. Girl, take your butt out there and go speak to her immediately. I promise you'll be safe. I'll listen by the door, the same way you were when I spoke to your mother. I saw your big feet." Naomi chuckled.

"Just in case I don't make it, always remember that I loved you. You're the bestest godmother a girl could have. You shall inherit the custom artwork that adorns my walls, should I not survive my mother's wrath. Be well, my not-so-fairy godmother." I looked down, trying to make a final appeal for Naomi to join me.

Instead, she pushed me right out the door. With nowhere to hide, I walked toward my mother slowly but not slow enough to annoy her.

"Manushka, *chita,*" my mother said, pointing to the chair beside her.

I proceeded to sit down as she watched my every step. I felt some relief because the shiny black belt was no longer in her hand; it was still within reach, though. I figured during her conversation with Naomi, my mother placed the belt on the chair. Before I could say anything, she spoke in Creole to make sure her message was fully conveyed; I just sat there with both hands on my lap and listened. There was no talking to my mother when she was this upset.

She cleared her throat before saying my full name again but this time, she included my middle name, "Manushka Marie Jean-Pierre?"

I wasn't sure how to respond. Was this a question or a statement? Was there a right or wrong answer?

"Um, yes, Mommy?" I responded while avoiding eye contact.

She asked the question I hoped to avoid, "*Ki kote ou te di mwen ou prale jodi a?*"

I had to be honest now because I was caught in a lie. "I told you I was going to the library, Mommy."

"Library!" she repeated. My mother made sure to emphasize every syllable in the word library.

"Manushka, you lie to me, Manushka, hmm!"

"Mommy, I'm not lying. I did go to the library first. And then—and then, I went out with my friend from school."

My mother's eyes were red. I wasn't sure if it was the result of anger, sadness, embarrassment, disappointment or all four. "Boyfriend, Manushka? I don't send to school for boyfriend, OK?" I remained both still and silent hoping the look on my face would trigger some degree of empathy. Wasn't she young and imperfect at one point? By her actions alone, I could tell there was no room for reasoning with my mother, at least not now. Confined to the chair, all I could do was watch, wait, and listen.

Huffing and puffing she reached for the belt causing my heart to leap into my throat. I instinctively placed a trembling hand over my chest while gasping for air. Wide with a mix of fear and anticipation, my eyes were fixed on her every move. The thought of running came to mind, but that would only make the situation worse. It was time to face judgment for my untruths but there was surely a better way to handle this situation, right? A loving conversation while sipping tea and eating crackers would be my preference but definitely not hers. My sweet mom was nowhere to be found. At this point, her actions were cloaked in unpredictability. She picked up the leather belt with a swift, decisive motion and deliberately placed it on the cold, hard surface of the kitchen counter, making sure it was within my visual field; she was sending me a direct message. Suddenly with a burst of energy, she aggressively grabbed a wooden chair slamming it squarely in front of me. The sound of the chair making contact with the floor echoed in the tense air between us. Without a word, my mother sat down, her eyes locking onto mine with an intensity that was both new and unnerving. The power in her prolonged gaze seemed to pierce right through my soul. This was the first time I had ever witnessed and experienced the look in my mother's eyes.

To be honest, my mother has only really threatened me with a spanking. I'm a good kid who never broke the rules until now. It was finally time for her speech, and as she spoke, I kept shouting, "I'm sixteen, and most people my age have a boyfriend. So why can't I? It's just not fair," in my head—the safest place for my thoughts. I only spoke up when questions were asked. My mother didn't care what other kids were allowed to do. During the speech, she said she didn't want me to make the same mistakes she made as a teenager. But what mistakes? I hoped for a moment of transparency, but that didn't happen. Being the eldest of five children really impacted my mother. She always felt the need to be strong and in control of everything, never wanting to accept help from others but always willing to come to everyone's rescue. She told me her dream was for me to be successful, to have more than she knew was possible. She told me to be careful with dating. I wanted to tell my mother that Devonte wasn't like other boys, but I knew in my heart it wasn't the right moment.

"Manushka Marie Jean-Pierre, *mwen pa janm vle tande pale de ou menm ak ti gason sa a ankò. Ou tande mwen. Mwen p ap di sa ankò, tande?*" Oh, no! My mother was serious about me not hanging out with Devonte again. She said she never wanted to hear his name again. "*Mèsi Bondye pou Sè Françoise,*" she continued. "*Si se pa t pou li, m pa t ap konnen.*" She just thanked God for Sè Francoise, the gossip. I had another thought about that woman, and thanking God was far from it. That woman ruined my life. I could feel my facial expression change as my mother mentioned her name, but I had to contain my feelings; I had no choice. The last thing I wanted was for my mother to think I was giving her attitude. Just when I thought she was done speaking, my mother said, " *Ou ka remèsye Naomi paske li sove w jodi a. Sentiwon sa te pou ou. Ou gen chans.* Hmm!" According to my mother, I should thank Naomi for saving me from a spanking. So, she did come through for me. I love my godmother. I would have to thank Naomi next time since she'd quietly slipped out the door while my mother was speaking.

Of course, she took my phone. From now on, I was required to give her my phone every evening at seven o'clock.

The weekend was so somber. I cooked, did homework, and attended church.

Who's the first person I saw after entering the church? You guessed it: Sè Françoise, the gossip. Unfortunately, I had to greet her with a kiss as my mother looked on. The truth is, I wanted to strangle the woman, but a less violent approach would be to pretend she was invisible. Sè Françoise hugged me and asked how I was doing as if she didn't know I had gotten into trouble because of her big mouth. The woman placed my life in danger but acted as though nothing happened. Oh, I forgot to tell you that the word *Sè* means *sister* in Creole. That evil woman is no sister of mine. Out of spite, I would love to expose her children's actions and that woman's lack of parenting skills to the entire congregation. In fact, as the pastor spoke, I envisioned myself in his position, speaking on the mic.

"Brothers and sisters of the congregation, we have one amongst us today, one who gossips for breakfast, lunch, and dinner. One who is so busy minding people's business that she doesn't have enough time to care for her own children. That woman is Sè Françoise. Everyone, turn to your neighbor and say, 'Sè Françoise is a gossip—'"

As I was about to finish the sermon in my head, my mother discretely pinched me hard enough to snap me out of my thoughts. This particular Sunday, she wanted to make sure I paid attention to the sermon as the pastor preached about lying. I mean, did Sè Françoise tell him? Did the whole church know about my indiscretions? My only ally at the church, Widelene, was nowhere to be found that Sunday. Her mother wasn't at church either, which was strange. As usual, I waited a couple of hours after church as my mother spoke to her friends. I was looking forward to school on Monday to fill my friends in on the weekend drama.

Chapter 10

I arrived early at the morning meet-up spot. Before I could say anything, Janae shouted, "Manushka, we've been calling you all weekend. Where the heck were you? Widelene and I had the craziest weekend."

"Whoa, slow down, girl. You wouldn't believe the kind of weekend I had. But go ahead, tell me what happened." I wondered what could have been crazier than my experience. Widelene stood quietly as Janae spoke, so I knew something was definitely wrong.

"Okay, so Widelene and I tried calling you to join us, but you didn't pick up the phone. So we went without you. While walking through the mall, those guys, you know, the ones who try talking to us all the time—"

"Yeah, yeah!" I was eager to hear what happened. "Go ahead!"

Janae continued, "So they tried talking to me and Widelene again, but this time it was different. There was a new guy with them. So, we politely said that we were busy and not interested. The new guy followed us as we walked away. He said, 'Yo, I wanna talk to you. What? You think you too good for me? Tryna act all bougie, sh** and you ain't that fine. I said come here; I wanna talk to you.' At this point, Widelene and I walked faster, practically running as this guy began chasing us. His friends laughed as though this was some form of entertainment they routinely indulged in. The guy grabbed Widelene's arm forcefully and then pushed her against a wall several times. We screamed, but the crazy thing is, people ignored us; I guess they thought it was a domestic dispute. Widelene and I continued screaming as I punched the guy, hoping it would hurt him enough to let her go. The more we screamed and tried to fight back, the angrier he became. Finally, one of the guys said, 'Let her go, man, she ain't worth it.' He said, 'Nah, man, this chick disrespected me, yo.' When I tell you, this guy was beyond scary: his eyes were dark and dead looking like he didn't have a soul. Pure evil was all I saw."

"Oh my God, Janae!" I exclaimed, taking a quick glance at a motionless Widelene.

Janae said, "Everything happened so fast. He took something out of his pocket at one point, then aimed for Widelene's face. I hit his arm as hard as I could, which caused his hand to move toward her shoulder." Janae stopped speaking for a moment, covering her face with her hands. I could see her chest rapidly moving up and down. I could almost hear every breath she was taking. She managed to calm down a little, then said, "God must have heard my prayers because a cop who happened to be shopping with his daughter heard all the commotion and immediately approached us. Out of fear, the guys ran off. The cop made a call, and before we knew it, four officers arrived. We gave them a description of the guys and then continued to speak to the cops. I looked over at Widelene, who was visibly shaking, and noticed blood steadily dripping from her hand."

When Janae mentioned the bleeding, Widelene began rubbing her hand. I couldn't believe what I was hearing. Janae made sure to fill me in on all the details. She said, "I immediately brought the bleeding to the officer's attention. He called an ambulance to take her to the hospital. Our parents met us there. Widelene ended up with stitches on her hand." Janae paused for a minute, waiting for Widelene to speak, but she didn't say anything. "Later that night, an officer called, letting us know all three guys had been arrested. Knowing they were in custody was a relief, but it didn't calm my fear or ease my anger. Poor Widelene had a huge bruise on her arm and stitches on her hand."

"Are you still in pain?" I asked Widelene, wanting to make sure my friend was okay. "How are you feeling?" Holding back tears, I waited for my friend to respond.

Widelene spoke in a gentle whisper as she avoided eye contact. "I'm still shaken up. That's why I missed church on Sunday. My arm and hand still hurt. You can practically see the guy's entire handprint around my arm. My mother said she doesn't want any problems but believes something needs to be done. I always thought of myself as super strong, but right now, I feel so weak and vulnerable. Why couldn't I fight back instead of freezing up?" She sounded discouraged.

"You were attacked by someone physically stronger than you. Feeling vulnerable, weak, and scared is normal. I learned in class that people respond to trauma differently. The responses are fight, flight, and freeze. Like many people, your body froze and that's okay." I hoped my words would be somewhat encouraging.

Widelene shook her head in agreement. "My mother wanted me to stay home, but that would mean crying all day. Being at school with you guys is a good distraction, I guess. I'm tired of crying. I need to talk about a different topic, like your date with Devonte? Go ahead, spill the details."

As much as I wanted to share my weekend drama it was obvious that my friends needed support. "I'll tell you during lunch," I said. We did a quick group hug before parting ways.

Still devastated about their experience, I struggled to focus in class. I was happy they were safe, but also couldn't imagine the fear they'd experienced. *Something needs to be done about those guys. What gives them the right to mistreat and disrespect women?* Had the police officer not been present, who knows what could have happened? *It's only a matter of time before those guys attack someone else.*

I was in the midst of these thoughts while walking between classes. When Mrs. Franca stopped me to get an update on the art competition submission, it was a good distraction because my mind was so scattered.

"Manushka, have you finalized a concept for the competition yet?" Mrs. Franca asked, curiously. "Be sure to mail the preliminary draft before the deadline."

"Yes, I finalized the concept and color scheme. I completed the preliminary draft of the painting and mailed it out over the weekend," I said, still feeling a little nervous.

Sensing my nervousness, Mrs. Franca said, "In twenty-one years of teaching, you're by far one of the most talented students I have had. Like I said before, between your talent, passion for art, and undeniable gift, I truly believe you have a bright future. And I'll keep reminding you of your talent until you believe it. I'm looking forward to the competition. Oh, I forgot to tell you. There has been a last-minute change so our school will host the competition. We plan to use the gymnasium for the event. I'll create a sign-up sheet for volunteers later this week."

"I would love to help," I said.

As I walked away from Mrs. Franca, I thought about what she said. She was the second person to say that I have a gift. The thought of people believing in my talents made me smile; I temporarily forgot about my weekend drama and the craziness Janae and Widelene experienced. I made it to my next class right before the late bell rang, and completed a group assignment. There's always someone in a group who doesn't complete their share of work but still gets full credit. I hated being paired with those students, but it was inevitable.

I went straight to the cafeteria after class ended. Every second counted because we had so much to talk about.

"Hey, girls!" I placed my backpack on the table.

"Okay, tell us what happened this weekend," Widelene said eagerly.

"Well, Devonte and I had the best date ever. He took me to the Metropolitan Museum of Art, which I absolutely loved. Then we went to a fancy restaurant. Between the candles on the table and fancy chandeliers, the atmosphere was so romantic. I mean, everything was just perfect until his mother called. Don't get me wrong, his mother is nice and all—"

Janae interrupted. "Wait! You met his mother? You official, girl, that boy likes you!"

"OK, so after his mother left, we ended up kissing each other briefly. And when I opened my eyes, Sè Françoise from the church was right there, staring at me. Now, you already know, before I even got home, my mother knew what happened. She pretty much took my phone. I have to turn in my phone every night. No more late-night calls with Devonte. He doesn't even know what happened. I need to tell him now." I scanned the cafeteria for him. "To be honest, I knew it was a matter of time before my mother found out because I was becoming a little reckless with the weekly dates." I waved at Devonte.

Janae said, "Wow, Manushka, seems like you had a tough weekend. The bright side is that you're still alive to share your story."

We all laughed. I was happy to see my friends laughing even though it was short. I could tell Janae was still hurting by the way she laughed. Janae was one of those people with the loud laughs you could hear from across the room. This time was different. I could barely hear her even though she was standing in front of me. Surprisingly, Widelene laughed a little more than I expected, but then again, she was one of those people who could find joy in any situation.

"Catch you later; time to fill Devonte in," I said, walking away.

Devonte quickly walked toward me. Before I could even say hello, he said, "Manushka, I tried calling all weekend, but you didn't pick up. Did I do something wrong? Did I say something that made you upset? Seriously, what happened?"

"No, you didn't do or say anything wrong. I enjoyed our date. You put so much effort into making it special, so I appreciate it. Someone from my church saw us kissing and immediately told my mother. My mom was mad and took my phone—no more late-night phone calls. I'm sorry," I said, embarrassed.

"Sorry you got in trouble. Since we can't have weekend dates anymore, we'll just have to hang out at lunch. We can spend the last ten minutes of lunch together. What do you think? I mean, it's the least I could do since I'm the reason you got in trouble." The look on his face was apologetic.

"I can't let you take the blame for this. It wasn't your fault. I should have known someone would see us together at one point and tell my mother." I reached out for his hand to comfort him. "Hanging out during the last ten minutes of lunch sounds like a great idea. That gives us time to hang out with our friends and each other." I was so relieved that Devonte was supportive and understood my situation.

We hugged right before walking to class. I guess we'd have to consider walks along the hallway and lunch together in the cafeteria to be our new version of dates. Knowing Devonte and I were able to work something out made the day a little better. The last thing I wanted was to lose my phone *and* my boyfriend.

Surprisingly, French class was getting better. It still wasn't easy, but I put more effort into studying, which improved my grades. A change in attitude also helped. Instead of saying that I hated French, I now considered it the class I really, really disliked. See, a slight shift in perspective makes a world of difference. The school day ended. I met up with Devonte for a few minutes before meeting up with my girls.

"Hey, wait for me!" I shouted, running toward Janae and Widelene.

"Oh, we waited a few minutes and thought you left," Janae said.

"Sorry, I was talking to Devonte. After this past weekend, I don't want to get caught talking to him outside of school, it's too soon.. I'm not trying to get in trouble again. Since my mother won't let me go to the library anymore, would you like to come to my house this Saturday?" I asked.

"Sure," Widelene said.

"I'm down, but make sure you have some of that black rice for me." Janae rubbed her stomach and smiled as she thought about my mother's cooking.

"I'll try to make you a little something," I said.

"Thanks but no thanks, Manushka. Now you know you can't throw down in the kitchen like your mom."

"Janae, even though you just insulted me, I'll still ask my mom to hook you up." We all laughed before parting ways.

Janae and Widelene had to meet with a police officer and their parents after school, so they took the train in the opposite direction. When I arrived home, my mother was the only one there, which was a relief—no neighbors or people from the church. I walked in cautiously, not wanting to say or do the wrong thing. She didn't need any more reasons to be mad at me. I felt guilty and angry because of the whole Devonte situation. If my mother had been open to the idea of me having a boyfriend, I wouldn't have had to lie. I mean, other girls my age were allowed to date. I greeted my mother with a kiss on the cheek, then proceeded to engage in a little small talk.

"Mommy, Janae and Widelene are coming over on Saturday. We're going to do our homework together. Is that okay?" I asked with a smile. "Oh, and Janae wants to know if you can make diri djondjon with shrimp. She said you make the best rice."

My mother took great pride in her cooking and loved feeding people. She showed love through actions, whether it was cooking, cleaning, making donations, or helping others. In fact, many of her relatives in Haiti, both young and old, relied on my mother to send food, clothing, cellphones, you name it. Being able to help others gave her something to be proud of, you know, a sense of accomplishment.

"Okay, I make the rice for Janae."

Since getting into trouble, I made more of an effort to speak to my mother a little more every day. She was still guarded about certain topics, which made me curious to know if my parents dated as teens, but I could tell she was taking that secret to the grave.

"Mommy, the art competition is coming soon. I can't wait to show you what I made. It's going to be a big surprise." I tried to contain some of my excitement.

My mother's response was more of a half-smile as she continued wiping down the kitchen counters. Her reaction—or lack of reaction, I guess—was disappointing. Since this was my first competition, I hoped and expected more excitement from her.

Chapter 11

Thankfully, the week passed quickly; it was time to have my friends over. Naturally, I woke up early to clean my room, bathroom, and living room before Janae and Widelene arrived. I helped my mother clean the kitchen and then gave her a hug. I always initiate embraces because physical displays of affection from my mother are rare. She loves me, but hugging just isn't something she does often.

As soon as the bell rang, I ran downstairs to open the door for my friends. "Hey, just a reminder. Whatever you do, don't mention Devonte's name."

"Don't worry, girl, we know better," Widelene said while placing a hand on my shoulder.

"Devonte, oops, I mean, I will not mention the name. I'm just trying to get to your mother's food. Now get out of my way!" Janae playfully pushed me aside then began walking up the stairs.

"Hello, Mrs. Jean-Pierre," Janae and Widelene said simultaneously; they almost sounded like a choir the way their voices harmonized.

"Janae, I make the rice for you," my mother said with a proud smile.

"Thank you, Mrs. Jean-Pierre. I've been thinking about your rice since last night." Without hesitation, Janae hugged my mother. I could tell by the widening of my mother's eyes she was momentarily taken aback, but she reciprocated the hug.

"Are you guys ready to start studying?" I asked. As much as I wanted to study, I also wanted to find out what happened when Janae and Widelene met with the police.

"Girl, I have to eat first!" The seriousness of Janae's tone and the look on her face made us all laugh.

"Okay, Janae, we'll eat first," I said.

My mother quickly sprang into action, placing food onto our plates. When Janae and Widelene told my mother the food was enough, she added two more spoons of rice as though she was feeding a hungry football team. For a moment, everyone was silent as we all enjoyed the food.

"Janae, I put some rice for your mother." Mommy always makes to-go plates for Janae.

Both Janae and Widelene thanked my mother before heading to my room.

Before we could sit down, I asked, "What happened when you met with the officer?"

"He told us that the new guy is still in jail." Widelene sighed. "It turns out that he'd attacked other girls earlier that week but managed to get away before the cops arrived. The attacker cut all the girls with a razor blade, probably the same one he used on Widelene. One of the girls was cut on her face. The officer said we may have to testify if he doesn't take a plea. Even if he's sentenced, I'm sure he won't be in jail long. Sentencing can be anywhere between three months to two years since he's a minor."

Seeing her look of despair, I sat beside Widelene, gently placing my arm around her shoulders.Feeling and seeing the pain in her eyes, Janae immediately joined in putting an arm around her shoulder also. We held our friend tight, reminding her she wasn't alone.

"Sorry, I hate to spoil this moment of silence, but what happened to the other guys?" For some reason, Widelene didn't mention them.

"Seems like they had a good lawyer. Technically, since they didn't attack me, there were no grounds to keep them in jail. So, I don't plan on going to the mall anytime soon. It's just not safe anymore."

Janae began pacing back and forth while biting her fingernails, which she only did when upset or in deep thought. "Something has to be done!" As Widelene and I looked in her direction, Janae continued without hesitation. "We should be able to shop at the mall without fear of being harassed and attacked. I couldn't sleep last night. This situation has been replaying in my head almost every day." She sat down across from us. It was a somber moment until, in usual Janae fashion, she decided to tell a joke. She said, "Hey, if I don't go to the mall anymore, where in the world will I get pretzels and Cinnabons? Those frozen pretzels and Cinnabons at the supermarket just don't hit the spot. You know I'm right!"

Her joke was right on time. Laughter was much needed.

Standing to regain our attention, Janae said, "All jokes aside, I've been brainstorming all night about what we can do. The only idea I came up with is getting whoever owns the mall to install some kind of emergency alert system in a few areas. It would be like the outdoor emergency towers we saw when we toured college campuses last summer. If they can have those outside, why not make an indoor version?"

"That sounds like a great idea, Janae! So, what's the plan? How can we help you make this happen?" I was eager to show support. I didn't want to be on the sidelines; I wanted to be a part of the change. I looked at Widelene, who seemed a little more comfortable as she listened to Janae and I speak.

"Well, based on information online and what I learned in some student government classes, people respond to numbers. The first step would be to get a petition going. I figured starting with an online petition would be more effective because we can reach people faster. We can also stand in front of the mall to get signatures. I spoke to my mom about the petition; she thinks it's a good idea. Are y'all in?"

Between the smiling, standing, and hand gestures, Janae's excitement was undeniable. She wanted to be part of a change that would positively affect everyone.

"Girl, you know I'm in," Widelene said." If there is a way for me to stop this from happening to someone else, I will do whatever I can to help. To be honest, I like the idea of doing an online petition because I'm afraid to go to the mall right now."

"I'm down too!" I looked directly at Widelene, confirming she wasn't alone. "You know I got you! When one of us hurts, we all hurt."

"Okay, we need a name for the petition. I've been trying to think of something since last night. How about Shop Safely, Keep Our Girls Safe, Mall Safety for All? What do you think?" Janae eagerly awaited our response.

"They all kind of sound good, but not catchy enough," I said with some degree of apprehension. As a friend, I had to be honest. I hate it when people are dishonest! I've seen girls hanging out with their friends, wearing some of the craziest outfits, I mean real crazy. I've seen mismatched outfits, boobs hanging out, too short, too tight, and just ratchet. Who lets their friend go out that way? How did they manage to say, "Oh, girl, you look good," with a straight face, knowing they were lying? I think honesty should be an unspoken agreement between best friends. Shifting focus back to my friends, I could see Widelene and Janae thinking about possible names for the petition.

"My Body, My Time, My Decision – Mall Safety Petition," Widelene shouted.

"That's it, we have a name! I don't know about you, Manushka, but I love it," Janae said approvingly.

"It's catchy and attention grabbing; I'm feeling it too."

Janae, Widelene, and I all sang, "We have a name, we have a name," as we danced together.

The celebration was cut short as Janae shifted our focus back to the details of the petition. As we continued to work, Widelene became a little apprehensive about sharing her experience with people she didn't know. "Guys, I want to be a part of making a difference, but what do you think people will say when they know what happened to me? Do you think they'll treat me differently or make fun of the situation? Do you think anyone will even care enough to sign the petition?"

Her questions took us by surprise; we didn't have any right answers. This whole petition thing was new to us. The only information we had was what we read, not personal experiences.

I wanted Widelene to know that her concerns were valid. "No matter what people say or think, we'll be right by your side." I sat beside her. "We can only hope and pray that people will sign this petition, especially since other girls were attacked at the mall."

Janae chimed in. "Yes, we'll be right by your side. We're doing this thing together."

After sitting silently for a few minutes, Widelene said, "Okay, as scared as I am to share my experience with strangers, let's keep going. Who knows? Something good can come out of this situation. And, like you both said, I'm not alone."

After Widelene spoke, we found a website to start the petition. Within the petition, we shared Widelene's experience and the idea of installing indoor emergency tower systems in the mall. The next order of business was to share the link with everyone we knew. Within two hours of making the petition live, we had twenty-five signatures, and three of the signatures were ours.

"Even though we don't have a lot of signatures yet, I'm still excited about this petition. And I'm so happy to have you two as best friends. We've been working on this for hours, so let's talk about something else." Widelene turned to face me. "Hey, Manushka, I know you always have something going on, so fill us in, girl."

"I told you guys pretty much everything," I said. "Oh, but I forgot to tell you I have a sister in Haiti, my father's daughter. She'll be moving in with us in December."

"Wait, hold up, girl, you never said anything to us about no sister. When did this happen?" Janae dramatically waved her hands in the air, pleading for answers.

"Well, I only know her from a few pictures. Her name is Fabienne, and she's eighteen," I said.

"You mean to tell me your dad was creeping on your momma? I didn't know Mr. Jean-Pierre had game like that." Seeing the look on my face Janae chuckled before saying,, "Girl, you know I'm playing."

"My father moved to the U.S. from Haiti when Fabienne was one. He was never married to her mother. Seems like my parents knew each other as teens back in Haiti. I guess my dad is kind of smooth; he got game," I joked.

Widelene was still slightly shocked by the news, considering our mothers often spoke to each other. "I know you always have something going on, but this news surprised me. I would've heard about this if my mother knew. So, when is Fabienne moving in?"

"Welp, she's arriving in December, around Christmas. My Christmas gift this year is a whole sister, not a baby sister, but an older sister. I barely have any space in this room, and sadly, I'll have to share it with Fabienne." I was feeling unapologetically selfish. I mean, did my parents even consider how this situation would affect me? How about my thoughts and feelings?

"You know, moving here from Haiti is not going to be easy," Widelene said. "Between learning a new language, getting acclimated to the school system, making new friends, and trying to understand the American culture, Fabienne is going to need all the support she can get. You already know that some people will make fun of her for being Haitian. I feel your pain, but Fabienne may have a hard time adjusting. When I moved here from Haiti, the first couple of years were rough, between learning the language and being bullied because of my accent. Try to be positive. Besides, you always wished you had a sister, and now you do."

"Yeah, Manushka, try to be positive. Widelene and I will support you."

"I guess you're right. I'll try my best to be positive about the situation." I silently thanked God for my friends because I seriously needed the positive vibes. But was I wrong for feeling a little selfish?

"Hey, my mother just texted me. She's on her way right now. Widelene, we can drop you off at home if you want. Let's go but I'm not leaving without my to-go plate. I'm taking my riri Joe-Joe with me."

Widelene and I both laughed at the way Janae pronounced the rice.

"Girl, repeat after me; it's di-ri d-jon d-jon," I said, slowly enough for her to catch on.

Janae laughed hysterically. "Listen, girl, I don't make the thing; I just eat it. Now give me my rice."

I grabbed the to-go plate and placed it in one of those tiny supermarket plastic bags, you know, the ones you get whenever you go shopping. My mother insisted on keeping them all: brown ones, white ones, even the ones with tiny holes at the bottom. She was convinced each one of them would come in handy one day. When her back was turned, I stuffed a couple of those bags at the bottom of the trash. There was no way she needed all of them as far as I was concerned. I walked my friends outside as we engaged in a final conversation. We had a great time together, as usual. We got a lot done but not any homework.

After hanging out with my girls, I spent some time with my mother before calling it a night. As I lay in my bed, I couldn't help but think about Devonte. I missed our late-night conversations. Now that we were spending less time together, I was beginning to feel a little insecure about our relationship. Would he lose interest in me? Would he break up with me to date a girl who could hang out more? Did he miss me as much as I missed him? Feeling down, I was at a loss over my relationship with Devonte; I just couldn't figure out what to do. As I continued to think about him, my mother, of course, busted into my room.

"Manunu, church tomorrow, wake up early. Here is your phone, be careful, okay," my mother said authoritatively. No more words required. I fully understood what she meant.

I was elated to have my phone again. I mean, my phone was like an extension of my body, my outside brain, my third arm, my connection to my friends, and my portal to the world of art and fashion. Who can survive without a phone?

"Thank you, Mommy. You can trust me," I said with a huge smile. As much as I wanted to call Devonte, I knew it was the wrong thing to do, at least right now. I didn't want to betray my mother's trust so soon, but next week is another story. I didn't have any plans to break up with my boyfriend. I just needed to be more careful.

"Hmm," my mother said as she walked out the door, shaking her head. For a moment it felt as though she was reading my mind, which was a little scary.

That night, I fell asleep, hugging my beloved phone.

Chapter 12

Bright and early in the morning, I was awakened by my mother's voice telling me to wake up because it was almost time to leave. "Leve leve, leve, Manunu! Li prèske lè pou n ale."

I quickly rolled out of bed, showered, and dressed for church. I didn't want to give my mother another reason to take my phone again, so I was standing by the door, waiting, by the time she put on her coat for our weekly trek to church. Today was especially cold, so my legs were freezing. My mother never allowed me to wear pants to church. Rather than having a debate, I accepted the rule and wore skirts or dresses. Of course, I made sure my outfits were cute from head to toe.

We made it to church in time and found our assigned seats. Seats weren't actually assigned, but everyone found their preferred seats over the years. As I prepared for my mind to drift during the testimonies, I noticed Sè Françoise making her way to the front. There's no way I was going to miss this drama. I quickly shook my head to refocus and sat up straight; full attention was required right now. For the first time, I wanted to sit in the front row. Sè Françoise dramatically approached the front of the church. She grabbed the microphone and then faced the congregation. Wearing her Sunday best with a cloth on her head, she began to speak. What was she going to say this time? Wait, was she planning on exposing me to the entire congregation? My palms began to sweat. Suddenly, I was nervous about the nature of her speech. I discreetly looked over at my mother, who was very attentive.

As I turned my head back to face the altar, our eyes met. Sè Françoise was staring directly at me, and it wasn't my imagination. Unsure of how to react, I awkwardly smiled. Sè Françoise smiled back. Out of all the people in the church, how did our eyes meet? Why was she looking at me? Was this intentional? I slid to the edge of the seat, prepared to listen to every word she spoke.

I was safe—no mention of my indiscretions. I took a deep breath before sliding back into my seat. Blah, blah, blah, followed by sharing the goodness of God. She talked about her children being a blessing. Sè Françoise's testimony was general, but the theatrics that accompanied it were hilarious. At one point, I couldn't contain my laughter. My mother's immediate pinch, quickly accompanied by the look of death, reminded me that I was in church. The temporary moment of fear and throbbing on my forearm had caused some discomfort, but not enough to stop laughing. I looked over at Widelene, who signaled me to meet by the bathroom.

"Excuse me, excuse me, excuse me." I eagerly made my way past the people seated beside me. Exiting the row always felt awkward, but I was on a mission. As I walked out of the sanctuary, I heard shouts of *amen* and *hallelujah* as Sè Françoise continued her testimony.

"Yo, Manushka, wait up, yo."

I turned around only to see Sè Françoise's son, Claude, trying to catch up to me. "What do you want?" I asked with an attitude, hoping he fully understood that I was not and would never be interested in him.

"You been lookin' real good lately," he said, licking his chapped lips, mistakenly thinking I would find him sexy. "Listen, I been watchin' you, waitin' for the right time to ask you out on a date."

"I got a man, and besides, your mother is sharing a testimony. Shouldn't you be in there listening?" I asked, curious about his response.

"I love my mom but she probably lying. Image is everything to that woman."

I smiled at him for the first time ever, but only briefly. I didn't want Claude thinking I was in any way entertaining the idea of going on a date with him.

Seeing Widelene behind him, I ran my hand over my head, signaling her to come and save me. Understanding the signal, Widelene walked over. "Hey, Claude, I need to speak to Manushka right now. It's an emergency; you know, girl talk."

"Aight, Manushka, hit me up on my phone if you wanna go on that date."

First of all, I didn't even have his number. And I wish he would stop licking his lips and put some Vaseline, Chapstick, butter, or oil on those things, ugh. He was walking backward slowly, trying to look at me seductively, only to trip after three steps. Widelene and I couldn't help but laugh at him. In response to our laughter, he turned around and walked away fast.

"So, what's the emergency?" I asked. "Your acting was so compelling; you even had me convinced something was wrong with you." We both laughed on our way to the bathroom. "Thanks for saving me, girl," I added.

Once in the bathroom, we looked under the stalls to make sure we were alone.

"Yep, no one is in here," Widelene said. "I had to leave the service because Sè Françoise had me laughing. I think she missed her calling as an actress. And to top it off, everyone in there was shouting 'amen' and 'hallelujah,' knowing full well that lady was lying through her teeth. I had to leave before I burst out laughing. The last thing I wanted was for my mother to pinch me."

"I sure do wish I had as much self-control as you. I started laughing then my mother gave me the look of death, followed by a pinch. Not just a regular pinch—this was the pinch and spin version, the most painful one." Just thinking about the pinch triggered some pain that could only be soothed by rubbing my arm. "The pain wasn't enough to keep me from laughing, though." I chuckled.

"Girl, you're crazy. So, since when is Claude interested in you?"

"I don't know, and I don't even care because I'm not interested. Girl, you know how I feel about Devonte. To be honest, I'm nervous about our relationship now. Since my mom found out about him, thanks to that testimony-giving gossip and actress Sè Françoise, I haven't been speaking to him much. Girl, no more late-night calls. We pretty much only speak at school. I hope he doesn't lose interest in me."

"I've seen the way Devonte looks at you. You have nothing to worry about at all," Widelene said confidently.

"I guess you're right. Anyway, we need to go back before my mother comes out here looking for me."

As we reentered the sanctuary, Sè Françoise was just finishing her testimony. At that moment, our eyes met again, this was beginning to feel very intentional. Why was she staring at me? Everything in me wanted to yell at that woman or at least ignore her, but since I didn't want to get in trouble, I politely waved. The pastor preached, but this time around, I paid attention. The sermon was interesting. The pastor talked about gifts from God and using our unique gifts for His glory. His message made me think about the upcoming art competition, which was only two months away. I had mixed emotions: confidence, nervousness, fear, self-doubt, and excitement. I must admit, this was an on-time message. I may try to pay attention to the sermons more often.

Finally, church was over. Of course, I had to wait for my mother to finish her conversation with the ladies. This time around, Widelene had to leave early, so I was left alone waiting until Claude decided to join me. "What up, girl! You thought about what I asked you earlier?"

I had to scramble and think of a way to get rid of him. The only way to do it was to talk about something he really disliked. Knowing how much Claude avoided school, I knew that would be the only topic to make him leave me alone. I said, "I was thinking if we hang out, we should do a study date, you know, like at the library. I really love school, and my grades are important to me. How are your grades? What's your favorite subject? Do you plan to take any advanced courses? I absolutely love science; learning about DNA, RNA, mRNA, cellular replication, and photosynthesis is intriguing. I especially love the atmospheric genealogy of hybrids. So, what do you think of the atmospheric genealogy of hybrids?"

Truthfully, I just put those three words together to sound smart. I don't even think this branch of genealogy is a real thing, but it worked.

I could see Claude scrambling to come up with an answer, but I had to play it cool. "Well, um, I find the atmospheric genealogy of hybrids interesting also," he said. I could see sweat beads forming on his forehead with each passing second. Claude repositioned himself on the chair— an indication of discomfort. I had to keep going; this was an opportunity to make sure he would never approach me again. I needed him to get the whole idea of us going on a date out of his head immediately and completely.

"Really? What part do you find the most interesting?" I was eager to hear his response.

"The part about—oh, I think I hear my mother. Gotta go, catch you next time," he said, moving quicker than I had ever seen him move. By the time I blinked, Claude was gone. That was the absolute last time Claude would be asking me on a date. Mission accomplished!

Finally, my mother's conversation ended, and it was time to go home. The pastor's wife offered to drop us off this time since it was raining. I was grateful for the ride, considering we didn't even bring umbrellas.

Chapter 13

I met my girls at our usual meet-up spot in the morning. After glancing at my watch, I couldn't help but smile. "Good morning! Have you both noticed I've been early every morning for the past few weeks? That's grounds for a celebration." I placed emphasis on the word *early* to get my point across. But a moment of silence was not what I anticipated after the announcement. I mean, they should be excited too. Did I miss something?

"Okay, but you're supposed to be early," Janae said. "What do you want? A parade or something?" Cupping both hands around her mouth, she shouted, "Manushka has been early for school for the past three weeks. Yes, ladies and gentlemen, three whole weeks. A parade for this great achievement will be taking place soon. Please stand by for details."

After we all laughed, Janae continued, "I'm just joking; I'm proud of you, Manushka."

"You know, being early actually relieves some of my morning stress," I said. "Listen, I have to cut my lunch with the both of you a little short today to catch up with Devonte. I hope you understand."

"I know you haven't been speaking to him much since your mother found out about your little rendezvous," Widelene said. "I have to retake a test during lunch, so I'll catch up with you after school."

"I won't be at lunch either," Janae said. "I have to work on a speech today with a couple of people from the debate team."

"Seems like we're all busy. Catch you later," I said before walking away.

"Manushka, please stop by my room before you go to lunch," Mrs. Franca said as we walked past each other in the hallway.

I nodded as my mind raced. If my submission was accepted, why wouldn't she just tell me? Or maybe my submission wasn't accepted, and she wanted to gently break the news to me.

I couldn't focus in class no matter how hard I tried. All I thought about was meeting with Mrs. Franca.

My heart skipped a beat as Devonte approached me in the hallway between periods. "Hey, Manushka," he said with a smile.

"Hey, Devonte," I was smiling ear to ear. It had been a while since we had one of our lengthy conversations.

"I missed you, and I miss speaking to you every night. Are we good?" he asked.

"Of course, we're good. You know my mother flipped out when she heard I was hanging out with you. Just to clarify, it's not you, it's just the idea of me having a boyfriend. That is not something she wants to entertain anytime soon. She's been walking into my room more than usual. Since I don't want to get in trouble again, I decided not to use my phone at night," I explained, hoping he'd understand my rationale.

For a moment, Devonte looked disappointed. "Listen, the last thing I want is for you to get in more trouble because of me."

I reached for his hand. "Hey, I think we need to talk a little more. Can we hang out together for the whole lunch period?"

He shook his head in agreement. "Cool, that works for me."

"Okay, meet me outside of Mrs. Franca's room. She needs to tell me something about the art competition," I said right before entering the classroom.

"Hello, Manushka," she said. *Enough with the pleasantries. Share the news now,* I thought. "Well, I heard from the art committee," she said. A long pause followed. *Hurry up and say it: they hated my submission.* Why was she making me suffer? *Why did I even consider entering the competition? What was I thinking?* "Manushka? Manushka, are you okay?" she asked, interrupting my thoughts.

Squeezing the straps of my backpack tightly, I responded, "I'm fine, just anxious to hear the news."

"Well, the committee provided me with feedback regarding your submission. And they absolutely loved it! I had no doubt they would. You made it!" she said with both hands in the air.

"Are you serious? They loved my submission?"

"As serious as a heart attack. A friend on the committee said everyone was impressed with your work."

"Oh, my gosh! Really? Thank you so much for believing in me, Mrs. Franca."

"When you're a famous artist one day, make sure you remember me," she said with a smile and hint of seriousness. Mrs. Franca believed in me, so I wanted to make her proud.

I rushed out into the hallway to share my news with Devonte.

"Wow, I'm so excited for you. I knew you'd make it," he said, hugging me.

We made our way to the lunchroom, where we found a somewhat quiet area to sit. I didn't want to delay the conversation; I needed answers.

Getting straight to the point, I said, "Do you want to break up with me since I can't go on dates or call you as much as I used to?" I spoke so fast that I needed to take a deep breath afterward. Without allowing him to speak, I continued, "I know other girls can go on dates and stuff, unlike me. So, are you still interested? Has the thought of breaking up crossed your mind? I mean, the thought hasn't crossed my mind at all. But I was wondering how you felt. Would you rather date a girl who can go on dates and hang out with you more? I would go on as many dates as possible with you if I could." At one point, it felt as though I was rambling. I couldn't stop speaking out of fear of what he would say.

"Manushka, Manushka!" Devonte said as he tried to get my attention.

"Yes?" I finally focused on him rather than my thoughts.

"I understand that your parents are strict; you explained that to me at the beginning of our relationship. To answer your question, the thought of breaking up with you hasn't crossed my mind. No, I don't want to date anyone else. I got one girl, and that's you," he said. Devonte gently placed his hand on mine, and I finally felt some relief. He was still interested in me. I was still his girlfriend. And he was still my boyfriend.

He continued, "I do miss our dates and phone calls, but we can't do anything about that now. Let's just hang out at lunch together whenever we can."

I replied, "That works for me. I mean, for now, school is the only place I can hang out with you without getting in trouble. Speaking of hanging out, did you ever get to speak to your parents about spending more time together?"

"Yeah, thanks to you, I ended up speaking to them last week," he said with a smile. "Surprisingly, they felt the same way. My parents said they plan to make changes so we can spend more time together. I have no idea what the plan is, but I hope it works." As Devonte spoke about his parents and their conversation, he seemed hopeful. I was glad he took the time to talk to them.

"Oh, Devonte, what about your grades? How is that going?" I asked.

"My grades are good. I have all As and Bs right now. I've been studying at night and turning in my assignments on time this quarter," he said. By gestures alone, I could tell Devonte was incredibly proud of himself.

"Not only are you smart but fine too," I said jokingly, tapping him on the shoulder.

"Well, you not so bad yourself. Nah, just joking. My girl is beautiful, smart, and talented. I think that's called a triple threat." He laughed.

Devonte and I continued to enjoy the lunch period together until the bell rang. I felt so elated, even Mr. Dupont couldn't spoil my mood. I stepped into his class confidently, ready to answer questions. Just like I expected, five students walked in before me, yet Mr. Dupont didn't say anything to them; he didn't have any demands of them. But the moment I approached the class, he just had to say something to me. *"Bonjour, Manushka. Comment vas-tu aujourd'hui?"* he said.

"Je vais bien aujourd'hui," I said with a little attitude mixed with confidence. Boom! Take that, Mr. Dupont.

"Très bien," he said. Mr. Dupont wasn't ready for me today. I was responding to him in French without hesitation.

"Merci beaucoup, Monsieur Dupont," I said.

"Manushka, wow, very impressive. Great job on the pronunciation. I knew you had potential," he said.

Wait a second—he never indicated that I had potential before. Harassment is not a form of encouragement. Knowing someone has potential and encouraging them means providing some positive feedback. I know for a fact Mr. Dupont never gave me any positive feedback. Instead, he made me hate the class. If I didn't run out of bathroom passes, I wouldn't be in the classroom right now. I nodded to avoid getting in trouble, then sat at my desk. After my quick responses, Mr. Dupont didn't ask me any more questions for the rest of the period. Class went by fast, along with the other periods. I was looking forward to meeting with my girls after school.

"Hey, Janae and Widelene," I said when I found them patiently waiting for me by the exit.

"Hey, Manushka," Widelene said. "How was your conversation with Devonte?"

"Everything is fine. Thank goodness he doesn't want to break up with me because I was worried. So, instead of going on dates and having late-night phone calls, we figured we'd hang out at school more."

"Girl, you had nothing to worry about. That boy is into you. Okay, enough about you and Devonte. We need to talk about this petition right now." Janae could barely contain her excitement as her eyes widened. She started pacing. "We have a total of 2,753 signatures."

"Ahhh!" Shocked by the news, Widelene and I joined Janae in jumping as we celebrated.

After we calmed down, Janae shared more information. "All thirty of my friends on the debate team wanted to help, so they shared the petition with everyone they know. And my mother has been spreading the word, too; she has a lot of connections between work and all the networking groups she attends. We're still far from our goal of 10,000 signatures, but this is definitely progress. We need more signatures, so let's go to the mall with a few signs and stand outside. I think the term is picketing. I figure that would get us signatures and bring more attention to the petition. My mother and uncles volunteered to join us for safety," Janae said with increased excitement. "What do you think?"

"Well, this is for a good cause, but I'm scared. Suppose something happens again?" Widelene was still clearly shaken up by the incident.

I tried to reassure her. "You have every right to still be afraid. If you choose not to go, we understand. If you decide to go, this time will be different. Janae's mother and uncles will be there."

"Alright, I'll go," Widelene said.

"Great!" Janae said. "How about we meet at my house on Saturday at ten o'clock? That will give us enough time to create signs before going to the mall."

During the train ride, we discussed more strategies to make mall safety a reality for girls like us.

The week went by fast, and we went through the motions of attending school, taking exams, and completing homework assignments.

Chapter 14

My mother allowed me to join Janae at the mall for picketing because her mother was chaperoning, and Widelene was going, too. My mother's only advice was to be careful. Understanding the potential impact of picketing at the mall, Widelene and I met early Saturday morning to head to Janae's house.

Janae's mother greeted us and immediately led us to a colorful breakfast display: Danish pastries, donuts, fruits, croissants, muffins, and eggs. "Girls, I hope you enjoy the breakfast I prepared for you. Seems like my ambitious daughter isn't interested in eating right now." She cleared her throat, looking directly in Janae's direction. "I want all of you to grab a plate and eat a little before you start. This is going to be a long day."

Without hesitation, Widelene and I placed food on our plates. Before we could even take a bite, Janae spoke excitedly. "I couldn't sleep last night, so I made some extra signs in case people decide to join us. I think this may get our petition the attention it needs to make a change. If I remember anything from economics class, companies don't like losing money, and negative attention is bad for business."

I couldn't wait to eat. "Girl, I don't know about you, but I plan to eat first, and you should do the same." I took a bite of my buttered croissant. Widelene was too busy eating her eggs to speak. Instead, she shook her head in agreement.

"I'm too focused to eat right now. Are you all ready? It's time to go." Janae walked toward the door with a box full of signs.

Taking control of the situation, Janae's mother interjected, "We're not leaving until you eat something. Trust me, you'll thank me later." A defeated Janae placed the box down before walking toward the table. "Eat this and eat all of it, or you'll be picketing right here from this couch, young lady." Her mother placed a plate on the table. In all my years of knowing Janae's mother, I've never seen her like this; she's usually laid back.

We all watched as Janae finally took a bite of her food. "Um, this egg sandwich is delicious. Mom, can you make me another one? In fact, can you make me two more?"

We all laughed at Janae's request, considering she didn't even want to eat. But once breakfast was over, Janae was back at it again with the instructions. "We need to leave now. Widelene, you can grab that box. Manushka, get the extra signs from my room; it's better to be over-prepared than not. And I'll carry the clipboard and petition sheet."

Together, we loaded the car and then sat down. "Girls, please fasten your seatbelts before I start driving. My brothers should be here in a few minutes," Janae's mother said. Between the look on my friends' faces and the fact that the car was momentarily quiet, I knew we were all nervous. Janae's uncles pulled up alongside the car, with one of them signaling it was time to leave as he pointed forward.

Nervous and all, we arrived at the mall just as the entrance doors were being unlocked. A fierce Janae led the way. She firmly planted her feet on the ground, held a sign above her head, and shouted, "My Body, My Time, My Decision, Mall Safety." Holding Widelene's hand, we stood beside our fearless friend and future leader.

I whispered in Widelene's ear, "I know you're scared, and that's okay. Thankfully, we have Janae's body-building uncles looking out for us, and I don't think anyone will mess with them."

Without saying a word, Widelene held her sign up high and shouted along with Janae. With each word, a tear ran down her face.

Seeing the pain in her eyes, I joined in. The more we shouted, the more people stared. As people looked on, a fast-thinking, Janae quickly approached the onlookers to provide information about the petition. Within an hour, nine teenage girls joined us. These girls were also tired of feeling unsafe at the mall. Progressively, more people joined, but most stared as they passed by. Some people took pictures of us while others recorded.

After a couple of hours, I was tired, but Janae wanted to keep going. Thankfully, her mother stepped in. "You all did a great job. In fact, a couple of people asked me about the petition. I would say you got your point across today. It's time to leave now."

Surprisingly, Janae didn't object; I guess she was tired, too.

During the car ride, we checked the petition signatures online. Astonished, we simultaneously said, "4,557." We began singing and dancing in the car. But was that enough to help our cause? By the time Janae's mother dropped me off at home, I was beyond tired. I spoke to my mother briefly, then went straight to bed.

Chapter 15

For the first time in a long time, I didn't have to go to church in the morning. My mother was called into work to cover someone's shift. As much as my mother loved church, she never turned down an opportunity to make extra money, which she used to send barrels of food and clothing to Haiti.

I was in a deep sleep when the phone rang. Not wanting to wake up, I slowly picked up to see who was calling. It was Janae.

"Hey," I said in my morning voice.

"Girl, wake up! I can't believe you're still in bed. It's one o'clock in the afternoon, girl. Wake up!" Based on how fast she was speaking, I knew Janae wanted to share some important news. So, I found enough strength to sit up. "You wouldn't believe what happened," she continued. "I was home just minding my business when my phone rang. I ignored the call the first time because I didn't recognize the number. The person called back two more times, so I finally decided to pick up the phone. Hello, is this Janae Peterson?" Janae took a long pause.

Fully awakened by how this story was unfolding, I was now anxious to find out the details. I urged her to say more. "What's with the long pause? You woke me up from my beauty rest, so fill me in with the details faster."

"You wouldn't believe who called me, you gotta guess," she said excitedly.

"Girl, you just woke me up, so I can't think of anything right now." I really wanted to guess but couldn't think of any names.

"A reporter from Channel 15 news called. Not just any reporter: Darryl Cunningham, the fine one I always talk about. Yes, he's interested in doing a story about our petition. He wants to interview us! We're going to be on the news!" Janae shouted.

"Wait. What? The news?" Shocked by what I just heard, I needed more clarification. "They want us to be a guest on the news?"

"Yes, girl, that's what I said! They want us to be guests on the news. With this kind of exposure, we may achieve our goal of having emergency towers installed at the mall." Janae continued speaking nonstop. But I was still a little confused.

"How did he get your number, and when does he want to interview us?" I needed more clarity.

"Well, an intern from the news station saw us at the mall. I had no clue she spoke to my mother that day. My mother gave her my number and shared the fact that I was a major Darryl Cunningham fan. I can't believe she didn't say anything to me. I guess saying something would've made the call less of a surprise. I can't believe he wants to interview us Tuesday morning, which would mean missing the first three periods of school," she said.

"Is there any way he can interview us after school, so we're not marked absent?" I asked.

"I'm willing to make an exception this time. The goal of making the mall safer for teenage girls and women is a worthy cause. So, are you available to meet tomorrow to prepare for the interview?" When Janae has a vision or believes in something, she's like a freight train; nothing can stop her.

"I should be able to, especially since it's for the news, but let me double-check with my mom. Since the whole Devonte date situation, she's been stricter." Preparing for any interview is important, and there's no way I'll allow myself to look like a fool on TV.

"Great, I know Widelene is at church, so I'll fill her in later. See you tomorrow," Janae said. I could feel pride in every word Janae spoke.

Staying home on a Sunday was extremely rare, so I planned to take full advantage of it. After speaking to Janae, I slept for another hour before finally rolling out of bed. I showered and then ate dinner for lunch. (Sounds confusing, right? Well, even though it was only three o'clock, dinner was already made. My mother woke up extra early to cook.) Satisfied with the meal, I then sat on the couch under my favorite fuzzy blanket, to catch up on missed episodes of *Bandits of Rage*. This was by far one of my favorite shows. It had a great mix of drama, humor, and thought-provoking scenes. Of course, the best part of the series was the costumes. After watching about four episodes, I called Devonte.

"Hey, Devonte!"

"Manushka!" he said, sounding surprised. "I didn't expect you to call me at this time. Did your mother change her mind about letting you have a boyfriend or something?"

"Nope, I can promise you, that won't happen any time soon. She's at work and won't be home until this evening," I said with a smile. Don't get me wrong, I love my mother, but it was nice to have a conversation with Devonte without having to whisper the entire time.

"Well, in that case, I'm glad you called. I was thinkin' about you, and I miss our dates. Spending time at lunch together is cool and all, but ten minutes isn't a lot of time. I might just have to tell your mother she needs to accept our relationship."

I needed to get that crazy idea out of his head immediately. "Trust me, that wouldn't work. My mother may be short, but trust and believe she might just drop-kick you with one of those wrestling moves."

"So why do you think your mother is so against dating?"

"Well, she has a lot of faith in me. My mother wants me to be a doctor and pretty much live a good life. She believes having a boyfriend is a distraction that will ruin those plans. One of her biggest fears is me getting pregnant before graduating from college. So, dating is not an option right now. Sometimes, I wonder if the rules would be different if I were a boy."

"My parents are okay with me having a girlfriend, but my sixteen-year-old cousin Vanessa isn't allowed to have a boyfriend. So, I guess the rules about dating are different for guys. We'll just have to keep hanging out in school."

"Devonte, you wouldn't believe what happened today!" Knowing he'd never guess, I just kept speaking. "Darryl Cunningham from Channel 15 news called Janae this morning. He wants to interview us about the petition this Tuesday. Can you believe it?"

"Wow! I Can't wait to see my girl on TV. Can I get your autograph?" he joked.

"Going on the news is exciting, but I hope the exposure helps us get emergency towers installed at the mall. I want to feel safe when I shop. Every girl should feel safe when shopping. We shouldn't have to worry about being attacked because we're not interested in some random guy with horrible and sometimes offensive pickup lines."

"What happened to Widelene was crazy. Being on the news is a big step, so it should help get the message..." Devonte stopped speaking mid-sentence for some reason.

"Hello, are you still there? Is everything okay?" I asked.

"Hey, I gotta go. My parents just called me downstairs. They want to talk about something. See you at school tomorrow." Devonte was spending more time with his family, which he was excited about. His parents were supporting his goal of being an astronomer, so they booked a trip to Florida to visit the Kennedy Space Center.

After speaking to Devonte, I focused on getting some homework done. Dragging my feet, I walked toward the room as slowly as possible. I pulled out textbooks, notebooks, and supplies, then plopped my body on the bed—math, French, science, and language arts, followed by art, my favorite class. I got my work done right before my parents got home. We spent a little time together. I had to eat the same thing again; I had no choice. My parents wouldn't agree to let me go out and buy food.

During dinner, my father reminded me that Fabienne would be arriving soon. I couldn't avoid it anymore. It was time to begin the countdown: thirty days to go. As much as I didn't want to share the room, I was determined to have a positive attitude about the whole situation.

Chapter 16

Bundled up in layers of clothing, Widelene and I decided to meet by the turnstile in the train station. The combination of snow and ice was always challenging to navigate. Two pairs of socks were no match for this weather. All I wanted to do was put my feet under hot running water or near the radiator but that would have to wait later. We made it to school after what seemed like an hour's walk. OK, I'm exaggerating; the cold made the five-minute walk feel more like an hour.

As soon as I approached the school, I saw Devonte standing by the entrance. He seemed unusually agitated. "Hey, we need to talk."

No hello or hug. This must be serious. "Devonte, is something wrong? What do you want to talk about?"

As if on cue, the bell rang. "Catch you later at lunch!" He walked away before answering my questions.

Oh, no! 'We have to talk' is what people typically say before a breakup. Was Devonte planning on breaking up with me? We had such a great conversation yesterday. Did I say something to upset him? I mean, we had a great conversation as usual. What could possibly be wrong aside from not being able to go on dates?

"Girl, are you okay?" I heard a voice say. When I turned around to find Janae was staring at me.

"Yeah, I'm okay, I think. Devonte said we need to talk, but I have no idea what he wants to talk about. I think he wants to break up with me. What else could 'we have to talk' mean?" I was so confused; I didn't know what to think.

"Why are you always so quick to jump to conclusions? Just relax, girl." She put a hand on my shoulder. "You know how much Devonte cares about you; I doubt he wants to break up, so chill out and wait."

"I guess you're right."

Thank God I had no tests that day because I would have totally bombed. All I could think about was my upcoming conversation with Devonte. I made it through the first couple of periods. As soon as the bell rang, I rushed straight into the cafeteria. Across the room, I could see Devonte looking around anxiously while twiddling his thumbs. I wanted to run toward him, but I also wasn't in a rush to hear whatever he had to say. Not sure if I should smile, I walked over to the table. "Are you okay?" I asked, reaching for his hand.

Devonte moved back with a serious look on his face. Oh, no! It's about to happen. *Breathe, Manushka. You can't cry over a breakup at school, especially in the lunchroom where everyone can see. Cry in your room, that's a safe space.* After giving myself a quick pep talk, I waited for Devonte to speak.

"No, I'm not okay. Remember when we were talkin' the other day, and I told you my mom was calling me?" he asked.

"Yeah, I remember."

"She got a promotion, which means more money," he said. "She'll also be able to spend more time at home."

"Well, that sounds like great news. You wanted to spend more time with your parents, right?"

"No, Manushka, you don't understand," Devonte said, still visibly upset. "This is bad news."

Conflicted, I couldn't understand why he was so worked up. His mother would be able to spend more time with the family and make more money. Devonte was trying to speak but couldn't get the words out of his mouth. "It's OK, speak to me, please," I urged.

"My mother took the job, but that means I'm moving at the end of the month." He looked down. "We're moving to Long Island. I'll have to go to a new school. Being the new kid at any school is always hard. And I won't get to see you much."

I wanted to scream, cry, bang on the table, and tell him not to go, but this moment wasn't about me. Devonte needed the same kind of support and encouragement he's given me through my drama. "I'm sad you have to move," I said. "I'll miss seeing you at school, but we can make our relationship work." Honestly, I had no idea how we'd manage being so far away, but I figured it was the right thing to say. "Your mother is taking the job because she wants to spend more family time, which is something you wanted, right? I'm sure everything will work out fine for everyone. I know it!" I reached out to hold his hand. "Oh, and you're right. Being the new kid at any school is hard. It'll take some time, but you'll eventually make some friends."

"I guess we can make our relationship work," he said with a partial smile, which was kind of reassuring. "I'll try to come down on weekends or special events to see you. We still have family in Brooklyn, so I won't be a stranger."

We spent so much time talking that we barely had time to eat. We only had about five minutes left to stuff our faces.

"I forgot to ask. When are you moving?" I secretly hoped he wouldn't move until the end of the school year.

"Christmas break. My parents think starting a new school right after winter break is a good idea."

Christmas break, I thought. My boyfriend is moving this Christmas, and I'm getting a new sister. I wondered what other surprises the holiday season would bring.

"Manushka, are you OK?"

"Oh, sorry, I was just thinking. That means you'll be here for another month." I was trying to sound encouraging, knowing I was crying inside.

Devonte and I walked toward my next class, hand in hand. This time, walking with him felt different. I knew our time together walking along the halls was coming to an end. Could our relationship survive the distance?

Sluggishly, I made it through the next couple of classes, then met my girls by the exit to go to Widelene's house. As Janae and Widelene talked about the interview, I could only think about Devonte. I didn't want to share my latest drama since they were both excited about the interview.

We made it to Widelene's house around 3:45 p.m. We discussed and wrote down our talking points to make sure everything was thoroughly addressed. We decided that Janae would be the main person speaking during the interview. Finally, it was time to discuss our outfits.

Widelene looked in my direction. "Manushka, you're the fashionista in the group. What do you think we should wear?"

I had a surprise for my friends. "Well, I decided to make something special for us. Last night, around eleven o'clock, I couldn't sleep. Probably because I spent most of the afternoon relaxing. So, I made us matching shirts with the name of our petition on it." I pulled the shirts out of my bag.

To make a statement, I'd used yellow shirts with block letters. The words *My Body, My Time, My Decision* were positioned right across the front. Of course, I had to make the shirts a little extra special by adding a couple of white rhinestones. I handed the shirts to Widelene and Janae, who both screamed.

"I knew you would have ideas about what we should wear, but I had no clue you'd make something," Janae said as she started to cry.

"Why are you crying? I know the shirts are amazing, but—-" I tried to make a joke to lighten the mood. "Seriously, why are you crying?" I asked again.

"I feel guilty about what happened to Widelene," Janae said as she continued to cry. "I'm the one who wanted to go to the mall. I tried to help her but didn't do enough; I just couldn't. If I could go back in time, I wouldn't have gone to the mall at all. Widelene, I'm so sorry."

"Girl, you did what you could. That guy was bigger and stronger than both of us. Even though everything happened so fast, I saw you hit him with your bag, I heard you scream, and I still remember the terror on your face. As painful as the experience was, you decided to do something about it rather than complain and wait for someone else to take action. That is what this petition is about and what the interview will be about tomorrow." She smiled. "Because of your passion, I know you will be a great Supreme Court Justice one day. Just make sure I'm your plus one when you get invited to the White House. No, but seriously, it wasn't your fault. You don't have to apologize." Widelene gave Janae a tight hug, and I couldn't help but join in.

After our emotional group hug, it was time to leave. We had our action plan for the interview. Since Widelene's mother agreed to let her go on the news, my mother also agreed. She was looking forward to seeing me on TV.

The morning of the interview, I woke up early to prepare. The custom shirt I made was paired with black jeans and high-top black and gold sneakers. Small gold hoop earrings and a gold bracelet were the perfect accessories to compliment my outfit. My mother inspected my clothing, checking for wrinkles and ensuring the fit was right. Thankfully, my attire met her expectations even though she really wanted me to wear a dress. Before I could finish breakfast, the bell rang. It was Janae and Widelene. I was ready, but nerves kicked in, so I had to run to the bathroom. I took several deep breaths, then ran out the door after kissing my mother goodbye. Without them saying a word, I could tell how my friends were feeling. We sat silently until Janae's mother began to speak.

"Girls, I'm so proud of you!" she said. "Don't take this moment lightly. What the three of you managed to do required a lot of courage and dedication. During the interview, try to relax and, above all, just be yourselves."

We drove to the news station downtown, where Darryl, the reporter, waited for us by the entrance. He was fine, just like Janae said. Darryl was off limits; he looked about twenty-five years old. He escorted us inside, gave us a quick tour, and reviewed questions he planned to ask during the live interview. We were all nervous, but there was no turning back now.

"This is Darryl Cunningham with News 15 on the one and only Channel 15, always bringing you the latest news—news that matters in your community, my community, our community. Our first guests are high school students who took matters into their own hands to make a difference in their community after an unfortunate event."

We were all mesmerized by how effortlessly he spoke on camera. One by one, we introduced ourselves, smiled, and waved.

"I'm impressed by the three of you and your story. Janae, can you share what made you start this petition?" Darryl asked, looking directly at her.

Without hesitation, Janae began to speak as though she'd been on television before; she was a natural. "A couple of weeks ago, Widelene and I went to the mall, which is a place we tend to frequent, you know, our hang-out spot. When we go to the mall, it's not unusual for guys to approach us, but this time was different. A new guy made advances at Widelene, who politely indicated that she was not interested. He followed us, so we walked faster. His anger increased with each step. Suddenly, he grabbed Widelene's arm and attacked her. I tried to help, but we were no match for him. People looked on, but no one intervened. We yelled, cried, and fought as much as we could. Fortunately, there was an off-duty police officer who happened to be shopping with his daughter. He heard the commotion and immediately stepped in. Who knows what could have happened if the officer had not been at the mall? Widelene ended up with stitches. We haven't shopped at the mall since. And we don't plan to go any time soon unless measures are taken to keep shoppers safe." Janae maintained her composure as she relived the experience.

"Wow, I'm so sorry to hear what happened to you," Darryl said. The look on his face was sincere. "I understand the three of you had a brainstorming session to figure out ways to increase mall safety, to prevent anyone else from being attacked. You decided to start a petition. So, what is the overall goal?" he asked. "Do you have a specific recommendation to increase safety at the mall?"

"The only idea we could think of was installing emergency alert systems at the mall," Janae said. "In fact, they should be installed at every mall. We figured the only way to get the attention of whoever owns the mall was to start a petition."

"As of this morning, do you ladies know how many signatures you have for the petition so far?" Darryl asked.

We said in unison, "Six thousand, seven hundred, ninety-four." The fact that the three of us spoke simultaneously made us giggle.

"Wow! That is a great accomplishment. Another question: How did you come up with the name?" Darryl asked.

Before the interview, we all agreed that Widelene would answer this question. She said, "My Body, My Time, My Decision is the name of the petition. I was attacked because I declined someone's advances. Not wanting to spend my time speaking to him was seen as a form of disrespect. Because he did not respect my decision, that individual decided to cause harm to my body."

"Well thought out! That name is what caught my attention. Just so you know, I signed the petition. I have one more question. Where did you get your shirts? They look pretty trendy!"

I was utterly shocked; I had no clue Darryl would ask about the shirts. He didn't mention it before the live interview. Widelene and Janae both looked at me, waiting for a response.

"Um, I made the shirts," I said shyly.

"You did a phenomenal job. You have a bright future, young lady. In fact, you all have a bright future. Thank you for being a part of this segment." Darryl shook our hands one by one. Then, he looked directly into the camera. "Adam Lane will share the weekend forecast after a brief commercial break. Stay tuned."

Darryl walked us to the entrance. "I will be following your story closely. Again, thank you for joining me on air today. I'll make a few calls during the week in hopes of helping you girls accomplish your goal. I strongly feel that something good will come from this situation." Darryl handed Janae's mother his business card before returning to the news station.

Since it was already noon, we opted not to go to school. Janae's mother took us all to a Thai restaurant. To my surprise, everything was delicious. I had spring rolls, crab rangoon, potstickers, and pad thai. Janae's mother said we could order anything, and she meant it; she encouraged me to order more food after I initially selected one item. I ate so much that I wanted to unbutton my pants for some room to breathe, but figured it wasn't appropriate.

My parents greeted me as soon as I arrived home. They were beyond excited to see me on the news. Of course, my mother had notified all her church friends about my being on television. I shared all the details, including the ones that seemed insignificant. My mother cooked my favorite meal. Even though I was full, I didn't want to disappoint her, considering the time it took to cook. Don't judge me; I told you I eat a lot.

During dinner, we discussed the necessary preparations for Fabienne's arrival. A new bed was scheduled to arrive over the weekend. I was tasked with rearranging the room to accommodate the new bed. I had to remind myself to be positive. I hope Fabienne is nice, considering we have to share a space.

Chapter 17

Three more weeks until Fabienne's arrival. Three more weeks until my Devonte moves to Long Island. Will Fabienne and I get along? Will we have anything in common? I had so much on my mind. Would my relationship with my boyfriend last, considering the distance? Would it be a long-distance relationship even though we only lived a few hours apart? Question after question crossed my mind as I sat in class. Oh, and the art competition. Would my submission be good enough for first place? A trophy would be nice, but my goal was the summer internship. I can't imagine how great it will be to have a mentor. I have to get my presentation together for the art competition.

"Manushka, comptez-vous vous joindre à nous aujourd'hui?" Of course, none other than Mr. Dupont interrupted my thoughts. Caught off guard, the only response I could think of was, "Huh?" This time, I had absolutely no clue what he said. By the smirk on his face, I knew Mr. Dupont intentionally said something he knew I wouldn't understand. "I said, do you plan to join us today?" This time, Mr. Dupont asked me the question in English, which was a first. He said each word slowly, as if I didn't understand English. But seriously, his question was ridiculous. Why would I even be in class if I didn't plan on joining?

I said, *"Oui oui!"* I had to reposition my body to make sure I was focused. The last thing I wanted was for Mr. Dupont to ask me another question. Out of all the students in the class, I was the only person he would pick on; at least, that's how I felt. While pretending to pay attention, I watched the clock intently. I didn't want to spend an extra second in Mr. Dupont's class.

As I clutched my bag, the bell rang. I grabbed my notebook and left the classroom as fast as possible. Devonte was absent from school today. His parents were taking him to see his new neighborhood and the school he would be attending.

I met Widelene and Janae after school. As we were walking to the train station, Janae received a call from her mother. It turns out that a representative for whoever owns the mall heard about our petition and saw us on the news. Installing several emergency towers was too expensive—the mall would place one on a trial basis. The representative also mentioned sending us some information through express mail, so Janae's mother provided them with our addresses.

For the next two days, we all anxiously waited for the delivery. Finally, the packages arrived, and we decided to open them together.

"My letter is halfway opened, so I'll read first," Widelene said.

Dear Widelene,

We're sorry to hear about the incident at the mall. Although words alone cannot ease the pain you experienced from the attack, please know we're taking this situation seriously. An emergency tower will be placed at the mall. With its installation, I hope you will feel safe enough to continue shopping at Willow Creek Mall. You're a valued customer. We applaud your courage in sharing your story. Thank you for bringing this situation to our attention. Please know that this is just the beginning of the measures we plan to take to increase safety for all customers.

Enclosed, please accept this small gift on behalf of our organization.

Please feel free to call us to address any questions and/or concerns. We look forward to speaking with you in the future.

Sincerely,

Bradley Hemingsworth

CEO, Greater Malls of America Corp

"They gave me a $200 gift card to use at the mall, ahhh!" Widelene screamed. I was pleased to hear the excitement in her voice, considering what she experienced. It was the first time I saw her this happy since the incident.

Next, it was Janae's turn. I figured it was only fitting for her to go second since she was there on the day of the attack. Janae read her letter.

Dear Janae,

We're sorry to hear about your recent experience at Willow Creek Mall. It was a regrettable event, and we thank you for bringing it to our attention. Due to your dedication, we were made aware of the lack of safety. Because of your efforts, we will place an emergency tower at the mall. As time progresses, and with feedback from customers like yourself, we plan to prioritize mall security. Also, we were highly impressed by your ability to articulate your concerns and the quick manner in which you created the petition. For this reason, we invite you to consider serving as a volunteer this summer with our community relations department.

We look forward to hearing your response. As summer approaches, we will contact you regarding the internship.

Enclosed, please accept this small gift on behalf of our organization.

Please feel free to call us to address any questions and/or concerns. We look forward to speaking with you.

Sincerely,

Bradley Hemingsworth

CEO, Greater Malls of America Corp

"I have a $200 gift card too, ahh!!! As much as I love shopping, I'm even more excited about possibly having a summer internship with the community relations department. That opportunity will be very impressive on my college applications. Okay, Manushka, it's your turn now."

Dear Manushka,

Although you were not present during the regrettable situation at the Willow Creek Mall, you've shown dedication in supporting your friends. Because of your support, we will install an emergency tower. While watching the interview, we were impressed by the shirts you created. We found them to be trendy while making a statement. On the day of the emergency tower reveal, we would like to provide you with a booth to sell some of your shirts, given you are interested. We will be in touch with you soon to work out the details.

Enclosed, please accept this small gift on behalf of our organization.

Please feel free to call us to address any questions and/or concerns. We look forward to speaking with you.

Sincerely,

Bradley Hemingsworth

CEO, Greater Malls of America Corp

"I got a $200 gift card, too, and they want me to sell shirts at the mall. Oh, my goodness! But how—"

Before I could even finish the sentence, Widelene spoke. "But nothing, this is a great opportunity. Don't even start doubting yourself now. We'll help you make the shirts, and we'll help you sell them. Don't worry, girl, we got you!"

"Thanks! You read my mind, and I can use all the help I can get. Are you doing anything on Saturday?" I asked, hoping they would be available.

"Nope, I'm free," Janae said.

"I'm free too," Widelene said.

"Great! I'll pick up all the supplies Friday after school."

After the phone conversation, I rushed to the kitchen to share the news with my mother. I could tell by the look in her eyes that she was both excited and proud. Surprisingly, my mother gave me money to purchase materials to make the shirts. She wanted me to use the gift cards to buy clothing and accessories from the mall. I hugged my mother so tight that she almost lost her balance. Within seconds, I heard my mother on the phone as I walked to my room. I knew she would call all her church sisters to share the news. Knowing that I made her proud brought me joy. It was just the beginning of making her proud.

Chapter 18

I was looking forward to hanging out with Devonte, so as soon as the bell rang, I went straight to the lunchroom. Without saying a word, I hugged him as tight as I could, knowing our lunch dates would soon end.

"Hey, I have a little something for you that'll make you smile," he said.

I wondered what it could be..

"Close your eyes and open your hands."

Eager about the surprise, I quickly complied. Devonte placed a paper in my hands. I made sure to hold on tight but gently enough not to cause any damage.

"Okay, you can open your eyes now."

Devonte's surprise left me speechless for a moment. I tried to contain my laughter as I stared at the paper. Green, blue, red, tan, and yellow were just a few of the colors he used. The colors didn't blend at all; they more so overlapped each other. I could see a distinct sun mid-page. Underneath the sun, he attempted to draw a frog. I assumed it was a frog because of the green coloring. Knowing Devonte wasn't artsy, I knew this took him long.

"What do you think of my masterpiece?" he asked.

"It's a piece all right. I love your, um, um, creativity—yeah, that's the word: creativity. Since I don't want to misinterpret this wonderful work of art, can you explain it to me?" I asked.

Clearing his throat, Devonte continued, "Well, since you asked, this is an abstract illustration of us seated under a cabana on the beach, watching the sunset as we hold hands."

"Oh, that sounds so romantic," I said right before laughing hysterically. I couldn't contain it anymore. "First off, this is not abstract art. And why in the world do I look like a frog with a hat? And you look like a flying stick figure." I was still laughing.

"This piece was inspired by that movie, you know, *The Princess and the Frog*," he joked. "You know I can't draw. I just took art to get an easy A, and it's not working out as planned. Besides, I just wanted to make my girl smile." He reached for my hand.

"Since you put so much effort into this masterpiece, would you kindly autograph it for me?" I asked, rummaging through my bag to find a pen.

Devonte created some super fancy signature to make his drawing look somewhat official; at least, that's what he thought. "Don't lose this; it may be worth millions one day. Consider it one of a kind."

We both laughed, knowing how bad the drawing looked.

"Devonte, guess what?" Not giving him an opportunity to speak, I continued. "Janae, Widelene, and I received letters from the CEO of the mall. He plans to install an emergency tower on a trial basis and gave each of us a $200 gift card. And you wouldn't believe this next thing; I still can't believe it."

"What is it?" he asked patiently.

"Well, he's allowing me to sell my shirts at the mall on the day of the emergency tower reveal," I said, speaking every sentence faster than the one before. "I'm excited, nervous, and scared at the same time."

"Hey, slow down and breathe. Don't worry; I know your shirt will be a hit. In fact, I'll be your first customer. I can pay you now. How much are you selling the shirts for?"

Oh, my goodness, pricing was the last thing on my mind. "I have no clue how much to sell the shirts for," I said frantically.

"Relax, just do a quick search online to see how much people typically sell shirts like yours. Give me a second while I check for you." He pulled out his phone and looked at a series of items. "Okay, it seems like the average cost for a shirt is between twelve and twenty dollars. How much are you comfortable with charging?"

I took a long pause. "Well, I guess I can sell the shirts for fifteen dollars; that's reasonable. Thanks to you, that was easier than I expected."

"Feel free to pay with cash or check for my services," he joked.

There was no way to avoid the next topic. Being the caring girlfriend I am, it was only right to ask. "What did you think about your new neighborhood and school?"

His face dropped. But as much as Devonte wanted to avoid the conversation, it was a reality. He needed to talk about it. *We* needed to talk about it.

"Well, the school is aight, and the neighborhood is nice."

That was all Devonte said, and based on his response, I knew not to ask him any more questions. He needed more time to accept that he was moving in a couple of weeks. *Just two more weeks.* I wanted and needed to go on a date with him. I had to be creative. I thought if we just happened to end up at the same place at the same time, it would be considered a coincidence rather than a deliberate date. I just had to stay far away from the hospital, or anywhere else I could run into Sè Françoise.

"Devonte, how about if I told you that I was going to the library, and you just so happened to end up there on the same day at the same time? I was thinking after school this Friday."

"I get it. You wouldn't get in trouble since it wouldn't be an official date. In that case, I'm down!" Devonte initiated a fist bump.

Once the lunch period was over, he walked me back to class as usual. This time was different as the reality of him moving struck me. As we walked through the halls hand in hand, I knew it was time to start the countdown.

At the end of the day, I met my friends, and we walked to the train station together.

"Hey, girl, we missed you at lunch," Janae said.

"Okay, girl, fill us in. What's going on with you?" I could always count on Widelene to ask me questions. Some would consider her nosy, but since we're friends, I'll just call her curious.

"Devonte is leaving in a couple of weeks. I feel like we're running out of time, so I plan to meet him at the library on Friday. I figure if we both happen to be there at the same time, it wouldn't be considered a date, right?"

"Girl, you're either the bravest person I know or just crazy. I don't even want to imagine what your mother will do to you if she hears about you being out with a boy again," Widelene said.

"I know, but Devonte is moving. The chances of us breaking up because of distance are high, so he's worth the trouble. And besides, we're meeting at the library; I'll be sure to wear some kind of disguise. The library is filled with people our age. If anything, I'll pretend Devonte is a stranger who was asking for help. Don't worry, girl, I planned everything out," I said, reassuring my friends that I would be careful.

"I get what you're saying, Manushka. Have fun, but please be careful," Janae said.

Chapter 19

After school, I headed straight to the library. No cutesy outfit for me. This time, I wore a coat, hoodie, jeans, sunglasses, boots and a hat. I found Devonte at the library, waiting for me.

"Hey, Devonte," I said, waving. For some reason, he didn't respond. "Hey, Devonte," I repeated. Again, but still no response from him.

In New York, most people avoid speaking to strangers. I guess my disguise was so good that even my boyfriend didn't recognize me.

"Hey, Devonte, it's me, Manushka," I whispered.

Once I caught his attention, Devonte's immediate response was to laugh. Although that wasn't the response I wanted, I totally understood to the point of joining him in the laughter.

"You look like a celebrity hiding from the paparazzi," he said, still laughing.

"Trust me, Sè Françoise is worse than the paparazzi." I cautiously looked around for familiar faces. Thankfully none spotted.

Devonte and I walked around for a few minutes until we found the perfect spot. I took out my art supplies and began to draw as we talked. I positioned myself so Devonte couldn't see what I was drawing. As much as I wanted to hang out, I had to keep track of the time since I was planning to purchase supplies to make the shirts, and I was nervous about being seen by someone.

"Okay, Devonte, you surprised me the other day, so now it's time for me to surprise you. Close your eyes and open your hands," I instructed. "Close your eyes, not *eye*." I laughed as he tried to get a sneak peek. "Do you need me to help you close your lids?" I asked jokingly.

"I'll take any opportunity I can get for you to touch me," he joked.

"You so crazy," I said before reaching across the table to gently close his eyes. I placed the canvas in his hands. "When I count to three, I want you to open your eyes. One, two, three, open."

Devonte opened his eyes, stared at the drawing, and then at me. "This is—I mean, how did you make something so beautiful in such a short time?"

"Oh, this is just a little something for you to keep in your room, you know, something to help you remember me." Knowing his interest in becoming an astronomer, I drew Devonte staring at the stars. "I hope you don't forget me when you're at the new school." I couldn't hide my sadness. I didn't want to be selfish, but I couldn't help myself. "I wish you didn't have to move. Since we won't see each other much, I know we'll eventually break up; it's just a matter of time, I can feel it."

Devonte placed his hand on my chin, repositioning my face so we could make eye contact. "Manushka, trust me, there is no way I could ever forget you. We just have to find a way to make our relationship work. I got you, and you got me!"

I couldn't hold back the tears as I got the feeling this would be the last time we hugged. For the first time since we met, Devonte and I sat together silently for a few moments. "Manushka, I promise I'll find a way to make our relationship work. I don't plan on breaking up with you."

I felt terrible about turning our possibly last date into a tear fest. I didn't feel like talking anymore, at least not today, so I left a little earlier than planned. Even though Devonte insisted, I didn't let him walk me to the train station. I needed some time alone. Rather than going straight home, I went to the fabric and craft store to pick up shirts and the remaining materials.

I couldn't help but think about the fate of my relationship with Devonte. Naturally, I wanted to cry again but held back the tears; the last thing I wanted was for my mother to start asking questions. Once home, I avoided eye contact as much as possible. Since my mother knew I had to make the shirts, I headed straight to my room after dinner. Based on what I had at home and what was purchased, I could make seventy shirts. I sorted all the letters and embellishments to make the process less confusing and more efficient since Widelene and Janae would be helping. Lord knows we'd be talking about more than just the shirts. That night, I made seventeen shirts to get a head start on the process.

The next day, Widelene and Janae arrived bright and early. Janae bought some donuts for us to eat for breakfast.

"Alright, time to get to work," I said, clapping to get their attention. "I want this to be fun, but we have to focus on getting all the shirts done."

"Hold up, wait a minute! I don't remember signing up for the military," Janae joked, waving her hands.

"Well, just call me Sergeant Jean-Pierre. Now, I will iron on the letters and rhinestones. Janae, I need to remove the clear plastic off the rhinestones. And Widelene, I need you to fold the shirts and place them in the box. Got it?"

"Yes, sir—I mean, ma'am," Janae said, placing a hand across her forehead.

"You guys are too funny. I'll start the music," Widelene said.

We laughed, danced, and talked all while working. By 12:30, we made a total of forty-seven shirts. For lunch this time, my mother made a dish called legume, which is a mixture of cabbage, eggplant, spinach, and other vegetables mixed with shrimp and blue crabs. She also made some white rice to go with the legume.

"Manushka, this is not riri Joe-Joe, but it tastes just as good," Janae said before putting a fork full of food into her mouth. "Man, anything your mother cooks is delicious, so you already know I'm not leaving without a to-go plate."

"Now, you know my mom is always ready to hook you up with some to-go plates. Look over there," I said, pointing toward the bag.

"See, now that's why I love your momma. And I think she loves me too. Widelene, how come you never seem too impressed with the food?"

"Well, that's because I'm probably going to have the same thing for dinner tonight," Widelene said, laughing. After eating, we returned to my room. By eight o'clock, we completed the remaining shirts, yes, seventy in total. Getting the shirts done a week before the event relieved some of my stress.

Widelene's dad picked both her and Janae up. I was so tired I could hear the bed calling my name. I decided to go to sleep early, especially since we were going to church the next day.

Chapter 20

The day of the emergency tower reveal arrived, and I was filled with mixed emotions: excited about selling my shirts but nervous about people's response to what I created. Most importantly, I was nervous about how Widelene and Janae felt. This would be the first time they entered the mall since the incident. My dad just so happened to be off this weekend. He drove me to the mall, where I met up with the girls.

I could tell by Widelene's stance and her facial expression that she was scared to walk in even though her attacker had been sentenced to two years in prison. Unfortunately, the other guys with him were not sentenced to jail time. Janae was also scared, but she never allowed fear to stop her from doing anything, especially something she believed in. After a quick prayer, we walked into the mall together, followed by our parents.

As soon as we entered, a woman approached us. "Hello, my name is Angela Danszlee, and I will be representing the Willow Creek Mall corporation today. Please let me know if you have any questions so I may address them immediately. I recognized the three of you from the news interview, and I must say I was truly impressed. We have a booth set up for you. Please follow me."

As Angela spoke, I analyzed her outfit. She wore a red two-piece pantsuit with black patent leather heels. I was drawn to a beautiful rose gold flower brooch with what appeared to be diamonds along the right side; I could tell it was high-end. Her hair was pulled back into a slick ponytail, allowing her diamond earrings to shine without obstruction.

After Angela escorted us to the booth, I looked around. The moment was so surreal, knowing this all started with an idea. The mall was filled with lights, balloons, and cameras. Behind the curtain, right in the middle of the mall, stood the emergency tower waiting to be revealed.

Darryl, the reporter, was there to cover the event. "Girls, look at what you managed to accomplish. Because of your hard work and dedication, safety will increase for all shoppers at this mall and other malls in the future. I'm so happy to have met such outstanding and driven young ladies. Oh, and Manushka, a little birdie told me that you're selling shirts today. Before they all run out, I would like to purchase twelve for friends and family. How much are you selling the shirts for?" he asked.

"Um, I'm selling them for fifteen dollars each," I said hesitantly.

Would people think fifteen dollars was too expensive? I took a deep breath as I waited for Darryl's response.

"Great, here's $200. Keep the change. Set the shirts aside for me. I'll pick them up after our interview."

I couldn't believe my eyes as I stared at the money in my hands. Not only did Darryl buy shirts, but he also gave me a tip. People entered the mall one by one and stood around the emergency tower covered by a huge gray curtain.

The mall representative, Angela, stood before the emergency tower as people gathered, whispered, and took pictures. She adjusted her blazer before speaking. "Greetings, everyone, and thank you for joining us. Here at the Willow Creek Mall, a regrettable incident occurred. This unfortunate incident is not limited to the Willow Creek Mall; it is happening at malls and stores throughout our country. But here at the Willow Creek Mall, we value our customers and decided to take swift action. We thank Janae, Widelene, and Manushka for bringing their experience to our attention. As we begin the countdown, please remember that we at the Willow Creek Mall value all our customers; your safety matters to us."

Angela signaled to the DJ behind her to stop the music before beginning the countdown. "Ten, nine, eight, seven, six, five, four, three, two, one."

Finally, the moment we all waited for had arrived: the curtain was removed, and the emergency tower was in plain view for all to see. I could hear cheers from people throughout the mall. I turned to see Darryl walking toward us with his microphone as the camera crew followed him.

"Hello, ladies. I'm sure everyone remembers you from the interview a few weeks ago. Thanks to your efforts, the mall will be a little safer for everyone. As an organizer of the petition, Janae, how do you feel looking at the emergency tower?" Darryl quickly placed the microphone in front of Janae.

"I'm in absolute awe knowing our petition was taken seriously despite our age. I would like to thank everyone who took the time to sign the petition. And thank you to everyone who picketed with us in front of the mall. And, of course, special thanks to you, Darryl. Allowing us to be on the news brought more attention to our cause." Janae sounded like a seasoned politician.

Darryl quickly transitioned to Widelene. "Do you feel a sense of closure?"

"Although my experience was traumatic, I'm glad some good came out of it. Seeing this emergency tower makes me feel hopeful that shopping at the mall can be an enjoyable experience again," Widelene said.

"I would like to thank you, young ladies, for making a difference. And thank you for giving me an opportunity to be a part of the change. To everyone planning to shop at the Willow Creek Mall today, stop by and purchase one of Manushka's shirts. I already purchased a few, so I'm sure these shirts will run out soon. Stop by her booth; let's support and encourage our youth. After all, they are our future," Darryl said as he ended the news segment.

Once he left, Widelene, Janae, and I silently stood in front of the emergency tower while holding hands. At that moment, I could see tears filling Widelene's eyes. I decided to hold her hand tighter; I knew she was experiencing a personal moment that didn't require words from me or anyone else.

Following the silence, we went to my booth, where our parents all waited. They took pictures and purchased a few shirts. After reassuring them that we were okay, they decided to walk around until we were done. Man, I couldn't believe the level of support people provided. One after the other, they lined up to purchase the shirts. For a brief moment, we let our guards down to enjoy the ambiance of the mall. I collected the money, Janae distributed the shirts, and Widelene bagged them. We created the perfect assembly line. Music played in the background as we danced, chatted, and served our customers.

"Psst, it's them," Widelene said in a whisper.

"Them who?" I asked, counting money.

In a shaky voice, Widelene said, "The guys who were with the monster that attacked me."

On high alert, Janae clenched her fist while Widelene grabbed her phone.

"There's a lot of people at the mall today, so I doubt they'll do anything stupid. Just in case they try something, Janae, I want you to run to the emergency tower; we need to put it to use." I had to take over. I could tell my friends were reliving the trauma of the attack.

When the last customer left, the two guys approached the booth. "Yo, we good?" one of them asked. Really? That's the only thing he could say? Of course, we're not good, you damn idiot. I had to keep that thought to myself to avoid causing a situation. "Listen, we didn't know he was gonna wild out like that. We wanna buy two shirts," he said, handing me the money.

"You stood there and watched him attack me," Widelene said, fuming. You didn't even have the guts or decency to stop him. Had the cop not shown up, who knows what that monster would have done to me? And you want to stand here talkin' bout we good. As far as I'm concerned, that is not an apology. Buying fifty shirts still wouldn't equate to an apology."

"Next time, try a real apology," Janae added. "In fact, why don't you do your part in keeping people safe at the mall? If a girl isn't interested in you, just let it go."

"Aight, we hear you, you right. Sorry about what happened. You got my word. Next time y'all shopping, you don't ever have to worry about us," the guy said as they walked off. The little one in the back appeared more remorseful; I could tell by the look on his face. Once they left, we felt relief.

Right before packing, our final customer arrived. This customer was tall, handsome, fine, and all mine! Standing right beside Devonte was his mother, so I had to address her first. "Hello, Dr. Robinson," I said with a smile.

"Hello, Manushka. Devonte told us all about the great work you girls are doing. I wanted to come out and show some support."

"We appreciate your support." This was my chance to speak to my boyfriend. I had to be extra careful since my parents were at the mall. "Hey, Devonte!"

"Hey, Manushka! Business is looking good! Seems like you're making some money," Devonte said with a hand gesture indicating money.

"How many shirts do you have left?" Dr. Robinson asked.

"I have about thirty-seven left."

"What is the total for all thirty-seven shirts?"

Why would Dr. Robinson ask me that? I didn't want to seem rude, so I gave her the total: $555."

"Okay, I'll buy thirty-seven shirts."

What? Did I hear correctly? Did Dr. Robinson just say she wanted to buy all thirty-seven shirts? Seriously! Devonte looked on with a smile as he watched my reaction.

"Um, are you sure you want all, um, thirty-seven shirts?" I wanted to be respectful but cautious not to say the wrong thing.

"Yes, you heard correctly. I want to purchase all thirty-seven shirts. I volunteer with a non-profit organization that works with at-risk teenage girls. Our goal is to help them develop self-esteem and understand that dreams are possible. Your shirts would be perfect for them. I love the message they carry. I also think wearing a shirt made by a fellow teenager would be encouraging to them. In fact, I would love to have you and your friends as guest speakers at one of our monthly meetings," Dr. Robinson said.

"That sounds awesome! We would love to be guest speakers. Just let us know when you need us there." I took the liberty of answering for my friends. I knew they would support me.

"Wonderful! I'll get your number from Devonte if you don't mind." She handed me a check for the total amount of $555.

"I appreciate the support, Dr. Robinson." I reached out to shake her hand.

"Manushka, come here, child. I do hugs not handshakes." As we hugged, I looked over at Devonte, who was laughing.

"See you at school on Monday," Devonte said before walking away with his mother.

After they seemed far away enough, I turned to Janae and Widelene. "Oh, my goodness! I can't believe she just bought the rest of the shirts and invited us to be guest speakers." I could barely contain my excitement. The shirts were officially sold out.

"Girl, it seems like Devonte's mom likes you," Janae said.

"This day was hands down amazing," Widelene said. "I can't believe what we were able to accomplish together. I love my best friends."

"We love you too!" Janae and I said.

After packing up, we called our parents, who met us at the booth. On the drive home, my mother was surprised by how much money I made. I told my parents it was only right for me to share some of the profit with Janae and Widelene. They both agreed with the idea.

Part II

Chapter 21

The dreadful! It was time for Devonte to move and time to welcome Fabienne. That Friday, I didn't want to go to school. I didn't want to face Devonte and pretend that everything was OK. I knew containing my pain would be difficult, but I didn't want to be selfish. Devonte didn't want to move, but he had no choice. Everyone knows how difficult it is to be the new guy at school. Since it was right before winter break, teachers gave us free time. In most classes, we watched holiday movies. I wanted my last lunch period with Devonte to be special, so I bought him his favorite white powdered donuts.

"Hey, Devonte," I said, staring into his eyes.

"Hey, Manushka."

"Well, since this is our last lunch together at school, I figured I'd bring you a little something." I reached into my backpack. Darn it, the donuts had fallen to the bottom of my bag and gotten crushed; my little surprise was ruined.

"Crushed, whole, I don't care. You know how much I love these donuts," Devonte laughed hysterically. He unwrapped the donuts and ate.

I laughed as he got some of the powder from the donuts on his nose. I reached out to clean his face. I didn't want the moment to end; I didn't want our relationship to slowly dissolve. Devonte was perfect for me.

"I don't want to sound selfish, but—"

"You never have to be afraid to tell me anything," Devonte said, trying to encourage me to continue speaking.

"I'm nervous—no, I'm *scared* that distance will cause us to break up. Suppose you find some girl at your school who can go on dates and have late-night phone calls. If that happens, I know we'll break up for sure. A lot of couples break up because of distance."

"I hear you, but I'm only moving a couple of hours away. And I'm not interested in dating anyone but you. You my girl, and that's it! I'll come down to Brooklyn as much as I can, so you have nothing to worry about. Trust me."

I heard everything he said, and it felt good, but I couldn't ignore the nagging feeling that everything was ending. The sound of the bell interrupted our final lunch period together. We walked hand in hand as always, but slower than usual. Mr. Dupont was absent, so I didn't need to rush to class. Devonte hugged me tighter than he ever had, so I reciprocated the hug. Everything about being in his arms felt so right; I felt safe, appreciated, respected, and loved.

"Break it up, kids, break it up. Where do you think you are? The bell just rang, so go to class right now before I send both of you to the office," said the random teacher who stood outside the classroom door with her arms crossed.

I wanted to explain that Devonte was moving, and it was our last hug in the halls of Paul Millerson High School, a moment that I would remember for the rest of my life. I needed this moment. As I contemplated sharing my thoughts and feelings with the teacher, her stance and facial expression were all I needed to remind me to be quiet. As Devonte and I released our embrace, we held hands while slowly taking steps away from each other. As our hands slipped away, I felt pain in my heart with every step.

I didn't enjoy the movie or the free time the substitute gave us. I just sat at my desk alone, doodling on a piece of paper. Devonte's parents decided to pick him up from school early because they planned to drive to the new house that night. I wouldn't see him again.

Widelene and Janae met me after school. "Manushka, we know you don't want to talk about Devonte moving now," Widelene said. "When you're ready to talk, we're here for you." Janae nodded in agreement.

As soon as I arrived home, my parents reminded me to clean my room because Fabienne would be arriving in the morning. This seemed like one of the longest nights of my life because I couldn't stop thinking about Devonte. And soon, I would be sharing my room with Fabienne.

I cleaned my room well enough to meet my mother's standards. After finally falling asleep for what felt like an hour or two, I woke up to my mother yelling. "Manunu, Manunu, wake up, your sister coming today," she shouted from the kitchen. As usual, she woke up extra early to cook. My mother wanted to make sure Fabienne had a decent meal when she arrived. I dragged myself to the bathroom and got ready. I still had to make sure there was no indication I was sad about anything before joining my parents in the kitchen. After eating, we all left. It was time to pick up Fabienne.

Living with a stranger was all I could think about. We never had any conversations. I didn't even know if she looked anything like the pictures I saw.

My father found a parking spot, and we all walked into the airport. As we waited, I wondered if I would recognize the girl from the photos. Should I greet her with a hug or handshake? I could tell my father was nervous: he clasped his hands and swayed side to side.

The moment finally arrived: Fabienne was standing right before me, looking exactly like her pictures, except taller. I looked at her from head to toe. We were about the same height and possibly wore the same clothing size. Fabienne's skin tone was lighter than mine. Her long hair was parted down the middle, with each side equally falling on her shoulders. Her hairstyle perfectly framed her face, complementing her high cheekbones and full lips. Fabienne wore a pair of stud earrings that perfectly matched her necklace. She was in a long blue dress with stockings and shoes. If Fabienne's life was anything like mine, I was 100% sure her mother influenced the outfit choice.

She seemed a little hesitant about approaching us, which I understood. Fabienne was probably a toddler the last time she saw my father. My mother, of course, nudged me to walk forward. I stumbled a little but caught my balance to avoid hitting the floor.

"Fabienne, Fabienne," my father called out with open arms.

She stared in our direction for a few minutes before finally taking a few more steps. "Bonjour, Papa." She reached out to hug my father—I mean *our* father. She then kissed my mother on the cheek and waved to me. I was happy she waved because I wasn't in the mood to hug her, at least not yet. The look on her face was sad.

My father asked her a ton of questions. My mother also asked questions but wanted my father to take the lead. Walking toward the car, I kept analyzing Fabienne without being too creepy. After we sat in the back seat together, I looked over as she stared out the window. As much as I didn't want to share my room, I felt terrible for her. Leaving everyone and everything she knew had to be difficult, so I decided to make the best of the situation to help Fabienne adjust to her new life.

When we arrived home, I took Fabienne to our room. I can't believe I just said, "our room," without being bothered. I could tell by her smile she was pleased with the space. I don't want to brag, but everyone loves the aesthetics of my room, everyone in my age range, at least. Pushing my pride about the room aside, I showed Fabienne where to place her belongings before returning to the kitchen to eat. After brunch, she took a long shower while I tried to figure out the best way to start a conversation. When Fabienne returned to the room, I could tell she'd been crying because her eyes were so red. I needed to reassure her that I was available if she needed someone to speak to. "*Fabienne, si w bezwen yon moun pou pale, mwen la.*"

Through tears, she said, "*Mèsi Manushka, men mwen pa sou pale kounye a.*" Fabienne was thankful I asked, but she didn't feel like talking.

That night, I listened as she cried herself to sleep. As much as I wanted to provide some comfort, I respected her decision to be left alone. Understanding the difficulty of the transition, my father took the weekend off to spend some time with Fabienne. After a couple of days, she warmed up a little, letting her guard down. On that Sunday, we went to church as a family; surprisingly, my father joined us. I could tell by the stares that the congregation was surprised as well. We took our usual seats but needed a little more space this time around. The pastor preached about marriage. Since I wasn't married, at least not yet, I drifted off with thoughts of Devonte until Fabienne tapped me on the shoulder. She wanted me to walk with her to the bathroom. Seeing us make our way outside the sanctuary, Widelene signaled, indicating that she would join us in the lobby. As we waited for Widelene, I saw Claude approaching us, but he was looking directly at Fabienne this time.

"Hey, who's your friend, Manushka?" he asked.

"She's my sister, so don't get any ideas," I said, trying to be as stern as possible in hopes that Claude would just walk away. Fabienne and I weren't close yet, but there was absolutely no way I would let her get mixed up with someone like him.

"Damn, girl! Why you actin' like that? I know how to treat the ladies. And you know the ladies love Claude." He licked his lips again as though it was attractive. Why in the world was he referring to himself in the third person now?

"I heard about how you treat the ladies; in fact, everyone knows. That's exactly why I'm telling you my sister is off limits," I said, slightly raising my voice.

"Seems like you a little jealous, especially since your boyfriend left town. Do you want some attention from Claude, too? Claude has enough love for all the ladies. Devonte probably has a new girl already. So, I think you could use a little attention from Claude." He adjusted his clothing as if someone was checking for him.

His mentioning Devonte was upsetting, but I had to stay in control. "I don't care if you were the last male left on the planet; there is no way I would be interested in you. Now, move out of my way! I have someone important to speak to." I pushed right past him.

I made sure to grab Fabienne's hand to get away from Claude. I explained to her why my attitude toward him was so bad, and that she should never consider dating anyone like him. After another five minutes, Widelene finally showed up.

"Girl, what took you so long?" I asked.

"My mother wanted me to hear a part of the sermon. Is this your sister?" Widelene asked.

"Yup, that's Fabienne," I said. I introduced them to each other before returning to the sanctuary.

Since my father joined us for church, my mother didn't stay long after the service.

I thought about what Claude said as I lay in bed. How long would it take before Devonte found a new girlfriend? That night, I cried myself to sleep, knowing an end to my relationship with Devonte was coming soon. I was afraid to share my feelings with Fabienne. Could I trust her? Should I trust her? I wasn't willing to take the risk, at least not yet. I needed more time to get to know her.

During winter break, I didn't hang out with Janae and Widelene much. I spent most of my time with Fabienne. Since she needed new clothing for school, I took her to my favorite spot. You guessed it, the thrift store. Fabienne's face lit up as we shopped. I was happy to know we shared the same enthusiasm about clothing. After shopping, I took her to a pizzeria. My parents were surprisingly generous with the money they gave us for shopping. I was determined to make the best of it. We ended the last part of our trip at the mall to pick up some sneakers. Shopping at the mall without Widelene and Janae felt kind of weird; this was one of our hangout spots. Since Fabienne didn't speak English, I spent a lot of time translating.

Once we returned home, I could tell by the look on my parents' faces they were happy we were getting along. I pretty much spent all of the winter break getting to know Fabienne. Between watching movies and talking, we were getting along better than I expected. And, of course, bonding much faster than I imagined. Winter break went by quickly. Soon it was time for Fabienne to start school.

Chapter 22

I didn't meet Janae and Widelene at our morning meet-up spot because my father drove Fabienne and I to school to complete the registration forms. She was placed in the twelfth grade. Since the paperwork needed to be processed, Fabienne would have to start school the following day, and I could tell by the look on her face that she was relieved.

With that settled, my father and Fabienne left, so I went to class. As usual, art was the best part of the day. Mrs. Franca wasn't like other teachers. She took time to listen to our concerns and answered all of our questions, even the ones that seemed silly. "Manushka, I would like to speak to you after class," she said, interrupting my thoughts. When the bell rang to signal the end of the period, I walked toward her desk. "The competition is around the corner. How are you feeling?" she asked.

"I'm a little nervous—no, actually, I'm extremely nervous."

"That's to be expected, considering this is your first competition. Try your best to relax and think positive." Mrs. Franca patted me on the back as I walked towards the door.

Following her advice, I took a deep breath.

The next class was language arts. That was one of the classes Devonte and I used to have together. I couldn't help but stare at the empty chair beside me—no more note-passing or smiles. Devonte was gone. Overall, the day was a little difficult as I tried to adjust to the reality that my boyfriend no longer attended the same school. The only thing that could make me feel better was speaking to Devonte, which I planned to do right after school. My mother was more comfortable working longer hours since I wasn't home alone. Besides, since Fabienne couldn't fully speak and understand English yet, there was no way she would know what Devonte and I were talking about. I managed to get through the first couple of periods before lunch, which was going to be one of the highlights of my day. I was looking forward to catching up with my friends.

As I walked over to the table where Janae and Widelene sat, I couldn't help but look at the table where Devonte and I used to have lunch together. "Manushka, get over here, girl," Janae shouted as she waved.

"Based on the way you're waving me down, you better have some juicy news to share." I placed my backpack on the bench and sat down.

"You know that guy I've been crushing on for the last couple of months, captain of the debate team, Patrick Monty? Well, he finally came to his senses and noticed me. He asked me out on a date. So, I'm gonna need you and Widelene to hook me up." I'd seen Janae happy before, but nothing like this.

"What! Girl, you know I got you. When is the date?" I asked.

"This Saturday. In fact, it's a double date because his twin brother Melvin is interested in Widelene."

I looked over at Widelene, who sat there smiling from ear to ear. "When did this all happen?" I asked out of curiosity.

"We had a substitute during second period who pretty much gave us free time. While I was talking to Widelene, Monty decided to sit right beside me. He gave me a few compliments before asking me on a date. His exact words were—Are you ready for this? Staring into my eyes, Monty said, 'Janae, I've been watching you for a bit, and you always look fine. Unlike a lot of the girls at this school, you're not only fine but intelligent, too. You're the perfect combination of beauty and brains. So, I'm wondering, would you like to go on a date with me?'"

Barely able to contain her excitement, Janae said, "Girl, it was hard, but you know I had to play it cool. So I said, 'I've been watching you for a bit too. You're not like the other guys at this school; you take your grades seriously. I'm trying to be a Supreme Court Justice one day. I can't hang out with just anyone. Oh, and you're kinda fine, too.'"

"What! So, when did Melvin ask Widelene out?" Fully captivated by the story, I wanted to know more about all of the details.

Eager to share her part of the story, Widelene said, "Monty had to nudge Melvin to get him to speak. Then he eventually said, 'Widelene, would you like to go on a date with me? I figure we can go on a double date to the movies; I mean, if that's okay with you. But if you don't want to, I mean, I understand.' I could tell Melvin was nervous; he was fidgeting with his pen. I quickly said, 'I would love to go on a date with you, Melvin.' I had to respond fast because all this fidgeting with the pen was even making me nervous. Girl, if he clicked that pen one more time—I don't know what I would've said or done!'"

"You got Melvin feeling all nervous. Well, I'm so excited for the both of you," I said.

"How are you feeling, you know, with Devonte being at a different school and all?" Widelene asked with concern.

"Well, today is a little difficult. When I was in language arts, I looked over to where Devonte used to sit. I'm going to miss him in class, at lunch, and, of course, I'm going to miss our walks in the halls together." I let out a deep sigh.

"I know it's difficult now, but it will get a little easier over time," Widelene said. "Besides, you guys have a great relationship. If there's any couple that can survive a long-distance relationship, it's you and Devonte." She was actually more hopeful about my relationship than I was.

"Hey, Manushka, how is it having a new big sister?" Janae asked.

"Actually, it's not bad at all. Fabienne seems nice so far. We've been getting along well. We went shopping together during the break. Turns out we have similar tastes in clothing. She's starting school tomorrow."

"Wow, I'm happy you guys are getting along well." Janae said. "I sure do wish I had a sister, too. Being an only child has its benefits, but it can get a little lonely sometimes."

Just like that, lunch was over, and it was time for French class.

I hoped Mr. Dupont was in a good mood today. Oddly, he was not standing by the door. I entered the class with a smile, thinking he was absent. Unfortunately, he was seated at his desk with a look that was more serious than usual. I guess he had a bad weekend. *"Bonjours, les étudiants,"* Mr. Dupont said. Uh oh, he had a stack of papers in his hand. According to Mr. Dupont, he'd graded our assignments over the winter break and was highly disappointed with our performance. Seriously, does he not have a life? Why in the world was he grading papers during a vacation? One by one, he returned our assignments. When he got to my desk, Mr. Dupont stopped to whisper, "You could use some tutoring." Fuming, I thought, *Tutoring? How about you try being a better teacher? In fact, how about you try a whole different profession?* I looked at my paper only to find red marks everywhere. My grade was a D+, a D+! It was official; Mr. Dupont hated me, and I finally had evidence that couldn't be denied. How in the world did I get a D+? And what was the point of the +? Failing is failing! I spent hours working on this assignment just to earn a failing grade. Bathroom pass or not, I needed to leave the classroom before I said the wrong thing. Without a word, I walked out.

"Hey, Manushka, what's wrong? I bet Claude can make you smile. You know the ladies love Claude, and Claude loves the ladies." Out of all the people I could possibly run into, I ran into Claude. I was shocked to even see him at school. This definitely isn't the time to entertain his foolishness. I walked right past him without saying a word. Between time in the bathroom and the hallway, I finally regained my composure. I entered the classroom quietly. There was absolutely no way I was going to fail this class. I couldn't give Mr. Dupont the satisfaction, and the last thing I wanted was to attend summer school. Where in the world would I find a tutor for French?

French class always seemed like the longest period of the day. The school day was finally over, and I was looking forward to meeting up with my girls.

"Manushka, what's wrong?" Widelene asked as we waited for Janae, who had to meet with her debate teacher to prepare for a competition.

"I got a D+ on a French assignment. Mr. Dupont said I need a tutor. Where in the world am I going to find a tutor in time to resubmit the assignment?" I felt defeated. "One day, he says I have potential, but now I need tutoring. I'm so confused!"

"Have you thought about asking Fabienne for help? I mean, she attended school in Haiti. There's a chance she'll be able to help, so ask. You never know," Widelene said.

"You know, that's a great idea," I said, hoping Fabienne would be the answer to my prayers.

After about fifteen minutes, Janae walked out of the school building with a huge smile.

"Hey, girl, we've been waiting for you forever. What took so long?" Widelene asked.

"Well, after speaking to Ms. Carrington about the upcoming debate competition, I found Monty waiting for me, so we talked about a few things. I looked at my phone and realized how much time had passed. I'm so sorry," Janae said, genuinely apologetic.

"Miss Punctual had us waiting for fifteen whole minutes! I mean, did you think of how we felt waiting and worrying about you, young lady? I never expected this type of behavior from you of all people, Janae." That was probably my only chance to say something about her being late because Janae was always on time. Just before she could respond, I said, "Girl, you know I'm joking. Widelene and I had a few things to talk about."

Janae had a comeback. "Oh, you got jokes now that you've been early a couple of times. Okay!"

We all laughed, knowing it was only a matter of time before I was late to meet up with them in the morning.

On the way home, I gave them advice on the outfits they should wear for the date. Widelene had the hairstyles covered. The trains were slower than usual, so getting home took a little extra time.

I walked through the doors to find Fabienne crying. I gave her time before asking questions. Turns out she was feeling homesick. She missed her friends, family, boyfriend, and most of all, her mother. Wait! Did Fabienne just share the fact that she has a boyfriend? *Yes! I can talk to her about Devonte.* Putting my curiosity aside, I tried my best to console her. Fabienne felt guilty. She wanted to get to know and build a relationship with our father, but she also wanted to be with her mother. I told Fabienne she needed more time to adjust to the culture, lifestyle, and environment change.

I didn't want to be selfish, but since my mother wasn't home, it was the best time to call Devonte without getting caught. Even though my mother wasn't home, I didn't want to risk calling Devonte in the living room or kitchen. Rushing to my bedroom, I dialed his number eagerly, and he picked up on the first ring. "Hey, Devonte."

"Hey, Manushka, I'm surprised you called me at this time, but I'm not complaining." Hearing his smooth voice brought back memories of our many phone conversations.

"My mother isn't home yet, so I figured I'd give you a call. I miss you. How was school today? Did you meet any new people?" There was so much to catch up with. I wanted to know what he was thinking and how he was feeling.

"I miss you too. Lunch was kind of weird. I sat alone for the entire period. You know, it's not easy being the new guy. The teachers seem OK so far, I guess."

"It's only a matter of time before you make some friends." As much as I wanted Devonte to be back at his old school with me, I wanted him to have a good experience.

"Manushka, remember that non-profit organization my mother told you about? She's meeting with the girls next Saturday around noon. She wanted to know if you, Widelene, and Janae would be interested in being guest speakers that week?"

"I don't have any plans next Saturday, so I would love to be a guest speaker. I'll speak to Janae and Widelene tomorrow and then let you know. Do you mind if Fabienne joins us?"

"Wow! Seems like you and your sister are getting along well. Bring her. I'm sure my mother won't mind."

We stayed on the phone for about an hour before I left to do some homework. Turns out that Fabienne was able to help me with the French assignment. I learned more from her in thirty minutes than half a school year with Mr. Dupont. With the changes to this paper, there was absolutely no way I would get anything less than a B. I was looking forward to going to school. I imagined making a dramatic entrance into the classroom, then slamming my paper on the desk, staring directly into the eyes of the evil Mr. Dupont. Since my mother still believes in spankings, I'll just leave the thought in my mind.

Chapter 23

It was time for Fabienne to start school. We took the train and met up with Janae and Widelene. My girls were welcoming, which helped Fabienne feel a little more at ease. We went to the front office to pick up her schedule. I walked Fabienne to class, which made me late, but I didn't mind. Thankfully, we had the same lunch period, so she joined us. This would probably be the norm until she made her own group of friends. I instructed Fabienne to wait for me after each class to make sure she didn't get lost. After lunch, it was time for French, of course. I walked into the room and gently placed my assignment on the desk, even though I wanted to slam it.

"I would like to speak to you after class," Mr. Dupont said.

What in the world did this man want to say to me? Whatever it was, I wasn't interested, but I didn't have much of a choice. We worked through a couple of assignments then the bell rang. I hesitantly approached Mr. Dupont's desk.

"Manushka, were you able to find a tutor? I'm concerned with your performance on the last assignment. Considering your potential, I would hate to see you fail this class."

His smirk annoyed me. In fact, everything about Mr. Dupont annoyed me: his face, pencil-thin mustache, hair, outfit choices, shoes, glasses, voice, and the way he walked. I had to put my feelings of disdain aside and respond in a somewhat pleasant manner. "I did find a tutor. In fact, I learned so much in just one session. My tutor would really be a great high school French teacher. All the students would love my tutor." Take that, Mr. Dupont, I thought as I imitated his smirk.

"Oh, really? Where did you find such a great—"

I cut him off as I remembered Fabienne. Truthfully, I really didn't want to give him an answer. "Mr. Dupont, I have to go now. I don't want to be late for my next class," I said, rushing out the door.

From the look on his face, I could tell he was interested in finding out who the tutor was.

As I ran down the hallway to meet Fabienne, she called out, "Manunu, Manunu." Did she just call me by my nickname at school? Ahhh, I screamed internally! I hoped no one heard her, even though a few people turned to stare in my direction. I couldn't hold it against her; Fabienne had no clue I didn't want people to know my nickname. I walked her to the next few classes before the day ended.

After school, we met with Janae and Widelene, who were equally excited about their double date. "Hey, guys, Devonte's mother wants to know if you would speak to the girls in her non-profit organization next Saturday. Do you have any plans?" I asked.

"I'm down," Widelene said. "I don't have any plans on Saturday aside from packaging a few products."

"I'll just get my debate speech out the way early so I can be available," Janae said.

The week went by fast. It was already Friday. Surprisingly, Fabienne didn't need me to walk her to class. I was proud of her for making an effort to adjust so quickly.

I walked to class slowly, hoping Mr. Dupont was absent. Well, no such luck for me because he was standing in front of the classroom with a stack of papers in his hand. "Class, I decided to grade the assignments early out of curiosity.. Most of you did a great job making the necessary adjustments." He walked around, distributing the graded papers. "Surprisingly, some of you exceeded my expectations. I take great pride in my work as a teacher; I don't want anyone to fail this class."

He handed me my paper face down. I was so nervous; according to the syllabus, this assignment was 25% of my final grade. I took a deep breath and slowly picked up the edge of the paper. No red marks were detected. My grade was an A-, an A-! That's the highest grade I ever got in this class. I only had one red mark on the paper, yet he added the minus to my grade. With the failing grade, the D+ was written extremely big, but he had the nerve to make my A- almost microscopic. Seriously! Nothing was going to take this smile off my face today, not even Mr. Dupont. As I left the classroom, he said, "Manushka, tell your tutor they did a great job."

Unsure of how to answer, I said, "*Au revoir*, Mr. Dupont." I hope he didn't think I cheated. I would rather get a failing grade than cheat; I do have good morals.

Since I had nowhere to go on Saturday, I stayed home and hung out with Fabienne, who braided my hair. I was a little hesitant to let her braid my hair at first since she'd only worn her hair in a ponytail every day. I was so wrong. Fabienne had my hair looking amazing—not a strand out of place. We spent a lot of time talking about her life in Haiti, including her boyfriend, whom she has been dating for two years. As we enjoyed each other's company, I couldn't help but feel grateful for having a sister. Sure, I lost some privacy and a part of my room, but it was worth it. Our Sunday routine now included my mother, Fabienne, and I walking to church together.

I waited all weekend to get details about Janae and Widelene's double date. As soon as I got to our meetup spot, I hit them with a barrage of questions. "How was the date? What did you wear? Did you have fun? Are you going on double dates again or solo? Fill me in!"

Janae immediately said, "My date was amazing. The movie was great and all, but my favorite part of the date was talking to Monty. Man, he had so much to say. Turns out he wants to go into politics, so he's considering going the law route in college. Oh, and he was lookin' fine from head to toe. We plan to go out again. He spoke to my mom on the phone before we went out, and she got a good vibe from him, too. My outfit was cute, you already know. I'll show you some pictures later."

I looked over at Widelene, who didn't seem as excited. "All right, Widelene, tell me about your date," I said.

"Girl, with a name like Melvin, I should have known he would be boring. I felt like I was babysitting the entire time. He seemed so nervous, acting like I was a lion about to eat him for dinner. I initiated all the conversations. At one point, I decided to stop speaking. I think I won the prize for the worst date. He better not try to ask me out again." Widelene rolled her eyes. She was always a positive person who took the time to encourage everyone, so I was shocked by her reaction. The date must have been really awful if Widelene couldn't find a bright side to the situation.

I wanted to lighten the mood. "I guess Melvin was so captivated by your beauty and perfection that he was afraid to speak to you, your majesty." Curious, I asked, "Would you consider going out with him again? You know, give him another chance."

Widelene quickly said, "Absolutely not! Girl, didn't you hear me? Melvin was dry as a rice cake, and so was the date."

We all laughed, except for Fabienne, since she still didn't fully understand English. I translated the conversation so she didn't feel left out.

"Manushka, girl, your hair is looking good. I wanna get my hair done, too. Who hooked you up, and was it expensive?" Widelene asked.

"Give me her number also," Janae said. "I need to get my hair braided, too."

"Oh, Fabienne did my hair. I got the little sister hookup."

"I hope she gives me a family discount since we're best friends and all," Janae said as we all laughed.

And just like that, Fabienne got two new customers.

"Hey, remember, don't make any plans for Saturday. Devonte's mother is looking forward to having us as guest speakers." I wanted to remind them of the event. Lord knows I didn't want to disappoint

Devonte's mother. All I could think of that week was seeing his face. It had already been sixty-three days, seven hours, and fifty-one minutes since we last saw each other.

Chapter 24

Time to see my boyfriend, yeah, my boyfriend. I was singing and dancing in front of the mirror as I put on the final touch to my outfit, hoop earrings. Fabienne and I left early to give me extra time to hang out with Devonte before the event began. Widelene and Janae decided to meet us at the community center. When I arrived, Devonte was waiting outside the center. I wanted to run to him, but I was trying to be cute by wearing these uncomfortable boots. The last thing I wanted was to break my ankle, so I walked towards him to play it safe.

Without even saying any words, Devonte hugged me so tight it almost took my breath away. I matched his intensity with the same amount of love, energy, and strength. All thoughts escaped my mind entirely to the point of temporarily forgetting about Fabienne. It felt like the world had stopped, and we were the only two people on the planet. Right before Devonte's attempt to kiss me, I saw his mother from the corner of my eye—talk about bad timing.

"Good morning, Dr. Robinson," I quickly said, adjusting my clothing.

"I'm sure you two love birds missed each other," she said. "Come on in and have some breakfast. I'm happy you made time to join us today." She led us down the hall towards a small lounge area.

"Thank you for inviting us. I almost forgot: This is my sister Fabienne. She recently moved here from Haiti." I pointed toward Fabienne, who waved at both Devonte and Dr. Robinson.

Seated in the lounge, Devonte and I talked while periodically including Fabienne. As we spoke, I couldn't help but admire my handsome boyfriend. His personality, complexion, eyes, height, everything about him was still perfect. We had so much to talk about; as usual, there was never a dull moment when we were together. Devonte even seemed happier. Spending more time with his parents had a positive impact on him.

When Widelene and Janae arrived at 11:30 a.m., Dr. Robinson gave us a rundown of the day. "Considering you all are teenage girls, thank you for carving time out of your busy schedules to join us today. As I mentioned before, with this organization, we make it a point to encourage the girls to use their voices and share their stories. After lunch, each one of you will be set up in a breakout room to share your experiences with career aspirations, businesses, academics, and of course, the recent petition. No need to be nervous. I will stop by each room so you won't be alone. During the morning session, we will discuss teen dating violence, a problem that is too often overlooked. Once our guest speaker is done sharing her story, we'll create an open forum for discussion and provide everyone with some preventative strategies and resources."

The whole idea of teen dating violence was a little strange to me. I didn't even think it was a thing. Dating as a teenager is supposed to be fun, not dangerous. Going on dates to the movies, walking hand in hand in the hallways, having long conversations on the phone, balloons, chocolate, and teddy bears on Valentine's Day— that's what comes to mind when I think about teenage dating. I heard of domestic violence, but that only happened in adult relationships; at least, that's what I always thought.

We all followed Dr. Robinson into a large room where several girls were seated. Devonte sat way in the back at his mother's request. He was the only guy there. It seems like he was also operating the speaker system. Dr. Robinson passed the microphone to a girl who looked about sixteen or seventeen years old. She cleared her throat before speaking..

"Hello, everyone, my name is Nicole. Dr. Robinson invited me to be a guest speaker today. I'm nervous because this is my first time sharing my story, so please be patient with me. Okay, here it goes." Nicole took a deep breath and briefly closed her eyes. "I was in the eleventh grade when I started dating this guy that all the girls wanted because he was tall, handsome, and popular. Instead of saying his name, I'll just call him R. I felt lucky to be R.'s girlfriend, you know, and I loved the attention he gave me. In fact, I needed the attention. See, my mom is what you would call a high achiever. She had high expectations of me, especially when it came to grades. I tried but couldn't meet her expectations since school was hard for me. Science, language arts, social studies—anything that required reading and writing was a challenge. No matter how hard I tried, I just couldn't get it. My dad, well, I never met him. He left when my mom was pregnant."

A woman in the front row repeatedly wiped a stream of tears running down her face. Based on her facial features, she was most likely Nicole's mother. Nicole continued speaking. "R. made me feel special. He was the first person to ever say that I was pretty and smart. So, I was willing to do almost anything he wanted. When I tell you, girls at my school were so jealous, some even wanted to fight me over R. We spent so much time together that I didn't have time to hang out with my friends anymore. They were mad, but I figured it was jealousy. R. and I used to cut classes to spend time together, so my grades slipped even more. My mother forced me to stay after school for tutoring, and that's when our relationship changed. I was getting tutored by the stereotypical nerdy guy, you know, one with big glasses and bad outfits. Well, after my first tutoring session, I noticed the look on R.'s face was a little different, but I didn't think anything of it. After my second session, R. said he was upset about me spending time with the tutor because he was a guy. I thought him being jealous was kind of cute and meant that he loved me. After about a month, he told me to quit tutoring, which I couldn't do. I wasn't trying to get into more trouble with my mom." She closed her eyes for a moment and placed a hand on her forehead.

Dr. Robinson said, "Take your time, Nicole. If you need to stop at any point, I'm sure everyone will understand." Her words gave Nicole the encouragement she needed to continue speaking.

"The look on his face and the sound of his voice were so scary that day. I didn't know that version of him, and I didn't know what to do. Of course, R. apologized and said I made him act that way because he loved me so much. You know, I've heard those stories before and even saw them on TV. I always thought those women were stupid because love wasn't supposed to hurt. Well, it turns out I was the stupid one. R. started getting mad about little things, like my clothing, people I spoke to, things that I would say—I mean just about everything. He hit me almost every time we were together for about five months, but I kept making excuses for him even though things were getting worse. I figured if I stopped making him mad, he wouldn't have a reason to hit me anymore. It was easy to hide the bruises because he never hit me on the face until—until I got the courage to tell him to stop. R. was so furious at the idea of me speaking up. I remember him punching me in the face so hard I must have blacked out for a few minutes. I tried covering the bruise with makeup, but no amount of makeup was enough to disguise the swelling. It was time to tell my mother the truth and show her all the bruises on my body. When she saw the bruises, my mother immediately took me to the emergency room to make sure there was no internal damage. I met Dr. Robinson in the emergency room that day. She wasn't like other doctors. Dr. Robinson took time to listen to me. Thank God, there was no internal bleeding, so we went home. I heard my mother cry herself to sleep that night. That was the first time I ever heard her cry about anything."

Nicole looked directly at the woman in the front row who was still wiping tears off her face. Dr. Robinson moved to the front of the room where she handed the woman a box of tissues while rubbing her back.

Nicole continued. "The next day, we went to the police and did the paperwork for a restraining order. I'm so confused right now. R. doesn't have a good relationship with his family. He needs a lot of help, he needs someone in his life who can love and support him. Even though R. hurt me, I still love…" Nicole started crying uncontrollably before finishing the sentence. The woman who had been crying quickly walked to the front of the room to embrace her. Together, they walked out the door.

Dr. Robinson picked up the microphone. "It took a lot of courage for Nicole to share her story today in hopes of helping other girls. Teen dating violence is real! Jealousy to the point of not wanting you to hang out with your friends is not love, and it ain't cute. One, abusers are often intentional about isolating their victims from friends and family to assure that you have no one else to rely on; this also limits if not eliminates the opportunity to seek help. Two, controlling all your decisions is not protection. You are an individual; therefore, you are entitled to have your own thoughts, feelings, and points of view. Three, hitting you for any reason is never justifiable. Do you hear me, never? You should not be in a relationship with anyone who thinks it's OK to hit you because the violence will only escalate. Four, don't expect people to change for you. Nicole, for instance, thought that changing her actions along with the love she demonstrated would change R. Despite everything she did, the violence continued to escalate."

Dr. Robinson looked at each girl in the room, intentionally making eye contact with us. She wanted to make sure we got the message about teen dating violence was fully conveyed. She cleared her throat and said loudly, "Please understand that genuine change comes from within. Change has to be internally driven, not solely based on the actions or requests of others. Five, don't ever think you're grown enough to handle this kind of situation alone. Please speak to a parent, teacher, counselor, or trusted adult. From the looks on your faces, I know this is a tough topic, so let's take a fifteen-minute break. After the break, we will open the floor for questions before lunch. Following lunch, our special guests Manushka, Widelene, and Janae will share some information with you all."

Dr. Robinson was speaking, but I couldn't process anything she was saying. I had no clue that some teenagers were in abusive relationships. Did the guy return, did something else happen, and was Nicole still scared? I had so many questions to ask, especially since she didn't finish sharing her story. The pain in her eyes as she spoke made my heart so heavy. I looked around the room, and everyone was quiet; the mood was a little somber. I guess I wasn't the only one wondering if Nicole would return and if she was OK. Dr. Robinson and another woman shared information about warning signs and resources for teen dating violence. Turns out February is National Teen Dating Violence Awareness and Prevention Month. I ended up learning more than I expected today.

After lunch, Widelene, Janae, and I were placed in separate rooms with small groups of girls. I shared fashion tips and information about upcycling. I had a display, including before-and-after pictures, so the girls could better understand the upcycling process. All the girls seemed to enjoy the Q&A. Although Fabienne was still learning English, she appeared interested also.

Once the event was over, Dr. Robinson walked us to the door along with Devonte. "Manushka, Janae, and Widelene, again, thank you for joining us today. Based on the feedback, the girls enjoyed your presentations. You're welcome to attend our future meetings. We have some more topics that I think you all would find interesting and enlightening. Manushka, please tell Fabienne she's also welcome to attend in the future."

Janae, Widelene, and Fabienne waited as I spoke to Devonte privately. Devonte held my hands. "I know we didn't spend much time together today, but I'm happy to see you."

"I'm happy to see you too."

Devonte kissed me on the cheek since we weren't alone.

"Enough with the mushy stuff," Janae shouted. "We're ready to go! It's cold out here, and my pinkie toe hurts."

We all laughed.

On the train ride home, we spoke about Nicole's story. "Guys, I don't know about you, but Nicole's story was a little scary," Widelene said.

Always with a plan, Janae said, "Let's make a pact. No matter where we are or what we're doing, let's promise to be open and honest with each other. If I see something in your relationship that makes me question your safety, I'm gonna say something even if you get mad. If I can't help you, I'll find the right person to speak to, whether it's a parent, a teacher, or even Dr. Robinson."

"Janae, that is a great idea," I chimed in. "I'll do the same."

Widelene nodded. "Yup, it's a great idea. So, I will do the same, too. But let's add a little more to the pact. How about promising to be best friends forever through the good and bad times?"

Liking Widelene's addition, we all shook hands and hugged to solidify our pact.

And before I knew it, it was Monday morning, just five days before the art competition.

Chapter 25

Everyone woke up extra early so we wouldn't be late for the competition. We were all seated in the car, getting ready to drive off, when my mother decided to go back in to make sure the stove was off. I was a little tense when she returned upstairs, but I understood the logic. My dad dropped me off in front of the school since he needed more time to find a parking spot. I stood in front of the building right before walking in. Saying that I was nervous was an understatement.

Students from high schools in all five boroughs entered the competition, totaling 100 contestants. The room was crowded, with everyone's artwork on display. Judges walked around, taking notes and having conversations about each piece. I tried to maintain composure by conversing with some other contestants. Did they like my art? Were they impressed? Did my piece measure up? Take deep breaths, Manushka, I reminded myself. Contestants were placed on one side of the gymnasium; family and friends were required to stay on the other side. After the first hour, results were released. I made it past round one, which was a sign that my art piece was at least decent.

I also made it past round two, thank God. My sigh of relief was so loud that it caught the attention of the other contestants, who turned around to look at me. I'm no doctor, but I was sure that my heart rate increased with every passing second. Sweaty palms, racing heart, restless, I could go on about everything happening within my body. My thoughts were racing, so much self-doubt. At that moment, I looked at

Mrs. Franca, who gave me a thumbs-up and whispered, "I'm so proud of you." One more round to go, but the final round was different. This round required that we speak to the judges to explain our work.

I was so lost in my thoughts that I didn't even realize he was calling my name until one of the other contestants tapped me on the shoulder. "Manushka Jean-Pierre, Manushka Jean-Pierre," a gentleman said. He looked about college-age. Startled, I stood up quickly but stumbled as I approached him. "Please follow me. I will be taking you to a room with three judges," he said. "I can tell you're nervous. Try to relax; I'm sure everything will work out just fine."

I picked up my painting and took it into a classroom. Once in the room, I placed the painting on an easel and analyzed the judges. Each had a visible badge with a number on it rather than a name. Judge 1 seemed like a bubbly middle-aged woman. Judge 2 was a younger man who wore a suit and glasses. He was overdressed for the occasion; I guess he wanted people to take him seriously since he appeared less seasoned. Everyone seemed friendly with a smile on their face except for Judge number 3, who happened to be a woman probably around twenty-five to thirty years old. I was impressed with Judge 3's choice of clothing; it was trendy. But the look on her face made me uncomfortable.

Judge 1 greeted me immediately. "Don't be scared. I promise we won't bite." I guess uncertainty and some degree of fear were apparent on my face and through my body language.

Finally, I found the courage to greet the judges. "Good morning, everyone," I said with a half-smile. *Breathe, Manushka.*

"We're impressed with your work," Judge 1 said. First, we would like you to describe your painting."

I quietly cleared my throat before speaking. "Um, the title of this painting is Brushed Between Cultures. I painted myself walking along an illuminated path toward my dreams with boldness and determination. In the background, one side represents Haiti, while the other side represents New York City. The paintbrush represents painting my reality and my love for the arts."

"Great! Now, would you kindly explain what inspired you to create such an amazing work of art?" Judge 2 asked, his voice shockingly deep, to the point that I was a little taken aback. Based on his size, I didn't think he would sound like that. Judge 3 remained silent as she stared at me.

It was time to begin my speech, so there was no turning back. Judge 1 repositioned her body in the chair and then adjusted her outfit; Judge 2 started fidgeting with his pen—all signs that I was taking too long to begin speaking. Judge 3—Well, I was way too nervous to look in her direction. I thought about how much Mrs. Franca believed in me, then took a deep breath before speaking. "Um, my parents were born in Haiti. They came to the United States with dreams of a better life, you know, achieving the American dream. There is so much to love about Haitian culture, like our art, food, and music. I also love our strength, determination, and pride." I took a deep breath and briefly glanced at my speech before continuing. "When people talk about Haiti, poverty is usually the only focus when, in fact, Haiti contributed to American history and world history. See, Haiti was a French colony named Saint-Domingue before the slave revolt. Pressure from the slave revolt caused Napoleon to sell the Louisiana Territory in what would be called the Louisiana Purchase. The Louisiana Purchase included about 830,000 square miles, which doubled the size of the United States. The land later became fifteen states. The impact and significance of the Haitian Revolution is barely discussed as part of history. Despite what some may say about Haiti, I'm proud of my Haitian Heritage. With me, I carry the Haitian culture and life lessons taught by my parents."

I got through the first part of my speech despite being super nervous. I could feel my palms sweating as I clasped my hands together. Just a few more sentences to go, and I'd be done. My speech was practically a ball by this point as I held the paper tightly. I quickly glanced at the judges. One was taking notes as the other two looked in my direction. Time for part two of my speech. I took another deep breath.

"American culture shapes my style, the way I speak, and many of my beliefs. The cultural norms are different from what my parents are accustomed to. I love music! Between Hip Hop and R&B, I can't go a day without listening to a few songs for inspiration and entertainment. I would like to explore some other aspects of American culture, but my mom is kind of strict so I'll have to wait a few more years. In closing, my submission honors my Haitian heritage while acknowledging that I'm also an American, Haitian-American." After the last word, I looked at the judges, unsure of what their reaction would be.

Suddenly, all three judges clapped. Judges 1 and 2 clapped at a fast pace, which matched their excitement about both my art and speech. Judge 3's clap was more like a slow clap as if she couldn't keep up with the others. Or was she totally unimpressed by my painting and speech?

"Manushka, thank you for taking the time to thoroughly explain the inspiration for completing such a superb work of art," Judge 1 said. "I feel at liberty to speak on behalf of all the judges. We're all highly impressed." Everyone was smiling except for Judge 3, who appeared serious, as though she had a lot on her mind. Based on her overall reaction, I concluded that Judge 3 wasn't impressed by me at all. She didn't appear interested in anything I had to say. I had to mask my feelings of defeat as I thanked the judges. I grabbed my painting and walked out of the room.

I could barely maintain my composure as I stared at the audience—at my parents, Fabienne, Widelene, Janae, and Naomi. All the way in the back stood Devonte with a bouquet of flowers. Distance didn't stop him from supporting me. Seeing him at the competition was a great surprise, but I was too nervous to focus on him.

It was time to announce the winner of the competition. Out of 100 participants, only one person would win the grand prize. I held my breath as Judge 2 walked toward the microphone. Yes!! I made it to the top 5. The winner would be based on a cumulative score; the maximum score for the competition was 100. *Breathe, Manushka, just breathe,* I repeated as Judge 3 used hand gestures to signal where we should stand. Judge 2 continued to speak. "All of you are such talented artists with an extremely bright future in this industry. Now, the moment you have all been waiting for has finally arrived. We will share the results for the top five contestants. Before I do, I just want all of you to be proud of yourselves. Hold your head up high, no matter the outcome; don't be discouraged. In fifth place is Jerica Samuels, with a cumulative score of 78. In fourth place is Sally Quong, with a cumulative score of 83. Now, we're down to the top three contestants. In third place is Michael Downings, with a cumulative score of 95. In second place with a cumulative score of 97 is Manushka Jean-Pierre," Judge 2 said.

I couldn't hear anything else. It was as though the world had temporarily stopped.

I had mixed emotions about winning second place. Second place wasn't bad, considering this was my first competition, but only the first-place winner would receive the grand prize. And naturally, everyone wants to be in the first place. Pushing through countless emotions, I had to contain my feelings of disappointment. "And the first place winner, with a cumulative score of 98, is Madison Jennings," Judge 2 said.

She beat me by one point. *One* point, really? Somehow, I found the strength to shake Madison's hand and congratulate her on the win. A summer internship in Italy with a famous artist, welp, I don't think my mother would let me go anyway. Saddened, I looked over to see Devonte in the crowd blowing me a kiss.

I slowly walked over to my friends and family. Mrs. Franca stood right there beside them. "Manushka, you should be proud of yourself," Mrs. Franca said. I know you didn't win first place, but this is your first time participating in this competition. Out of 100 students, you came in second place. That is a great accomplishment. I believe, without a doubt, that you have a gift. So please don't forget me when you're rich and famous." She continued to speak, but it was directed at my parents this time. "Mr. and Mrs. Jean-Pierre, you have a smart, talented, and respectful daughter. I love having her in my class. She has a bright future in the arts. I know you're proud of her," Mrs. Franca said as she shook my parents' hands before leaving.

"Girl, you know we're so proud of you," Janae said.

"Yes, your painting is amazing. I love how you represented with the Haitian flag. Hold your head up, girl; you should be proud of your accomplishments today. Here, take these beautiful flowers," Widelene said with a wink to signal that the flowers were from Devonte.

"I'm so proud of my goddaughter. You know you get your talents from my side of the family, right?" Naomi said with a laugh.

Sensing my pain, Fabienne hugged me without saying a word, which was exactly what I needed. Everyone wanted to say the right thing to encourage me, but I just needed a little time to process the whole experience. As Fabienne hugged me, I saw my parents staring at the painting. I saw my mother's eyes filling up with tears; she didn't say a word, but I knew she was proud of me. I knew the painting reminded her of the many great memories in Haiti she often spoke of. As we all walked toward the exit, Judge 3 approached me.

"Excuse me, Manushka Jean-Pierre, if you have a moment, I would love to speak to you," Judge 3 said.

With a nod, my mother signaled it was okay for me to speak to her. I briefly stared at her as we walked off to the side of the gymnasium. This time, her face looked a little different, almost approachable. Why in the world would she want to speak to me? I mean, when she had a chance to speak, she decided to give me a blank stare instead. What I really wanted to say was that I didn't have time to talk to her. And I wasn't interested in anything she had to say. Instead, I decided to be polite, especially since my parents were looking in our direction.

"Manushka, I was highly impressed by your painting. Every detail you created made me speechless, in case you were wondering why I didn't speak before and after your presentation. Like you, I was born in Brooklyn. My love for the arts began when I visited Haiti for the first time at age nine. The paintings, sculptures, creativity, and colors drew me in. From that moment, I knew I wanted to be an artist. As you spoke, I saw myself in you."

I couldn't believe it: Judge 3 was speaking to me, and she was actually nice. Astonished by her story, all I could do was listen and nod. This was the first time I met a Haitian-American artist.

"I related to everything you shared," Judge 3 said. "Although you did not win the grand prize of a summer internship with a well-known artist in Italy, I would love to offer you a full-time summer internship with me here in New York City. Here's my business card. Let's touch base sometime next week; call me one day after school. I can give you and your parents more details in English or Creole, whatever it takes for you to work with me this summer. By the way, my name is Stephanie Mondesir."

Wait, what? Was I hallucinating, or did the judge, who I thought hated me, just offer a summer internship? "Thank you, Ms. Mondesir. I'm looking forward to speaking with you next week," I said enthusiastically while holding her business card tightly. This internship may be the key to a future in the world of art.

"Great, but you can call me Stephanie. Speak to you soon."

I watched as she walked away. Ms. Stephanie was extremely fashionable from head to toe. Between her tailor-made pants suit, stiletto boots, purse, and coat, everything was perfect. To be honest, she looked more like a runway model than an artist. But that may not be a fair assessment since she was the first artist I've met in person.

Chapter 26

One point! I missed first place by one point. I didn't feel like going to school the next day, but staying home was never an option unless I was deathly ill. I managed to roll out of bed to make my way to school. I got through the first few periods sluggishly. Before entering art class, I stood outside the room, and for the first time, I was late to art class. With thoughts of defeat running through my mind, I contemplated leaving school early. I didn't want to face Mrs. Franca again, especially since she believed in my talent or what she called "a gift." Apprehensively, I pushed the door open to enter the classroom.

"Manushka, Manushka, Manushka!" chanted my classmates, who gave me a standing ovation. I was pleased by their excitement, especially since I didn't win first place.

"Settle down, class, settle down. As I told you all earlier, Manushka came in second place out of 100 students in her first art competition. She can only go up from here. She overcame all the fear and nervousness that almost stopped her from entering the competition. Even more exciting is that Manushka has a summer internship with a talented artist named Stephanie Mondesir. If you ask me, working with Stephanie is better than the first-place prize," Mrs. Franca said.

How did she know about the internship? How did she even know Judge 3, I mean Ms. Stephanie?

"Okay, class, it's time to get back to work," Mrs. Franca said as she clapped to signal everyone to return to their seats immediately.

As soon as class ended, I quickly approached her. "Mrs. Franca, how did you know about the internship, and how do you know Ms. Stephanie?" I asked eagerly.

"Stephanie is a former student of mine. The truth is you remind me so much of her. That's why I know you'll be a phenomenal artist in the future. Do you see the painting up there?" She directed my attention to the wall behind her desk. "Stephanie created it when she was in the 9th grade. Just like you, I immediately identified her gift. Stephanie was too shy and afraid to share her work. But with some pushing, I mean a lot of encouragement, she eventually entered an art competition. She came in tenth place one year, sixth place the second year, and finally first place two years in a row. Her first go-rounds were challenging and heartbreaking, but Stephanie never gave up, even though the thought crossed her mind several times. One day, I would love to put your artwork right above my desk, beside Stephanie's."

"How did you know about the internship?" I needed to know, especially since I hadn't shared the information with anyone yet.

"Well, I've been Stephanie's mentor since she graduated. We speak weekly. Make sure you call her as soon as possible. In fact, try calling her today."

After speaking to Mrs. Franca, I decided to call Ms. Stephanie that day. When I got home from school, I went to my room, closed the door, took a few deep breaths, then made the call. "Um, good afternoon, my name is Manushka Jean-Pierre. May I please speak to Ms. Stephanie Mondesir?" My nerves kicked in, and my voice was shaky as I spoke.

"Hello, Manushka. I'm so glad you called. And please feel free to call me Stephanie. Linette, I mean Mrs. Franca, told me to expect your call today. This summer, I'm participating in a community revitalization project in Brownsville, Brooklyn. I have been tasked with creating five murals representing love, hope, peace, laughter, and community. I could use someone like you with fresh and innovative ideas. The internship would be seven weeks long. This is a paid internship, in case you're wondering. The hours will be 9:00 a.m. to 3:00 p.m., Monday through Thursday. You would receive a weekly check in the sum of $200. Do you have any questions?"

A paid internship! I was excited about the murals, but now I was even more excited about making some money. I scrambled to think of questions but drew a blank. "I don't have any questions yet. The only thing I have to do is speak to my mom to get permission. Oh, and if you don't mind, I would rather call you Ms. Stephanie. My mother is adamant about me addressing adults correctly."

"I understand. You can call me Ms. Stephanie. How about I help you out? Let me speak to your mother if she's available. I'll give her some information about the program and let her know I'll make sure you're safe."

Speaking to my mother was a great idea. I placed the phone down briefly to see if she was interested in speaking to Ms. Stephanie. Thankfully, my mother was willing to talk to her. I handed her the phone then listened intently to the conversation. My mother was engaged as she asked a lot of questions. At one point, they laughed as they discussed topics other than the internship, which was a great sign. After my mother hung up, she agreed to let me do the internship. Her only advice was to be careful. I often heard the saying, "Never judge a book by its cover," but now it had personal meaning. Ms. Stephanie was super nice, friendly, and down to earth; I was completely wrong about her when we first met. Even though I was going to be busy the entire summer, I was looking forward to learning as much as possible from her. Countdown to summer break, only thirty-eight days left until the end of the school year.

With the help of Fabienne, my understanding of French and my grades continued to improve. Mr. Dupont gave us more pop quizzes, but it didn't matter because I scored either an A or a high B. He kept asking about my tutor since my grades improved, but I didn't tell him. Now that I was doing well in French, school became less demanding since it had been the only class where I struggled. As the school year continued, Devonte and I only spoke a little less every day because of his schedule. He'd taken a liking to Lacrosse and wanted to join the school team. Since tryouts for the next school year were going to take place in four weeks, his mother hired a private instructor. Devonte met with the instructor five days a week for a couple of hours per day. Between meeting with the instructor and homework, we didn't have much time to speak to each other. I missed our conversations, but there was nothing I could do to change the situation.

Chapter 27

I got through junior year with As in all classes with the exception of French, which was fine. It wasn't like I was planning on having daily conversations in French. Keywords such as *bonjour, oui,* and *merci beaucoup* were pretty much all I needed to know for now. Overall, this school year was eventful between having my real first boyfriend and entering an art competition. I did get into trouble for having a boyfriend, thanks to Sè Françoise, but the good definitely outweighed the bad this year. Janae was volunteering in the community relations department for the Willow Creek Mall. Widelene was making and selling more hair products. Fabienne planned to help Widelene with the products a couple of days a week and also make money braiding hair; I got her a few clients. Devonte was vacationing in Florida with his family; he was excited about visiting the Kennedy Space Center. Between Devonte's trip and Lacrosse practice when he returned, we wouldn't have much time to speak to each other.

As for me, it was time to begin the internship with Ms. Stephanie. Not wanting to be late on the first day, I left extra early that morning. unsure what to expect. Was the office big? What would be my first assignment? Was I the only intern? No matter what, I was ready to get started. Taking a deep breath, I entered the two-story building.

Ms. Stephanie met me by the door. "Good morning young lady. Very impressive, thank you for arriving early.."

"I'm beyond excited about this opportunity, so I plan to be early every day," I said with a smile.

She gave me a tour of the place. The first floor was an open space with tables and desks, a large TV screen, painting materials, and a fridge with snacks. Ms. Stephanie used this area to train students and to create her paintings. I thought she would give me a tour of the upper floor, but she didn't, which piqued my curiosity. I wanted to ask but figured it was a bad idea. As we continued, Ms. Stephanie motioned toward a desk. Yep, my very own desk. I was moving up in the world fast. Not only did I have a desk, she also gave me one of those fancy fuzzy fur chairs with wheels.

"Manushka, the first two weeks of this internship will take place in this office. Based on the painting you submitted for the art competition, this task is right up your alley: I want you to draw a sketch representing Hope for our first mural. Do you think you can do that?" Ms. Stephanie asked as she tapped the table with her pen while waiting for me to respond.

"Yes, I'll start working on it now," I said, grabbing paper and colored pencils immediately. I didn't want to give her a simple black-and-white sketch. After restarting several times, I created a detailed sketch within two hours. Apprehensively, I walked over to her desk. "Ms. Stephanie, I finished the sketch. Would you like to see it now?" I asked.

"Wow, you finished faster than I expected. Yes, I would love to see the sketch."

I analyzed her face as she held the paper, but Ms. Stephanie remained expressionless. As she wrote some notes on a sheet of paper, I didn't know what to think. The look on her face reminded me of the art competition.

"Okay, you're off to a great start," she said eventually. "Here, read these notes. As you consider the feedback, remember, I want your uniqueness to show through everything you create. Don't create what you think I want. Instead, I want you to create something from the heart."

The bright side is that the sheet of paper was small, so there wasn't much to fix. When I returned to my desk, I sat down for about twenty minutes, looking at the sketch and reading the notes. Ms. Stephanie was right. I liked the sketch, but I didn't love it. Before restarting, I thought about my family, personal experiences, and the many stories I heard over the years about hardships and hope for inspiration. Finally, I had the perfect sketch in mind. With a big grin, I completed the colored sketch within an hour.

"Um, Ms. Stephanie, thank you for the feedback. I took your advice and created something I love. I hope you like it." I handed her my paper with more confidence this time.

Immediately, she smiled. "This is it! This is exactly what I expected of you. I love it! As you work with me this summer, it will be a learning experience for you. I want you to be true to yourself. Never add your name to anything that you disagree with. Do you understand me? Never agree to support anything that you're not proud of or anything that goes against your personal beliefs. That is the first lesson I want you to learn from me. Got it?" There probably was a story behind her words, but I guess I'd have to wait.

"Yes, I got it!" I nodded. I wanted Ms. Stephanie to know I was listening and valued her advice.

"It's lunchtime. Did you bring food?" she asked.

"Yes, my mother packed me a large bowl of rice and chicken for lunch," I said, laughing. Ms. Stephanie joined in the laughter. The lunch my mother packed was enough to feed three hungry teenage boys.

After she left to pick up a meal at the local restaurant, I settled into a reverie about a future in the arts. Ms. Stephanie made me realize that a career in the arts was actually possible. Someone like me had the potential to be a successful artist. I hoped seeing Ms. Stephanie's success would help my parents one day accept my future goal.

After lunch, she told me there was a change in plans and that we would begin painting the Hope mural the following day, which was exciting. Since it was a last-minute change, Ms. Stephanie said she'd invited her nephew to help us out. This was going to be my first mural, so I was super excited. I went home that day with what felt like a permanent smile. Nothing would change my mood, not the crowded train, not someone stepping on my toes, not the person with the funky armpits standing too close to me on the bus. Nothing at all could wipe this smile off of my face.

When I got home, Fabienne was braiding my mother's hair. It was nice to see them bonding. I gave my mother a rundown of the day. Seeing my level of excitement made her smile. That night, I hung out with Fabienne a little before bed. I decided to sleep early because I didn't want to take the chance of being late.

Chapter 28

I left my house early again. Man, I was feeling mature, you know, kind of like an adult. Thankfully, there was an empty seat waiting for me on the train. After I sat down, I looked for my phone for entertainment but couldn't find it anywhere, not in my backpack or lunch bag. Oh no, my phone was a part of my body; we did everything together, including going to the bathroom. Could I even function without my beloved phone? The thought alone was overwhelming, but I didn't have a choice. There was no way my mother would get on the train to bring it to me. It was too late to turn back. Was this a sign that I would have a bad day? *Calm down, Manushka, just calm down,* I said to myself. The train was approaching my stop. I stood up right before the door opened, only to fall on the floor. It felt like everyone was staring at me, so I quickly stood up and exited the train. Yep, this was going to be a bad day for sure.

As I waited for the light to change, I noticed a familiar person, but I couldn't pinpoint where we met. He was tall, muscular, and dressed in all black despite the hot weather. The look on his face seemed a little intense, considering he was clearly a teenager. Just when I remembered where I met him, our eyes suddenly met.

Oh my God, I wanted to run, scream, or even call someone, but I didn't have a phone. The next best thing was to walk as fast as possible to make it to meet Ms. Stephanie. I speed-walked, practically running. The only thing I could use to defend myself was this tin lunch container my mother gave me. As much as I complained about it, this tin container may be the key to saving my life. My lunch container couldn't do much damage, considering his size, but it would at least slow him down a little. I turned around only to see him right behind me. Was he following me? Two more blocks to go. I was practically out of breath as I rapidly walked another block. Oh no, he was still behind me with a hand in his pocket! He was getting closer and closer, but I was still a few steps ahead. Finally, I could see Ms. Stephanie, I was safe.

"What took you so long to get here? You're late!" she shouted.

Late? Yes, I have a history of lateness, but that is a thing of the past, I've matured. I'm fifteen minutes early, and I can prove it. What was she talking about? Right before I responded, Ms. Stephanie spoke again. "Yohane, you were supposed to be here at 7:45 a.m.; you're an hour late. Seriously! I need you to be more responsible."

I was happy she wasn't talking to me. But who is Yohane? I turned around to see one of the guys from the mall. It was the guy who made passes at us, and he was there the day Widelene was attacked. The guy who stood there and watched as my best friend was savagely attacked. The guy who gave us the lame apology at the emergency tower reveal. Could this day get any worse?

"Manushka, this is my nephew Yohane. He'll be working with us to create the mural today. If he gets his act together, Yohane will help us with other projects this summer. From the look on your face, it seems you've already met. Do you two know each other?"

Before I could get a word out of my mouth, Yohane spoke. "Auntie Stephanie, I don't know her. In fact, we've never met until today. Manushka, it's a pleasure to meet you. I'm looking forward to working together," he said, preparing to shake my hand.

Great! He was trying to act like a gentleman in front of Ms. Stephanie when the truth is this guy was a loser, an idiot, a bully, a coward; I could go on. Oh, yeah, and a liar. He didn't want his auntie to know what happened at the mall. Instead of shaking his hand, I began coughing hysterically while staring directly at him. If I had superpowers, the look on my face would have turned him into either dust or stone. Ms. Stephanie was standing at an angle, so she couldn't see the way I was looking at him.

"Are you okay? Give me a moment while I grab you a water bottle from the cooler." Ms. Stephanie quickly opened a bottle and handed it to me. "How about you sit for a few minutes until you feel better." She led me to a chair inside the community center.

From the window, I watched as Ms. Stephanie had what seemed like a tense conversation with Yohane. The conversation ended abruptly when a tall gentleman wearing a suit joined them. As Yohane walked toward the door, I quickly readjusted my body, hoping it wasn't obvious that I was watching the entire time. Some may call it nosy, but I would call my actions during this situation curiosity and a desire to be informed..

"Aunt Stephanie is calling you," Yohane said, his voice tense.

Why was he giving me attitude? Choosing not to respond to his tone, I made my way outside. Although challenging, addressing his attitude wasn't worth jeopardizing the relationship with my mentor and losing a paid internship. Walking away was the only option, at least for now.

"Manushka, this is my boyfriend, Elijah. He stopped by to bring me lunch before going to work." Ms. Stephanie was holding onto his hand as she spoke.

"I've heard so much about you already. Based on what Stephanie has shared, you're quite the talent. I think you'll be a good influence on Yohane." Mr. Elijah appeared gentle and strong at the same time. He was wearing a dark blue suit and white collared shirt, with a gray and blue patterned tie. Between his short curly hair, hazel eyes, and soothing voice, I could see why Ms. Stephanie was gushing over him. She smiled the entire time he spoke.

Wait, did he suggest I would be a good influence on that Yohane guy? That was the last thing on my mind. There was absolutely no way I wanted to be associated with anyone like him.

Ms. Stephanie pulled me aside, far enough to have a private conversation. "Sorry about this morning. I could tell my response to Yohane's arrival startled you. Just so you know, he's extremely brilliant and was on track to graduate from high school a year early. He was even a championship fencer, winning first place for three consecutive years. After his parents died, Yohane made some poor decisions. He was involved in a recent incident at the mall. I don't know all the details, but thankfully, Elijah is a lawyer, so he took care of everything." Ms. Stephanie quickly looked around before continuing to speak. "Yohane may not be the easiest person to work with, but he's a good kid. I don't anticipate the two of you having any problems, but if you have an issue with him at any point, please let me know. Here he comes now. Please don't tell him I shared any of this with you." Ms. Stephanie sighed.

Bright, straight-A student, and a championship fencer? How could that be? He hung out at the mall all the time. He didn't even seem capable of putting a complete sentence together. Was he an imposter? Did his friends know the truth? Ms. Stephanie knew about the mall incident but didn't know my friends were involved. Should I tell her? My mind was running wild. I couldn't wait to call Janae and Widelene.

"Yo, here's the stuff Stephanie told me you needed," Yohane said, interrupting my thoughts.

"First of all, my name is not yo, it's Manushka. Please don't speak to me if you can't address me correctly." I made eye contact with Yohane as I spoke; I wanted him to know I was serious.

"Aight, Ma-nush-ka!" So he was trying to taunt me by pausing after every syllable in my name. This Yohane guy was really trying to push my buttons. "Here's the stuff Aunt Stephanie said you needed. Is that better? Does this manner of communication meet your satisfaction? For thy willist not dare say anything to offend thee." The sound of his laugh was sickening.

Without responding to him, I forcefully grabbed the materials one by one, placing them closer to the wall we would be painting.

As he walked away, Ms. Stephanie shouted, "Yohane, I want you to help Manushka paint. Make sure you do exactly what she says. I'll be over there in a few minutes."

I completed the first few steps required to prepare the wall as Ms. Stephanie instructed. She did say completing a mural for the first time was intimidating, which is why Yohane was there—seemed like he had experience with murals.

Yohane and I worked together without speaking, making the experience awkward. Since this mural was small, we were halfway done by lunch. I decided to eat inside the community center during lunch since it was such a hot day. I sat with my back to Yohane, although I couldn't see his face, I could feel him piercing a hole through my back with his eyes. I ate as fast as possible just to get away because the idea of spending another minute in the room with him literally made me feel sick.

The mural was coming along nicely, yes, my first mural. After I worked alone for about an hour, Ms. Stephanie joined me. "Manushka, you have made so much progress. I find it hard to believe you've never done this before. Since you worked so hard today, you can leave early. If possible, bring a sketch of your ideas for the laughter mural. That will save us a little time tomorrow." Ms. Stephanie patted me on the back. The thought of staying longer crossed my mind, but I wanted and needed to get home ASAP to call Janae and Widelene.

"Have a good evening, Ms. Stephanie! See you tomorrow." I rushed off quickly.

Thankfully, the train and bus were running on time, with no delays, yes!

My mother wasn't home yet. Fabienne was sitting on the couch watching a TV show; according to my sister, daytime talk shows and soap operas were helping her learn English. After a quick conversation with Fabienne, I went to my room, I mean *our* room. Just like I thought, the phone was on my bed. While doing a last-minute outfit change, I'd placed it on the bed but forgot to pick it up.

I didn't want to tell the story twice, so I made sure to have both Janae and Widelene on the line at the same time. "Hey, Janae, hold on a second. Let me get Widelene on the line, too. I need to tell you guys something."

Not waiting for Janae to finish her sentence, I immediately called Widelene. "You wouldn't believe what happened today. I needed both of you on the line together for this one. I accidentally left my phone at home today, I should have known it was a sign that the day wouldn't go well. So, when I got out of the train station, I noticed a familiar face. After a few minutes, I figured out who the guy was. To be honest, at first, I thought the guy was going to rob me. I had my tin lunch container ready to knock him out, but you know I was scared. I thought the guy was following me, but it turned out we were going to the same place. One of the guys from the mall, you know, the one who always tries to talk to us, the one who apologized the night of the tower reveal? Yeah, well, I have to work with him this summer during my internship." I spoke so fast that I practically ran out of breath by the last word of the sentence.

"What!" Janae shouted. "Wait, wait, wait a minute. How in the world did he get that kind of an internship?" I could imagine Janae waving her hand in the air as she spoke.

I quickly said, "Well, he's Ms. Stephanie, my mentor's nephew. Did you hear that? He's her nephew! So, even though I can't stand the guy, I have to be polite. When Ms. Stephanie said he was her nephew, I thought my eyes were gonna pop right out of my head. I mean, what's the likelihood? She even knows about the mall incident but has no clue I know both of you. Do you think I should say something at one point?"

"I know how difficult it was for you to hear about the mall attack and how much this internship means to you. Personally, I don't think you should say anything, at least not yet. Wait until the opportunity presents itself. The last thing you want to do is cause friction early into the internship. And girl, you better collect those checks, make that money." Widelene said.

As usual, Widelene had great advice. She was right. The last thing I wanted to do was miss this great opportunity. I was getting paid to learn and do what I love: anything related to drawing, painting, and just creating. All I had to do was get through it. It wasn't like I had plans to befriend Yohane; I couldn't stand the guy.

After speaking to Widelene and Janae on the phone, all I wanted was to call Devonte, but he was still on vacation in Florida with his family. Before going to sleep, I made three different sketches for the laughter mural. But it was hard to focus on laughter when all I wanted to do was scream. I had to work with Yohane all summer, as much as I couldn't stand him, and my boyfriend was too busy to speak to me.

There was no way I was going to forget my phone again; I made sure to put it in my backpack before leaving.. When I arrived at the community center, surprisingly, Yohane was there before me but Ms. Stephanie was nowhere to be found. I stood outside for a few more minutes, but she still didn't show up.

"Aunt Stephanie asked me to bring you to the next location for the mural." Yohane avoided eye contact the entire time he spoke. "It's about two blocks away."

"You watched me walk around and look for her. Why didn't you say something sooner?" I wasn't in the mood to play games with him today or any other day.

"Well, you didn't ask." His response was so nonchalant, it aggravated me even more.

"Seriously! Just take me to Ms. Stephanie or tell me the address. And by the way, I'm not stupid. You lied about not knowing me," I said with an attitude to include hand gestures while moving my head, you know, Brooklyn style.

"Actually, I didn't lie because I know nothing about you. There is a clear difference between knowing someone and seeing them once or twice. You're the girl from the mall, that's it. If you want to know where my aunt is, just follow me. I'm heading there now." There was no sense of urgency in the way he walked, but I had no choice but to follow him.

To avoid a potential argument, I kept quiet. Yohane was, in a way, right; we didn't know each other. Still, he did lie about never meeting me before.

Ms. Stephanie was waiting outside for us. Before I could settle, she said, "Good morning, guys. Manushka, sorry about the last-minute change of plans. I hope you're feeling better today. This is where I want the Laughter mural. May I see the sketches you're proposing?"

"Good morning, Ms. Stephanie. I guess you can say I saw a ghost or maybe even a monster yesterday morning. But I'm feeling much better today." I heard Yohane clear his throat when I said the words *ghost* and *monster*, which means he was listening. "Here are the three sketches I have in mind."

"Manushka, these are absolutely amazing. So amazing that I can't decide which I like best. Yohane, what do you think?" She placed all three sketches directly in front of his eyes.

"They aight," he said.

"Thank you, Yohane. I truly appreciate your extensive and well-thought-out response. Considering our timeline and the size of this particular wall, how about we pick the second sketch? I have a few phone conferences lined up, but I'll check on both of you throughout the day. I'm confident you can get the job done together. Everything you need is right here," Ms. Stephanie said as she picked up her pocketbook.

I can't believe I have to work with this guy again, and alone. Without saying a word, I began drawing my sketch on the wall as Yohane looked on. At one point, I kind of struggled to bring the ladder to the wall to reach the higher parts. Of course, he just looked on instead of helping.

"Yohane, you're supposed to help. Didn't you see me struggling with the ladder?"

"I figure ghosts and monsters don't like helping others. You were talking about me, right? I heard you." Yohane was shaking his leg and rubbing his hands together, so I could tell he was bothered by my comment.

"Well, what do you call a person who watches someone get attacked and does absolutely nothing? Doesn't sound too human to me. Didn't you hear my friends screaming?"

"Listen, Manushka, you don't know anything about me, so don't make any assumptions. You have a lot to say for someone who wasn't even there when everything happened."

"Well, I may not have been there, but I can still remember the terror on my friend's face as she talked about the incident. I wasn't there, but when she spoke about it, I felt her pain, I felt their pain. My friends are still traumatized by the situation. This could have been avoided if you and your friends had more respect for women. I can't understand why guys take it so personal when a woman says she isn't interested in their advances. As much as I can't stand you, I will not let you get in the way of this opportunity for me. We don't have to be friends, but we do need to get these murals done perfectly."

Surprisingly, Yohane didn't have any snarky responses. After what felt like a lecture, I climbed the ladder to complete the top portion of the mural. Within a couple of hours, I completed the sketch on the wall. Impressed by the progress, Ms. Stephanie took us out to lunch. To be honest, I did all of the work, but I guess she had to buy Yohane lunch since he was her nephew.

After lunch, I began painting the wall. Yohane must have had a revelation or spiritual awakening because he decided to help paint. I watched him discreetly from the corner of my eyes. I was shocked by his technique. He had skills, but I would never admit it.

"You guys are a great team, very effective together," Ms. Stephanie said. "Tomorrow morning, I have another meeting, so I will be in my office all day. I'd like both of you to finish painting the wall in the morning; it should take about two hours. Elijah will stop by to pick you up in the morning around 11:30. Yohane, I need you to pack everything up." Ms. Stephanie then directed her attention solely to me. "Manushka, Elijah and I will drive you home today since it seems like it's going to rain. He should be here in a few minutes."

I sure was happy to have her drop me off at home because I was extra tired today between the wall and my conversation with Yohane. Within fifteen minutes, Elijah arrived in one of those fancy two-door sports cars. "Wow" was the first word to come to mind when I saw the car. The words "Oh, no" quickly followed when I realized I would be in the back seat of that tiny car with Yohane. It was too late to decline the ride home, so I had no choice but to sit beside him.

"Yohane, be a gentleman and open the door for the young lady," Ms. Stephanie instructed.

As he opened the door, I heard Yohane mumble, "What young lady?" under his breath.

I responded in the most appropriate and mature way I could think of. As he held the door open, I stepped on his foot as hard as I could with a smile, then whispered, "This young lady" in his ear.

For a car this fancy and expensive, the space in the back sure was tight. Even pushing my body as close to the door as possible wasn't enough to keep our knees from touching. Rather than focusing on Yohane, I looked over at Ms. Stephanie and Mr. Elijah holding hands as he drove the car. Seeing her stare at him made me think of Devonte. I missed spending time with him. I thought about our dates and the many times we walked and held hands. I had no idea when I would see him again.

My thoughts of Devonte were interrupted when Ms. Stephanie called my name.

"It looks like someone was daydreaming about me," Yohane said as he laughed.

"I had no idea you were a comedian. Can't wait to hear more jokes tomorrow, Yohane. Mr. Elijah and Ms. Stephanie, thank you for dropping me off at home. I appreciate it."

"Any time, Manushka," Ms. Stephanie said as she and Mr. Elijah waved goodbye.

Vacation or not, it was time to call Devonte. I wanted and needed to speak to my boyfriend. As I prepared to walk through the front door, I heard laughter and a couple of voices. One voice stood out and sounded familiar, but it couldn't be; there was no way. I unlocked the door quickly, hoping I was wrong. Unfortunately, I was right. It was Claude sitting beside Fabienne on the couch, having a conversation. After a couple more steps, I saw it—I mean Sè Françoise in the kitchen with my mother. This day was truly turning into a nightmare. When my mother mentioned her name, all I wanted to do was suck my teeth, but my desire to live was far too great. Sucking my teeth in the presence of adults was considered a capital crime and subject to punishment.

Understanding my obligation, I greeted Sè Françoise with a kiss on the cheek followed by a little small talk, but all I could think of was Claude speaking to my sister. I greeted my mother, then quickly went into the living room to interfere with whatever was going on in there. Instead of interrupting, I made the last-minute decision to analyze the situation first. Oh no, Fabienne seemed way too comfortable with him. It was now time to interrupt.

"So, Claude, what's so funny?"

"You know Claude got game, and your sister recognizes greatness when she sees it. Jealousy is a sin, so please try to control yourself. It's just a matter of time before Fabienne becomes my lady." Claude adjusted his collar and licked those crusty lips of his.

"I'm not worried because my sister is way too smart to fall for your lame lines." I desperately wanted to believe Fabienne wouldn't fall for Claude, but I was concerned. She was smiling a little too much. I needed a plan to put an end to this madness.

"Stop blocking, Manushka," Claude said quicker than expected. "You had your chance but blew it. Just sit back, watch, and remember this could have been you."

Fabienne was watching Claude and me speak, hoping she could understand a word or two. Since Claude was fluent in Creole, there was no language barrier between them.

"Whatever!" I said as I walked toward my room. Since my mother was busy entertaining Queen Busy Body, Sè Françoise, I had time to call

Devonte. I locked the door and turned on some music for safety. With the music on, my mother wouldn't be able to hear the conversation. When I called Devonte the first time, the phone rang a couple of times, but he didn't pick up. I waited about two more minutes before calling again, but the phone went straight to voicemail. I guess he's too busy for me. While lying on my bed, I wondered what Devonte was doing and if he even wanted to talk. Did he miss our conversations? Did he miss having lunch together? Did he think about our first kiss as much as I did? Thinking about Devonte and being unable to speak to him affected my mood, and not in a good way. When I walked out of my room, Sè Françoise was standing right outside of the door. Really! The bathroom is near my room, but I just didn't trust that woman to be anywhere near me.

"Manushka, you very skinny. You have to eat rice and sòs pwa," Sè Françoise said with that evil smile. I hated that old folks felt the liberty to comment on people's bodies without even considering the damage their comments caused. Considering she's shaped like a barrel, I'm surprised Sè Françoise comments on anyone's body. I had nothing nice to say; I just smiled and walked away.

Claude was standing by the door, which meant they were about to leave, thank God. I don't think I could've handled another minute around him and his mother. As Claude walked out the door, he licked his lips again, but this time, he added a wink that he must have thought was sexy. Claude's wink was beyond awkward; he looked more like an insect landed right on his eyeball. I could always count on him to get a good laugh. I turned around to see my sister smiling. Later that night, I decided to speak to Fabienne about Claude.

Sadly, she admitted being a little interested in him. After all the warnings, she still managed to find a way to be interested in Claude, who wasn't even cute. I almost threw up in my mouth when I heard her say nice things about him. Turns out, Fabienne decided to break up with her boyfriend in Haiti. She didn't believe long-distance relationships worked. Was she right? Did that mean my relationship with Devonte was doomed because of distance? My relationship with him was different; I considered it a short-distance relationship since he was only in Long Island. After all, we still lived in the same state. That night, I decided to sleep with the phone under my pillow, hoping Devonte would call, but he didn't.

Chapter 30

I arrived extra early, hoping to get some work done before Yohane showed up, but he beat me to it.

"What time did you get here?" I asked.

"About an hour ago."

Since everything was already set up, including the ladder, I got started. I painted the top half of the mural. On the way off the ladder, my laces got caught. As I tried to pull them out, I lost balance, falling backward. Yohane came to my rescue as he caught me just in time. At that moment, we made eye contact for the first time. Without saying a word, he gently positioned me on the floor. A little shaken up, I decided to sit on the bench. Yohane handed me a water bottle, and then walked away, not saying a word.

I watched him paint. Despite working fast, he was doing a great job, kind of professional. Ms. Stephanie did say Yohane had experience painting murals with her in the past. I returned to painting but had no plans to use the ladder this time.

We finished the mural, but Mr. Elijah was running late, so we had no choice but to wait for him. Sitting in silence was a little uncomfortable. It was time to break the ice since he saved me from a potential injury.

"Yohane, thanks for catching me," I said. "I appreciate it. I could've hurt myself today."

"No problem! Next time you describe me, feel free to use the words *superhero*, *kind hearted*, *strong*, and *charming* instead of *ghost* or *monster*." Based on the laugh, I guess he found his comment amusing. But I, of course, ignored his sad attempt at a joke.

Just when I took my phone out to balance the awkwardness of our silence, it rang. Wanting some privacy, I took a few steps away from Yohane before looking at the phone's screen. It was Devonte! I picked up immediately. His voice sounded just as perfect as I remembered. "Hey, Manushka, sorry I missed your call. We've been so busy. How are you doing, and how is the internship going?"

Hearing Devonte's voice made me smile; I just couldn't help how he made me feel. "I figured you were busy, but I just wanted to hear your voice. I miss our conversations. The internship is going great, except for one thing, but I'll have to tell you all about it next time we speak."

I waited days to speak to my boyfriend, but now Yohane had to interrupt our conversation by shouting, "Yo, Manushka, Elijah is here. We gotta go!" Didn't he see me on the phone? Just plain rude!

"Who's that?" Devonte asked, sounding slightly concerned.

"Oh, that's just Yohane, Ms. Stephanie's nephew. I gotta go now, speak to you soon." I abruptly ended the conversation and then quickly grabbed my bag. I waved to Mr. Elijah, who cleared his throat to cue Yohane to open the door for me. I was happy to sit in the back of the car alone this time.

Mr. Elijah was pretty funny. He joked around the entire ride.

"Hey, guys, thanks for finishing the mural today." Ms. Stephanie greeted us at the door. "Lunch is ready."

"You made it sound like you cooked the meal instead of ordering it from a restaurant. How in the world did I end up with the only Haitian woman who can't cook, especially when I love Haitian food?" Mr. Elijah joked.

Ms. Stephanie playfully tapped him on the back. "I may not be able to cook, but I sure do know how to order the right meal."

We all sat down to eat together. The conversation was nonstop. Yohane even made a few funny jokes. At one point, I couldn't contain the laughter anymore.

"It's nice to hear you laugh, Manushka," Yohane said.

Laughing felt good because I'd been so guarded to the point of being angry whenever I was around him. To be honest, being guarded and angry all the time was becoming a little tiring.

After lunch, Ms. Stephanie gave us some work, but it wasn't art-related this time. We had to sort through and file a few documents while she was on the phone. A few times, I turned around to find Yohane staring at me. Or was I the one staring at him? I'm no relationship expert, but something told me Yohane was checking me out. Was he interested? I hoped not because I had a boyfriend. And besides, I still couldn't stand him.

As soon as Ms. Stephanie hung up the phone, she walked toward us. "I worked out the details with the director of the Gateway Community Center. Instead of painting murals, we'll work at a community center with seven- to ten-year-old children for the next two weeks. Once you're done filing the documents, I want to review my plans for the children with both of you."

Working with children is thrilling, but I was particularly excited about working indoors. Painting outside in 90-degree weather was kind of brutal. This was actually the best summer vacation, thanks to Ms. Stephanie. The day I received my first paycheck was special, a moment I'll never forget. I opened the sealed envelope to find a check with my name, Manushka Jean-Pierre, written right above the words two hundred dollars. I decided to deposit the check in the bank, you know, saving it for special occasions like going to the mall with my friends or back-to-school shopping. On the way home, I thought about my future: Would I live a life like Ms. Stephanie? Would I be as successful as her?

The phone rang as I drifted further into thoughts about my possible future life. "Hey, Manushka!? Is everything okay? Last time

we spoke, I heard you mention the name Yohane before hanging up."
Devonte sounded a little concerned.

"Everything's okay. Yohane is Ms. Stephanie's nephew, and we're
working together this summer. The crazy thing is he was with the guy
who attacked Widelene at the mall. Can you believe that? Well, I only
speak to him when I have to."

"Okay, I was about to fly out to New York. You know I gotta keep
my girl safe."

"I always feel safe with you. Devonte, I miss you. I hope we can see
each other sometime soon."

"I miss you too. Once I get back to New York, I have to practice
with the team almost every day. But, as soon as I have a break, I'm
coming to Brooklyn to see you even if I have to walk all the way there."

"I'll be waiting for you."

We spoke for a few more minutes before hanging up.

I arrived home to find my parents sitting on the couch listening
to the radio. Instead of interrupting, I went to my room, looking for
Fabienne. As soon as I entered, she abruptly put the phone down as if
I wouldn't notice. Without even asking, I knew who she was talking
to. The look on Fabienne's face made it so evident that she was on
the phone with Claude. Despite all my warnings, she just wouldn't
listen. Oh well!

On a brighter note, Fabienne was adjusting well. She was speaking
English with more confidence. I was happy to have a sister around,
especially since Widelene and Janae were so busy on weekdays. Since
it was still early in the day, Fabienne and I went to the mall to pick
up a dress I planned to wear to this Sweet 16 birthday party. Having
Fabienne around was great. My mother rarely said no to going places
since I wasn't going alone. Oh, the benefits of having a sister!

After going to a few stores, I found the perfect dress and, of course,
a pair of shoes. I was feeling a little generous, so I purchased a dress
for Fabienne even though I knew she had some money. We walked
around the mall a little. On the way out, I saw Yohane hanging out in

his usual spot, but he seemed a little different this time. When one of his friends made passes at us, I heard Yohane tell him to leave us alone, which was slightly impressive. I got home eager to try the dress on to show my mother. She liked the dress, only making one comment about the length. It's been a while since I attended a party, so I was beyond excited. I picked out the right accessories, and Fabienne hooked up my hair. That night, I fell asleep thinking about all the fun I would have and, of course, my amazing outfit.

Since my mother always conveniently forgot my requests and plans to go out, I decided to remind her again in the morning. "Mommy, do you remember the party I told you about? It's tonight," I said with a smile.

"I remember you tell me about the party. But I have a dream last night, Manunu, a very bad dream for you."

Why does she always have a dream right when I'm supposed to go out and have fun? Why? My plans were now ruined. The whole idea of her having a dream meant I couldn't go to the party. If I went out, I'd be too paranoid to have fun. My weekend was ruined, and there was nothing I could do about it. Instead of getting ready for a party, I was stuck doing chores on Saturday. Later that night, Fabienne and I watched a movie together before my mother reminded us about waking up early for church the next day.

We woke up Sunday morning, ate breakfast, and went to church. By the time we got there, service had already started. I tried listening to the pastor but was distracted by Fabienne as she fidgeted with her skirt. Within minutes, she mentioned having to go to the bathroom but didn't want me to join her, which was strange. After she walked out, I signaled to Widelene to meet me near the bathroom. When I walked out of the sanctuary, I wasn't surprised to see Fabienne and Claude having a conversation. Right as I was about to walk over to interrupt, I felt a hand on my shoulder.

It was Widelene. "Manushka, don't do it. Let Fabienne make her own decisions. Trying to stop her from talking to Claude may harm your relationship. The best thing to do is make yourself available if she needs someone to talk to. Knowing Claude, it's only a matter of time before he does or says something ridiculous."

After some thought, I realized Widelene was right. The last thing I wanted to do was argue with my sister over some old Claude. He wasn't worth it. "Thanks, girl, you always have the best advice at the right time. I miss hanging out with you and Janae. How are you doing?" I asked.

"Girl, my mother is working longer hours, so I have to spend more time with my little brother. You know he gets a little wild sometimes. Anyway, let's go back inside before my mother comes out here looking for me. And leave Fabienne alone. She can find her way inside."

I took one final look at Fabienne before going back inside. My mother didn't say anything about Fabienne not returning with me. In fact, my mother's rules didn't apply to her at all. Although it wasn't fair, I understood why. My mother felt uncomfortable enforcing rules on Fabienne since she wasn't her biological daughter. I guess that was her way of making sure nothing impacted her relationship with my dad.

After about fifteen minutes, Fabienne returned to the service. Knowing I disapproved of her relationship with Claude, she altogether avoided eye contact. Claude, on the other hand, didn't avoid eye contact with me at all. In fact, he intentionally made eye contact. I just can't stand that guy. As usual, Fabienne and I had no choice but to wait for my mother to have her routine conversations with the church ladies before walking home. Since the weekend was so boring, I looked forward to working this week. Strangely, the thought of working alongside Yohane wasn't as bothersome anymore.

Chapter 31

I arrived at the community center early, but Yohane beat me to it. He was there with Ms. Stephanie, setting up the tables and preparing materials for the day.

"Good morning, Manushka," Yohane said.

Wait, he just said good morning to me without Ms. Stephanie's prompting. Confused by his greeting and overall politeness, I could only smile in response.

"Yohane, I have to make a quick phone call," Ms. Stephanie said. "I need you to update Manushka on what I shared with you this morning."

He was more excited than usual and I wanted to find the source, I mean, he typically has an attitude or is angry about something. I wasn't prepared for this version of Yohane. He walked over to me and then began speaking. "Aunt Stephanie is going to start off with a game, you know, an icebreaker kind of thing. After the game, she's going to teach a brief lesson and then break the kids up into small groups. Then we'll start working with them. Oh, did you find what you were looking for at the mall?"

"Thanks for the update, and yes, I found exactly what I was looking for. I heard what you said to that guy. Honestly, shopping there hasn't been the same since Widelene was attacked." His facial expression immediately changed. "Even though there is an emergency tower, I still don't feel completely safe when I'm shopping," I continued, and I could tell Yohane was still embarrassed by his part in the incident.

Rather than making him feel more uncomfortable, which I would have done a couple of weeks ago, I decided to change the topic. "You seem a little happier today, Yohane. Are you OK? Should I call a doctor?"

He laughed before responding. "So, you're a stand-up comedian and artist, a woman of many talents. Well, there's a lot you don't know about me, at least not yet. I can be nice sometimes. If you're lucky, you may see the nicer side of me more often."

"Man, please. Let's get to work with the kids."

When Ms. Stephanie returned, she was accompanied by about twelve kids, who all appeared happy. She played a game with them and was surprisingly animated. Once the lesson was over, Yohane and I worked with the kids. He was happy, engaged, and patient; I could tell he was in his element. The kids couldn't get enough of Yohane; they all tried to get his attention. How could Yohane possibly be the same person from the mall? The more he worked with the kids, the more he let his guard down. Since Yohane was in such a good mood, we ended up having lunch together that day, and every day that followed until my internship ended. Slowly but surely, we began talking more, and surprisingly I enjoyed our conversations.

Yohane and I had one more mural to complete together. This particular mural was supposed to represent Peace. We devised the concept together, and Ms. Stephanie immediately approved it. Although I hate to admit it, I enjoyed Yohane's company. The following Monday, we painted together. To my surprise, he positioned the ladder for me without asking. We continued working until it was time to take a break.

During lunch, Yohane said, "Manushka, I've been thinking about this Peace mural. The truth is, I'm sorry about what happened to your friend. I didn't even know the guy. He's Mike's friend, and I met him on the day of the attack. Anyway, when he went crazy, I wanted to stop him, but couldn't. I was shocked to the point of not knowing what to do." He took a long pause. Puzzled, I patiently waited for him to continue. "I, I, I watched my parents get murdered during a home invasion. Ever since then, I just freeze whenever I'm scared."

I can tell Yohane was holding back tears because he covered his face. I knew words weren't enough to provide the comfort he needed. Rather than risking saying the wrong thing, I sat closer to him, rubbing his back. I couldn't believe Yohane and I were having a moment like this. I never would have thought we'd be sitting this close together without having a disagreement.

"I should have done something to help my parents. They probably would still be alive today." He fisted his hands and began shaking his leg. "I know Aunt Stephanie wants to help me, but counseling is not my thing. I don't see how talking to some stranger will take away my anger or pain. I mean, what's the point? It's not like the counselor can bring my parents back or change what happened that night." He stood up with fisted hands and began pacing back and forth. I could tell there was a change in his breathing pattern as I watched Yohane's chest rapidly rise and fall. "I had the best parents. Why did they have to be taken away from me so soon? I should have and could have done something. Anything would have been better than just freezing up." Seeing the passersby staring at him through the window, Yohane sat down again. With a rounded back and elbows positioned on his legs, Yohane rested his head in his hands, covering his face.

"Yohane, I don't know all the details of what happened to your parents, but chances are, you could have gotten hurt also. Although it's hard, try not to blame yourself. You didn't do anything because you just didn't know what to do. And the counseling Ms. Stephanie recommended may be helpful, so you should at least consider trying it when you're ready."

"Thanks for listening. I think we should get back to work now." Yohane looked sad as he walked toward the mural. I decided to put on some music to cheer him up a little. We continued painting while debating the top three rappers of all time. Between laughing and dancing, Yohane and I finished faster than expected. Ms. Stephanie and Mr. Elijah arrived just in time to see the final product.

"Wow, this mural looks amazing. I might have to call you two the Dynamic Duo. Which one of you is Batman?" Mr. Elijah was the only one laughing at his joke as all three of us stared at him.

"Stick to being a lawyer, man; I don't think comedy is your thing." Yohane shook his head and patted Elijah's back.

"The mural does, in fact, look amazing," Ms. Stephanie said. "I'm proud of both of you. Great job! And Manushka, we'll drop you off at home."

We all walked to the car together. Without having to be told, Yohane opened the door for me. As we sat in the back together, our knees made contact, but I didn't move away this time. At one point, Yohane reached for my hand. As our fingers made contact, I pulled away quickly. Devonte was still my boyfriend, so I didn't want Yohane to get the wrong idea.

"I'm having a little get-together at my house on Saturday. Since this is your last week, I would love for your family to join us. I'll call your mother a little later," Ms. Stephanie said.

"Thank you for dropping me off. I'll tell my mother to expect a call from you. "

Since it was raining, Yohane walked me to the door using an umbrella from the car, even though I asked him not to. As we walked, he said, "I'm sorry I tried to hold your hand. It just felt like the right thing to do at that moment. Don't worry, I won't do it again. I don't want to make you uncomfortable in any way."

Sensing his discomfort, I decided to lighten the mood by saying, "I guess you're not a monster after all."

We both laughed.

"I know you have a boyfriend and all, but if things don't work out between you, I hope you give me a shot," Yohane said as he held the umbrella over my head.

Speechless, I awkwardly took a few steps backward and waved goodbye. When he walked away, I felt a little conflicted. Why was I feeling so comfortable with him? How I felt around Yohane was familiar, kind of how I felt when Devonte and I first met. Smart, fine, and tall. Yes, Yohane was my type. I mean, Devonte was far. And he'd been a little too busy. No, whatever I was feeling and thinking needed to stop immediately. I couldn't let anyone get in the way of my relationship with Devonte, at least not now. After Yohane left, I went inside to find my mother watching TV on the couch.

I sat down and told her about the get-together at Ms. Stephanie's house. She was open to attending. While speaking to Ms. Stephanie, my mother offered to bring food to the event. Since Ms. Stephanie couldn't cook, she welcomed any dish my mother was willing to bring.

That night, I called Widelene and Janae. I had to let them know what happened with Yohane. "Hey, Janae and Widelene, you wouldn't believe what happened today. So, Yohane tried to hold my hand in the car. He said if Devonte and I ever break up, he wants me to give him a shot." Curious about what they would say, I waited for their response.

"A shot at what? He must be crazy! Please tell me you would never consider dating that guy. He stood there and watched Widelene get attacked by his friend." Janae raised her voice as she spoke while Widelene remained silent.

I knew they would be bothered by the news, but the intensity of their responses made me uncomfortable. "No, I'm not interested in ever dating Yohane because of the mall incident. But he is a nice guy who had a rough couple of years. Yohane didn't even know the person who attacked Widelene." For some unknown reason, I felt the need to defend him. If only they knew his story, that would change their entire perspective.

"Wait, are you making excuses for him? If you are, that could only mean a tiny part of you is interested in this Yohane guy. We've known each other since elementary school, but if you were ever to date him, I know without a doubt it would affect our friendship." Janae sounded serious. And since Widelene didn't have any input, I knew she fully agreed with Janae's stance.

"Calm down, girl, I'm not interested in Yohane. All I'm saying is that he's actually a nice guy. Also, Devonte and I are still together. We aren't breaking up any time soon." I needed to reassure my friends. The last thing I wanted to do was lose them by dating Yohane.

Chapter 32

The day had arrived for the get-together at Ms. Stephanie's house. I wore the nicest dress in my closet, even though I wasn't trying to impress anyone. My mother decided to cook her famous rice mixed with shrimp and blue crabs, baked macaroni, and chicken. Ms. Stephanie was excited to see how much my mother brought, especially since the food she ordered from the restaurant had yet to arrive.

I looked over to see Yohane standing by the door, all dressed up with a fresh haircut. I must admit he looked good, but it didn't matter since I still have a boyfriend, and I'm not interested in dating Yohane. He took the platter out of my mother's hand so she could hold onto the railing while walking up the stairs. It was time to see the top floor. The thought of running past my mother crossed my mind but only for a second. Finally!! The top floor of the loft was no longer a mystery. As I stood in awe of the décor, furniture, and the expansive openness of the space, my expectations were confirmed. After she gracefully placed the platter down, Ms. Stephanie guided us to the roof. Oh, my goodness, she has a rooftop patio! I had only witnessed it in films, yet here I was about to experience it firsthand. *It's official: I want to be just like Ms. Stephanie when I grow up.*

As I walked around and looked at the city landscape, I knew at that moment the life I so often daydreamed about could one day be a reality. I drifted further into thoughts of a prosperous future until Fabienne tapped me on the shoulder to make sure I was okay. Ms. Stephanie took my mother by the hand and gave her a full tour of her place. I sure hoped seeing Ms. Stephanie's lifestyle would help my mother accept that I wanted a career in the arts, whether as an artist, fashion designer, or anything art related.

Yohane joined us but seemed a little nervous for some reason.

"Are you okay?" I asked.

"Yeah, I'm fine," he said.

Fabienne was busy on her phone trying to text Claude discreetly. I reminded myself of Widelene's advice and let Fabienne make her own decisions about her dating life. As Yohane and I continued to talk, more people arrived. Soon, my mother was fully engaged as she spoke to a few ladies who appeared to be in her age range.

"Yohane and Manushka, please get the decorative plates and forks on my desk downstairs," Ms. Stephanie said.

As we walked down the stairs, Yohane said, "Manushka, you look beautiful in that dress."

Surprised by his comment, I immediately looked at him. Our eyes met as we stood at the bottom of the staircase. Yohane gently grabbed my hand. In the stillness of the moment, I could feel the warmth of his breath on my face as he moved closer. He smelled so good, and the moment felt right, but I resisted. To stop him from kissing me, I placed a hand on his chest as he stood inches from my face. "Yohane, you know I have a boyfriend. I would never do anything to disrespect him. I'm not that kind of girl."

I continued walking down the steps quickly, not saying a word to him. My heart was beating so fast. What just happened? Did I almost kiss Yohane? I mean, did I want to kiss him? This was all too confusing. I couldn't talk to Janae and Widelene about this situation. And I couldn't speak to Devonte about it either. Fabienne was too caught up with her dating situation with Claude. I'd have to deal with this on my own. The atmosphere felt tense as we quietly grabbed the items before returning upstairs. We handed Ms. Stephanie the plates and forks. I walked toward the opposite end of the patio to get as far away from Yohane as I could. I needed space to process what had just happened between us.

Mr. Elijah loudly cleared his throat. "Everyone, I have an announcement to make." Ms. Stephanie had a puzzled look. Whatever Mr. Elijah was going to say wasn't part of her plan.

Mr. Elijah continued, "Stephanie, I admire your faith, optimism, and ability to love people from all walks of life. As many of you may know, Stephanie and I have been dating for three years. She has given me unconditional love, laughter, and endless support in such a short time. Stephanie, you complete me because you're my soulmate. I know without a doubt that God created you specifically for me; you're my angel, best friend, and the love of my life. Before meeting you, I never knew a love so strong and pure could ever exist. Please make me the most blessed man walking on this planet by becoming my wife." Mr. Elijah got down on one knee, holding a small black box in which a large shiny ring was nestled. "Stephanie Mondesir, will you marry me?"

Ms. Stephanie was clearly surprised as she stood with both hands covering her mouth. After what seemed like a delayed response she replied, "Yes, yes, yes, Elijah, I would love to be your wife." As Mr. Elijah slipped the ring onto her finger, everyone was startled by the fireworks that accompanied Ms. Stephanie's acceptance of the proposal, the timing was perfect.

Just like a scene from a movie, Ms. Stephanie jumped into Mr. Elijah's arms as he romantically spun her around, followed by a lengthy kiss. They stood hand in hand, watching the fireworks display for a few minutes. Ms. Stephanie then made her rounds as everyone wanted a firsthand look at the engagement ring. I sat and watched as she spoke to everyone. She was glowing from every angle.

After making her rounds, Ms. Stephanie approached me. "Why are you sitting alone in a room filled with people?"

"Um, congratulations on your engagement. Seeing your joy and accomplishments made me think about my future," I said.

"Where do you see yourself in the future? What do you want to do in terms of a career?" Ms. Stephanie asked.

"Well, I love designing clothing, upcycling, drawing, painting. I guess I can do one of them." Would I have to pick one? If so, which one? I was confused and felt sad as I temporarily doubted the possibility of achieving my goals.

"What makes you think you can't design clothing and create beautiful art? People told me not to pursue a career in the arts. They said that if you want to make money, become a nurse, doctor, engineer, or do computers. But I didn't listen. After several unpaid internships and long hours, I finally reached this point. So, if you're genuinely interested in pursuing this career path, I will do whatever I can to help you."

"Thank you, Ms. Stephanie. I enjoyed the internship opportunity this summer, and I'll miss working with you."

Waving her hand dramatically, she said, "I'm not going anywhere. We will stay in contact! In fact, I have a little job for you if you're interested. I would like you to create a few paintings for my wedding. I'm not sure of the capacity; it's just an idea for now. What do you think?"

I couldn't believe what I was hearing. Lord, forgive me for being so wrong about her. Without thinking, I hugged her. "Thank you, thank you, thank you, Ms. Stephanie. I would love to keep working with you, even if it means sweeping the floor." My level of excitement was so apparent that a few people momentarily turned around to stare at me.

"Absolutely not! My protégée will not be sweeping floors. You will be creating beautiful works of art," Ms. Stephanie said in a tender voice as she returned my hug.

After speaking to her, I was beyond elated, to the point where I knew without a doubt that nothing could take my joy away. I couldn't wait to share the news with Devonte.

Chapter 33

I couldn't wait to share the good news with Devonte. He always knew what to say to make any situation extra special. Calling him now was the perfect opportunity since my mother was busy sharing the details about Ms. Stephanie's lavished event.

"Hey, Devonte, you wouldn't believe what just happened." Excitement got the best of me, without giving him the opportunity to guess, I continued speaking, " Ms. Stephanie got engaged today, and she wants me to create some paintings for her wedding. Can you believe it?" I said, expecting his response to match my enthusiasm.

"Great!" Expecting more I waited and waited, but he didn't say anything else. A one-word response is not what I expected from my boyfriend. What happened to *that's amazing, I'm happy for you, my girl got skills?* The tone of his voice didn't reflect any elation.

"Why do you sound so different? Is something wrong?" I asked, hoping he was okay while still feeling kind of disappointed.

"I'm actually in Brooklyn for the weekend and need to see you tomorrow before I leave. Can you meet me around six?"

"What! I had no clue you would be here. I can't wait to see you, but that's going to be hard. Since the library is closed on Sundays, I can't use studying as an excuse. But don't worry, I'll think of something." My mind immediately sprang into action as I thought of possible plans to meet Devonte. I needed a plan that wouldn't get me in trouble again. I felt special knowing he was making time to see me. "Oh, I have a plan! We can meet at the Stylish Threads & Kicks. Does that work for you?"

"Cool, see you at six," Devonte said.

I'm going to see my boyfriend, yeah my boyfriend! I sang and danced around the room for a couple of minutes before finalizing the plan. Shopping is the perfect cover, but I need an accomplice. Fabienne has to go to the mall with me. If she does, my mother wouldn't suspect a thing.

"Fabienne, *m pral wè Devonte demen a sizè. Ou ka vini avè m tanpri, tanpri, tanpri, sè m?*" I practically begged Fabienne to come with me to the mall to meet Devonte at six. I kept my fingers crossed, hoping she would agree.

Thankfully, she said, "*Pa gen pwoblèm. Mwen pral avè w, men fòk ou fè atansyon. Mwen pa vle manman w fache avè m si yon moun wè w ak Devonte.*" Fabienne agreed to go with me to the mall but wanted me to be careful. She didn't want to be implicated in my crimes, especially since Fabienne and my mother were still building a relationship. When a crime happens, the accomplice has to face consequences, too. So, I assured her that I'd be extra careful.

Now, it was time to pick an outfit. I chose something nice—nice enough to impress my boyfriend. I made sure to ask my mother about going to the mall since she was still in a good mood. As expected, she quickly said yes and continued conversing with my dad. My mother was now standing as she talked about the best part of the event. Hand gestures and all, she reenacted the proposal. Joining in on the fun, I grabbed the remote as a prop then got down on one knee pretending to be Mr. Elijah. "Yes, Elijah, I want to be your wife, I love you very much," said my mother as she attempted to impersonate Ms. Stephanie. As my dad's laughter grew louder, Fabienne joined us in the living room, making this a memorable family moment. Once the proposal was accepted, I stood up and held my mother's hands then we began to move in a circular motion, kind of like Ring Around the Rosie. To complement my mother's performance, I presented her with an award for Best Actress in a Leading Role, this time, the prop was a glass. She accepted the award followed by an animated speech. Being dramatic definitely came from my mother's side of the family.

Sunday morning, I woke up extra early to get ready for church and to remind my mother that I was going to the mall. I had to make sure she wouldn't conveniently forget. Thankfully, she remembered and didn't have one of those dreams that constantly interfered with my plans. The church sermon was interesting. The pastor talked about deception and honesty. For a moment, I thought about my meeting with Devonte. Was I lying? Well, technically, I wasn't lying. I just decided to omit the detail that included Devonte. So, the message didn't really apply to my situation but maybe someone else.

Fabienne and I arrived at the mall around six o'clock. Instead of following me into the store, she decided to shop while waiting. From the window, I immediately spotted Devonte as he nervously paced around Stylish Threads and Kicks. Between our last phone conversation and the pacing around, something was definitely bothering my boyfriend but what could it be? I wanted to ask him what was wrong but made the conscious decision not to ask. It's been a while since we last saw each other so I didn't want anything negative getting in the way. Whatever was bothering him would have to wait until the next phone conversation.

"Hey, Devonte." I couldn't stop smiling as I walked toward him.

"You look beautiful as usual," he said, leaning forward to hug me.

Yes, a hug from my boyfriend was precisely what I wanted and needed. I nervously looked around the store to make sure I didn't see familiar faces before embracing him.

"I can't stay too long," he said. "We're driving out to Long Island tonight."

Despite being a little disappointed, I said, "That's okay, I'm just happy to see you."

Devonte took a deep breath before speaking, which was unusual for him. And for some reason, he wasn't smiling anymore. He then said, "Well, I don't know how else to say this, but we have to break up. I didn't want to break up over the phone because you deserve better. See, my family really enjoyed our trip to Florida. We're moving to Orlando in the next six months. I have a lot going on, so our relationship isn't going to work right now."

My eyes widened as I listened in complete disbelief. Before I could respond, he continued, "My parents said we haven't established roots in Long Island yet, so now is the best time to move. And I kind of agree with them. We've been spending more time together, thanks to you. Anyway, we all decided that moving to Orlando would be a good opportunity for our family."

Since I can be a little dramatic sometimes, I gasped for air. I couldn't believe my ears. It was the inevitable breakup, an absolute nightmare. Sure, long-distance relationships can be challenging, but there was no reason to break up, at least not yet. I wanted to be sensitive to his needs, but this time, I decided to be completely selfish, anything to keep my boyfriend. "Devonte, I understand you're moving, but it's not like you're going to a different country. A flight to Florida is about two and a half hours. I know my parents would never let me fly out to see you, but that's not the point. Our bond is strong enough to make a long-distance relationship work. We can talk to each other every day." It was as though I was pleading my case to a jury in a courtroom.

"I thought about this before we spoke today," Devonte said. "In fact, I thought about this for a few weeks before saying anything, but life is about to be real hectic for me. I need you to understand that I have other priorities right now and I'm sorry, this relationship isn't one of them. Once life gets settled and back to normal, we can try dating again, but I just don't have time now." Based on his tone, he was sincere, but I didn't care, at least not anymore.

"You know what? I'm tired of being understanding! Goodbye! " At a loss for words, I knew it was time to leave.

He leaned forward to hug me again, but this time I stopped him. I wasn't in the mood. I got all dressed up, trying to be all cute, and took a trip all the way to the mall only to have him break up with me. To top it off, I kind of lied to my mom again—or omitted the truth is how I like to refer to it. But seriously! The more I thought about the situation, the more upset I became.

"I hope you're not mad at me," he said, reaching for my hand. "Let me walk you over to Fabienne. I want to make sure you're safe before I leave."

"Don't worry about me being safe. I can handle myself perfectly fine, thank you." I walked away quickly not wanting to make a scene or draw unnecessary attention. I tried ignoring him to avoid saying something I'd regret in the future, but he wouldn't stop following me.

"Manushka, slow down and talk to me. We can't end our relationship like this. Please say something."

"I'm not the one who ended our relationship. You did that. I understand you have a lot going on, but how do you expect me to feel, huh? What, you thought I'd just smile and wish you well? You didn't even consider my feelings! I was trying to be understanding, but the truth is I'm mad right now. You had me come all the way to the mall just for you to break up with me. You could've done that over the phone and saved me a trip and the embarrassment." My reaction surprised me, but bottling up my feelings was no longer an option. I turned around for a final look at Devonte. With each step away from him, more tears ran down my face. I was now boyfriendless. My boyfriend, I mean my ex-boyfriend shattered my heart into a million pieces.

I found Fabienne standing in line, preparing to make a payment. When she saw my face, Fabienne frantically dropped everything at the register and ran in my direction. "*Poukisa w ap kriye?*" she asked.

Naturally, she wanted to know why I was crying, so I explained the situation. Fabienne was slightly relieved, knowing I wasn't in physical pain, but she was sad about the situation. We took what seemed like a long train ride home. Fabienne made sure to stay right by my side the entire time. She didn't even respond to texts or calls from Claude. I had my big sister's complete attention.

"*Mèsi anpil. Mwen kontan genyen w kòm sè.*" I thanked Fabienne for the support and let her know how much I appreciate having her as a sister.

"*Mwen kontan genyen w kòm sè. Koulye a, siye figi w anvan n antre.*" Fabienne was happy to have me as a sister, also. She instructed me to wipe my face before going inside. The last thing we wanted was for my mother to notice anything.

That night, I curled up in my bed like a baby. Fabienne rubbed my back as I silently cried myself to sleep.

The next day, I called Janae and Widelene, who were both supportive. They were too busy to hang out. Truthfully, I wanted to wear pajamas and stay in bed all day, but that wasn't an option when my mother was home. Amid my sorrow, the phone rang. Unfamiliar with the number, I altered my voice and used a heavy Haitian accent just in case it was a telemarketer. Those telemarketers often had difficulty taking no for an answer, and today, I was not in the mood.

"Hello, beautiful," the person said.

It was clearly not a telemarketer, so I dropped the accent. Although I liked the sound of the words "Hello, beautiful," I still wasn't in the mood to speak to anyone. "Who is this?" I asked with a slight attitude.

"What, you forgot my voice already? It's Yohane. I was just calling to check up on you. I also wanted to tell you how much I miss working with you."

"Yohane, your voice sounds different on the phone. I had no idea it was you. Thanks for the compliment, but I don't feel like talking right now."

"What's wrong? Is there anything I can do to make you feel better?" He patiently awaited a response.

I held back tears before sharing the news about my breakup. "My boyfriend and I just broke up, so there's absolutely nothing you can do to make me feel better, especially since the breakup was totally unexpected. I gotta go. I just don't feel like talking anymore. Maybe next time. Bye!" I slowly hung up the phone and then covered my face using a pillow to mask the sound of crying.

This felt like the longest week of my life.

For the first time ever, I was looking forward to the new school year in a couple of weeks. I desperately wanted to get my mind off Devonte, even if that meant another French class with Mr. Dupont. And you know how much I can't stand that man.

Chapter 34

Time to start the most important year of high school. SENIOR YEAR! Fabienne and I took the train to meet Janae and Widelene. Everything was perfect between leaving on time and my outfit of course, but Claude had to ruin the moment. Who invited him to our meet-up spot? Oh, yeah, I almost forgot he was dating Fabienne. When Claude and Fabienne greeted each other with a hug and kiss, I seriously wanted to throw up, but had to be mature about the situation. How did she feel so comfortable kissing Claude in public? I mean, she wasn't even hesitant, no looking both ways or anything. I'm sure his mother, the gossip, wouldn't say anything to tarnish her dear son's alleged good reputation. Fabienne knew my dad felt guilty about not being present in her life when she was in Haiti, and my mother was still trying to nurture their relationship, so she took full advantage of the situation. Fabienne had a free pass to do whatever she wanted. Lucky her.

Claude approached me. "Manushka, I need to talk to you for a second."

Although apprehensive, I figured a brief conversation wouldn't kill me. "Alright, I have a minute. Go ahead and speak. I'm listening." With crossed arms and a little attitude, I waited for him to begin speaking.

Claude rubbed his hands together and adjusted his collar then said, "The moment I looked into your sister's eyes, I knew she was the one. I'm a changed man, Manushka, a changed man, I tell you. I know they're lots of ladies out there cryin' right now because they can't get with Claude no more, but I'm only one person. And I've decided to be a one-woman man now. Your sister is safe with me so you have nothing to worry about. We're family now." Well, he sounded a little more mature. I guess there was hope for him after all.

"I hear you but don't think for a second that I'm not watching," I said while rhythmically tapping my foot on the ground.

Claude's relationship with Fabienne wasn't a priority for me, at least not now. Besides, there was nothing I could do or say to stop them from dating. Fabienne made her decision and she was sticking to it. Just when I thought the conversation was over, Claude continued speaking.

"One more thing, I heard you and Devonte broke up. You know the saying, 'No sense crying about spilled juice. Right? "

"It's no sense crying about spilled milk, not juice!" I shouted. By this point, I was losing patience.

"I did not say juice, I said milk?"

"No, I clearly heard you say juice."

"No, I didn't."

"Yes, you did," I responded. There was no way I was going to lose this argument with Claude even though we sounded like preschoolers.

"Seems like I have to be the mature one in this situation. I obviously meant milk, not juice. Besides, my point is that Devonte wasn't the one for you, his loss. Maybe one day you'll get lucky and find someone just like me. I mean, dreams are possible," he said with a smile. In usual Claude fashion, he almost tripped while walking towards Fabienne. Strangely enough, she found him amusing instead of awkward.

That was definitely a failed attempt at encouragement. Funky-lipped Claude was still a jerk and would always be a jerk! I was trying to spend at least one day without thinking about Devonte, but Claude ruined it. Rather than saying something regretful, I bit my tongue and clenched my fists while watching the happy couple walk off hand in hand.

"Girl, don't mind him. You know he been saying crazy things ever since we were little," Widelene said as she placed her arm around my shoulders.

Janae chimed in. "It's time to get along with your future brother-in-law and mother-in-law. Between dinners and celebrations, you'll be a big happy family in no time." As usual, Janae always had jokes funny enough to lighten the mood.

We arrived at school right before the late bell rang. As I slowly walked along the halls, everything reminded me of Devonte, from the hallways to the lunchroom to the classrooms, just about everything. Thoughts of Devonte were interrupted by my nemesis, Mr. Dupont. Why did he feel the need to speak to me?

"*Bonjour, Mademoiselle Manushka. J'espère que vous avez passé un bel été,*" he said.

My immediate response was, "Huh," since I had no clue what he was saying.

"Manushka, I hope you had a great summer, is what I said. I see you have not practiced your French at all. Where is your mystery tutor? Did they quit? Seems like you need to retake my class," he said with a smile.

"I had a great summer, Mr. Dupont. The bell is about to ring, so I have to go now." I rushed off intentionally to avoid answering his question. There is absolutely no way I would tell him who my tutor was. Not knowing was bothering him and I intended to keep it that way. Besides, Fabienne was scheduled to take Spanish so they would never cross paths.

Despite having a great schedule, the first day of senior year was tainted by thoughts of the inevitable breakup. It wasn't supposed to be this way. Devonte and I were supposed to go to prom together, not to mention the senior trip and graduation. Sluggishly walking through the exit, I spotted my friends.

"Manushka, have you heard from Devonte at all?" Janae asked.

"Nope, not a call, text, or even an email. I haven't heard from him in like three weeks. To be honest, I don't even know if Devonte is in Long Island or Florida," I said.

Before I could finish the sentence, Janae assertively said, "Girl, get yourself together. One way of getting over Devonte may be to date someone else. Have you thought of that? I mean, do you know of anyone interested in dating you?"

Janae had a point: I needed to explore my options. But knowing how they felt about Yohane, I didn't mention his name. He'd been sending me the sweetest text messages. The thought of his messages made me smile, but there was absolutely no way I was telling Janae and Widelene. I didn't want to lose my boyfriend and best friends in the same year.

"I can't think of anyone interested in me." Yes, I lied, but I lied for a good cause, for the cause of preserving and protecting our friendship.

That evening, I did my homework and a couple of chores. Yohane sent his routine text message, "Hey beautiful, I'm thinking about you."

Typically, I didn't respond, but I made an exception this time. "Thank you for putting a smile on my face, especially today."

Within seconds, my phone rang. It was Yohane, and he sounded concerned. "Hey, Manushka, I read your message. Are you OK? Is there anything I can do to make you feel better?" he asked.

"I'm just feeling a little down. I can't seem to get over Devonte," I said.

Without hesitation as if he was waiting for this moment, Yohane replied, "He had more than enough time to work out your relationship. I know it hurts, but you have to move on at one point. Let's go on a date. If you don't have a good time, I won't ask you out again. Just think about it and let me know by tomorrow."

"All right, I'll let you know."

Once we hung up the phone, I started thinking about a possible date with Yohane. Just one date wouldn't and couldn't hurt, right? Besides, it wasn't like I had much of a social life. Janae was spending more time with her boyfriend as they prepared for an upcoming debate, and Widelene was putting more time into building her business. So, I agreed to go on a date with Yohane, just one date. Sadly, I couldn't ask my friends for advice on clothing; this date had to remain a complete secret. Since I wasn't interested in dating Yohane, there was no real reason to get dressed up. I managed to make it through the week. The only real highlight was looking forward to my date, or should I say "hang out" with Yohane. We decided to hang out at Ms. Stephanie's loft since I didn't want to take the chance of running into Sè Françoise.

Before I could even ring the bell, the door quickly swung open. Yohane was standing in the doorway with the biggest smile. "Um, hi, Manushka, I was about to go outside for a little air," Yohane said as he seemed a little embarrassed.

"Yeah, what a coincidence, if that's what you want to call it." I laughed. I walked in as he held the door open.

Ms. Stephanie and Mr. Elijah were seated at a table with a stack of papers. "Hello, Manushka, don't mind the mess," Ms. Stephanie said. "We're working on our engagement announcement cards and guest list. Trust me, it is not a fun process especially when your assistant is Elijah," she chuckled.

"Wait a minute, I'm not letting that slide. No one stuffs envelopes better or faster than me." Mr. Elijah stood up waiting for recognition.

"King envelope stuffer, I am highly honored to have your assistance."

"Thank you, madam Stephanie. No applause needed, I take this job very seriously." Mr. Elijah took a bow before returning to envelope-stuffing duty.

"Now that my husband to be has been thoroughly acknowledged, I can now say what I intended. Manushka, I'll need to touch base with you, possibly next week, to discuss what I want you to create for my wedding. In the meantime, have fun."

Yohane led me to the rooftop, where he had several board games on a table, along with food and drinks. "Okay, Manushka, which board game would you like to play? Just so you know, I'm the board game king, I have a box of tissues in case you decide to cry when I beat you." This was the most confident I had ever seen him.

"Man, please! Didn't anyone tell you I'm the queen of board games? Let's start with Scrabble." I dramatically stretched my arms and legs as if preparing for a marathon.

We played for about an hour. The game was intense as I strategized as many triple and double word scores as possible. Yohane was doing better than I expected, creating words I didn't know. I was a little nervous but played it cool. "Never let your opponent see you sweat," is a quote I heard in a movie one day. Today, I had every intention of implementing that quote. I kept my game face on the entire time. Yohane was next-level serious, not even a smile. Finally, the game was over, and it was time to calculate the score. I beat him by one point, but it didn't matter because a win was a win, and I officially earned full bragging rights.

"I told you I'm the queen!" Performing a victory dance was the only way to celebrate the win appropriately.

"A queen indeed," Yohane said as he smiled at me.

After playing Scrabble, we sat down and talked for a while. Our conversation was great, no awkward moments at all. We talked about almost everything. Seems like nothing was off limits.

"Since you mentioned your parents, do you mind if I ask you a question about them?"

"I don't mind. What do you want to know?" Yohane repositioned his body on the couch. I guess that was his way of preparing to answer my questions.

"What were your parents like?" I asked.

To my surprise, he didn't even hesitate before answering. "My parents were amazing. You know how some people say they can't talk to their parents about anything? That wasn't the case for me. No topic was off-limits for them. And they loved traveling. Twice a year, we went on some kind of family vacation. The best thing about my parents was that they loved to have fun. You couldn't be around them and not laugh."

"Wow, I love that you had such an open relationship with them. So, have you thought about going to therapy like Ms. Stephanie mentioned?"

"Nah, I'm still not interested in talking to some stranger about my business." Based on his response, I knew he would soon change the subject. "Before you leave, how about we play one more game like tic-tac-toe?" he said.

"Oh, I see. You can't handle the fact that I won. Seems like someone is a sore loser. Let's go. I'm always ready for a challenge."

After agreeing to play one more game, he scrambled to find a sheet of paper as I waited patiently to celebrate my soon-to-be win. Despite my previous victory, Yohane was still pretty confident. "I'm the master of tic-tac-toe, so get your tissues ready cause you're about to cry when I beat you this time. Besides, you're a little too confident about the Scrabble win. How do you know I didn't just let you win?"

He was trying to downplay my win so I needed to solidify the fact that I was a champion. It was time for no mercy or beast mode. Completely focused and quiet with the game face on, we challenged each other to the best of three. Whoever won at least two games would be the winner. We were neck and neck with two games each. Yohane had his game face on too. We were down to the final move. As expected, I won. While doing another celebratory dance, I glanced at my phone. It was time to leave.

"Yohane, I had more fun than I expected, but I have to leave now."

Taking two steps toward me, he asked, "Did you enjoy it enough to hang out with me again? Be honest, Manushka. I can see you trying to hold back your smile."

The truth is, I enjoyed every moment spent with him that day, but I wasn't ready to share that information. I didn't want to develop feelings for Yohane aside from a friendship. I couldn't; it was too soon. I took the easy way out instead. "How about we talk about that next time? I have to leave now. Bye!" Before Yohane could say anything, I made my way downstairs to avoid having to answer his question.

"Goodbye, Ms. Stephanie," I said, waving as I walked toward the door.

"I'm sure he was a perfect gentleman, right?" Ms. Stephanie said as she turned around and winked at Yohane. She continued, " I'll touch base with you soon to discuss specifics about the paintings I want you to create." Ms. Stephanie was writing and stuffing envelopes the entire time she spoke. To say she was busy was an understatement. There were papers on the desk, floor, chairs, everywhere. Mr. Elijah looked confused as he stared at his future wife.

"Can't wait to hear the details," I said. From the corner of my eyes, I could see Yohane standing on the staircase. Before he walked towards the door, I slipped out quickly.

On the way home, I thought about my time with Yohane. I truly enjoyed it, probably more than I wanted to. As I drifted off into my thoughts, my phone rang, and it was him.

"I know you purposely avoided my question today," he said. "Hey, I'm no detective, but according to my calculations, the way you left led me to believe you enjoyed spending time with me. So, how about admitting the truth? I know you're a pretty honest girl."

After a long pause, I had no choice but to answer his question.

"Okay, Detective Yohane, you solved the mystery. Spending time with you was all right. I mean, it wasn't as painful as I expected," I said with a chuckle. Honestly, I had a great time, even more than expected actually. "Did you recover from that beatdown I gave you? I'm the queen of Scrabble and tic-tac-toe." I believe a little bragging never hurts.

"You only won by one point."

"Man, like I said before, a win is a win. I'd celebrate even if I won by half a point."

We laughed before the conversation became a little serious.

"Okay, champ, chill out. I got it; you're a winner. How about we hang out again since we both had a great time? "

I tried to think of reasons aside from my friends not to hang out with him again, but I couldn't think of anything. He was smart, cute, tall, funny, and had real art skills. He changed his overall outlook on life; no more hanging out at the mall and getting in trouble. I was proud of him. Taking it all into account, I figured I could keep Yohane a secret until my friends realized just how nice he was.

"Alright, I'm down to hang out again."

That response resulted in spending more time with him than anticipated. Yohane and I managed to hang out every weekend for the next three months, thanks to my work schedule with Ms. Stephanie. She asked me to create unique canvas paintings for each table at the reception, which was a total of twenty-five. My family was even included on the guest list. Yohane helped whenever he could, but Ms. Stephanie didn't want any distractions since she was both nervous and excited. After working with Ms. Stephanie for about two hours, Yohane and I played board games and watched movies. I liked having him as a friend until one day when Ms. Stephanie stepped out quickly to pick up lunch. I guess Yohane thought it was the perfect moment to profess his feelings for me.

"Manushka, we've been hanging out for the last three months, and I like you enough to want you to be my girlfriend." Without warning, Yohane took a couple of steps toward me. Then it happened. He kissed me. And this time, I didn't push him away. Everything about the moment felt so right—until I thought about Janae and Widelene. What would they think? What would they say? I was keeping this secret from my best friends and wasn't candid with Yohane either. It was time to tell him the truth.

"Um, Yohane, I like you, and I want to be your girlfriend, but—" At that moment, I couldn't even look him in the eye anymore; I looked down. I was conflicted. Would I pick my heart or my friends? Was I jumping into a new relationship too soon? What kind of person am I?

"But what? You can tell me anything," Yohane said as he gently reached for my hand.

"Well, my friends can't stand you. So, they definitely wouldn't want us dating. And part of me wants to be your girlfriend, but I don't think rushing into a new relationship is a good idea right now. I need to make sure I'm completely over Devonte." At the mention of Devonte's name, I became a little upset. Why was I holding onto the possibility of dating him again after he broke up with me? "You know what, I'm over Devonte. I just don't want to lose my best friends; that's the only real concern." Was I really over Devonte, or did I let anger take over my thoughts and feelings?

"The only reason you won't be my girl is because of your friends. So, will you be my secret girlfriend? We can hang out at my aunt's place instead of going on dates. Then you can tell your friends about us when you're ready. What do you think?"

I couldn't deny the fact that I had feelings for Yohane. Even though dating him now felt too soon, losing my friends was the only thing really stopping me from being his girlfriend. So, if we only hung out inside, they would never know. I mean, how could they? I paused for a few more seconds, then responded. "Yes, I want to be your secret girlfriend. When the time is right, I'll tell Janae and Widelene about our relationship."

As Yohane was getting ready to hug me, Ms. Stephanie opened the door. Standing in the doorway, she said, "Yohane and Manushka, I hope you two are behaving yourselves."

"You don't have anything to worry about, Aunt Stephanie. I'm always a perfect gentleman, you know that." Yohane walked toward Ms. Stephanie and gave her a tight hug. He winked at me, indicating that our relationship would remain a secret. I worked on a couple more canvases before leaving.

I couldn't believe I said "yes" to Yohane, my second boyfriend. Hanging out with Janae and Widelene was sometimes awkward, especially when Yohane would send me those random "Hello beautiful, I miss you" text messages.

"I see you smiling after that text. Hmm, who is this mystery person?" Widelene asked out of curiosity.

"Yeah, I saw that too," Janae said.

Oh no, they noticed. I didn't know what to do. Would my secret boyfriend be discovered too soon? I needed to think quick. I needed help and didn't know what to do. Now was not the time to tell them about Yohane. I began to panic since I couldn't think of a way out of this situation.

Janae crossed her arms. "We're waiting for the details. Hey, when did you start keeping secrets from us, best friend?"

Just when I was about to tell the truth, Janae's phone rang. It was her boyfriend, Monty. As usual, there was something debate-related they needed to discuss. Thank God. Monty and the debate team to the rescue!

"Guys, I have to go," Janae said. "Being a leader isn't always easy. Monty and I have some debate team issues to resolve. Manushka, you're off the hook for now. Don't think I'll forget this conversation. Gotta go!" She took off, leaving me with Widelene, who awaited my response.

"Janae may be gone, but I still want to know who is sending those texts. It has to be a guy. Who is he, and does he have a brother?" Oh, my goodness, she was waiting for an answer.

Thankfully, I came up with an excuse to leave. "I have to go, too. Fabienne is braiding my hair today," I said, grateful for the opportunity to get away before my secret got out. Telling them about Yohane was inevitable, but I just wasn't ready yet.

Between school, chores, and working with Ms. Stephanie, I was busy almost every day. Yohane and I continued to exclusively hang out at Ms. Stephanie's place every weekend until she asked us to pick up a few items at the mall. Before leaving, I had a flashback of Sè Françoise. So, I quickly called Fabienne, asking her to meet me at the store. She agreed, but of course, she was hanging out with Claude, so he was going to join us, which, for the first time, was actually a good thing. Being with a group rather than hanging out with a boy alone was less suspicious and practically eliminated cause for concern by my mother. Yohane and I made our way to the art store together. While walking down the street, he held my hand and said, "I'll count this as a date."

Just when I was about to respond, I looked over in total disbelief. My cover was blown.

Chapter 35

Standing right in front of us was Widelene and Janae! Running toward my friends, I pleaded, "Guys, wait, I can explain. Just give me a chance."

"Manushka!" Janae shouted. "How can you do this to us? Not only did you keep your relationship a secret, but you're dating *him*? Out of all the guys in the world, you choose to date *this one*? What happened to the pact about being open and honest with each other? Did you forget that, too?" Janae had no plans to listen to my pleas.

I looked over at Widelene, who just stood there without saying a word. It was as though she couldn't move, frozen or even paralyzed in the moment. Watching the situation unfold and knowing his presence only made things worse, Yohane took a few steps back as he faded into the background.

"Widelene, please listen to me." I tried to get her attention only to see a tear rolling down her face.

Since Widelene couldn't speak, Janae continued with a barrage of insults. Understanding the pain I caused, I could only listen. Now was not the time to fight back, especially since I was wrong. As I continued to withhold my thoughts and feelings, tears burst from my eyes. Nothing I could say would make things better.

"Manushka, I never thought I would say this, but I can't be your friend anymore. I just can't trust you. You threw away years of friendship for that guy. Really?" Janae said furiously. She continued yelling at me, but I couldn't hear the words as I sank further into a new reality—the reality of losing my best friends. Widelene didn't utter a word in my defense, which meant she agreed with Janae.

I looked over at Yohane as he appeared horrified. Insult after insult, I took it all in as Janae continued to speak. I couldn't move. Just then, an unlikely hero came to my rescue: Claude. He said, "Listen, Janae, I know you're mad, but this is not the time or place for this. I can't stand here and watch you speak to my future sister-in-law like that. Everyone makes mistakes at one point in life. And everyone has the potential to change if they want to, like me. This situation isn't about me, although I know lots of people enjoy talking about me. I have a special effect on people. Some say I'm irresistible, but that's not the point. The point is you need to stop all this foolishness right now. Just go home and take Widelene-the-statue with you."

I never thought I would say this, but I was happy to see Claude. As he made sure Janae and Widelene walked off, Fabienne hugged me as I sobbed uncontrollably.

To get a final word in while walking away Janae shouted, "I hope he's worth it!"

When Janae and Widelene left, Yohane approached me apologetically. He said, "Manushka, I'm sorry. I know I'm the reason you and your friends got into an argument. I hope you can forgive me. I hate that you're in so much pain because of me. I know there's nothing I can say to take your pain away, but I plan to be right by your side if you let me."

As we hugged, I melted in Yohane's arms. For a moment, I felt safe from the reality of this situation. With each stroke of my hair and back, I felt safer and more confident that I made the right decision in becoming his girlfriend.

"My aunt will know you were crying. So, I'll take the supplies to her. You can go straight home. Don't worry about anything. I'll cover for you. Claude, man, thanks for helping my girl. I didn't want to make things worse by saying anything, especially since this entire situation is my fault."

After an elaborate male handshake, kind of a hug thing, Yohane left, and I headed home with Claude and Fabienne. It was time to thank Claude; considering our history, he had no reason to step in and help me.

"Claude, thanks for defending me today. I can see how much you've changed. I guess you'll be a great brother-in-law one day if you don't mess things up with my sister." Even the sight of Claude licking his lips didn't bother me as much as before, at least not today. I was genuinely grateful for his support.

As we walked home, I knew my life was changed. My best friends would now see me as an enemy. Despite the internal pain, I masked my feelings. There was no way I wanted my mother to have any indication that something was wrong. I could see her staring at me intensely several times, but I had to be strategic. Thankfully, Fabienne knew what was going on. She distracted my mother as much as she could.

Sunday arrived, and I knew it could be an opportunity to speak to Widelene. We arrived at church and sat in our regular seats. As usual, there were several testimonies from the same people in the same order. The pastor taking his position in front of the congregation was usually the cue Widelene and I used to meet in the lobby. This time was different. I tried to make eye contact, but after a few minutes, it was obvious that Widelene was avoiding me. Feeling defeated, I decided to listen to the sermon, which was surprisingly interesting. The pastor talked about God looking at a person's heart rather than outward appearances like man does. Listening to the sermon made me think about Yohane. He's a good person with a beautiful heart, but Yohane made some poor decisions because of the pain he was carrying after witnessing his parent's death. He deserved a second chance.

I couldn't understand why Widelene was completely ignoring me at church, of all places. What happened to forgiveness and grace? I guess we missed that sermon during one of our many trips to the lobby. Was she willing to throw away years of friendship without even giving me a chance to explain myself? At one point, I decided to hang out in the lobby, but after ten minutes it was obvious that Widelene had no plans to join me . I re-entered the sanctuary and looked at her one last time, hoping she would glance in my direction, but she didn't. Being unable to speak to one of my best friends at church was painful, but I couldn't do anything to change the situation. If seeing Widelene ignore me at church hurt this much, I couldn't imagine what school would be like.

On Monday morning, the alarm sounded. I must have pressed the snooze button at least three times in hopes of not having to go to school. The sound of my mother shouting, "Manunu, wake up, wake up, you have school today," forced me to roll out of bed. Fabienne was an early riser, already dressed and eating breakfast. I got ready quickly. Since I was nervous about the day, I couldn't eat breakfast. So, my mother packed a piece of avocado and Haitian bread for me to eat on the way to school.

That morning, I apprehensively approached our meet-up spot, and just like I thought, Widelene and Janae were nowhere to be found. Claude was the only one there waiting. This new reality immediately slapped me in the face, determined not to cry, I continued walking and remained silent. I was now Fabienne and Claude's third wheel. Since they were holding hands, I decided to stay a few steps behind them. Despite being determined not to cry, I could feel my eyes filling with tears with every step closer to the school building until the phone rang. It was Yohane. "Good morning, beautiful. I just wanted to check up on you. I didn't want to wait until after school."

"I'm happy you called because Widelene and Janae are still not speaking to me. They didn't even wait for me at the morning meet-up spot, so I'm pretty much walking to school alone. Claude and Fabienne are here, but I don't want to be a third wheel." Having your own crew is everything in high school. Without my friends, I'd be the kid sitting at a lunch table all alone, and no one wants to be that kid. I had no clue how I would make it through the day.

"I'll stay on the phone until you get to school, so you won't have to walk alone." Just like he promised, Yohane remained on the phone. His much-needed humor cheered me up. I went through the motions to get through the first few periods, dreading the thought of lunch. I walked into the cafeteria and immediately stared at the lunch table Janae, Widelene, and I once shared. They both looked at me, but only for a second. If looks could kill, I would've died on the spot. The disgust in their eyes was so unsettling that I couldn't stay in the cafeteria. I decided to find a quiet place in the hallway to have lunch, sadly, all alone. Walking down the hall, I heard Mrs. Franca calling my name.

She spoke faster than usual. "Manushka, Manushka, I have an exciting opportunity for you. An art club I belong to is hosting an exclusive competition for high school students."

She explained that the competitors would each have twenty minutes per round to craft a painting inspired by random words or concepts. The contest was structured to have four rounds, with eliminations occurring after each, based on the lowest scores. Only the elite would advance through the rigorous process. Interestingly, this competition was unique in its exclusivity; only those specifically invited could participate. And I'd been identified as a worthy contender. Participation was free of charge. The last artist standing would receive a $500 scholarship.

"I really believe you can win this," she said, radiating positivity.

Based on her excitement, there was no way I could say no. "Mrs. Franca, thanks for entering me in the competition. And thank you for believing in me." Mrs. Franca's positive energy made me feel a little better.

Before I walked away, she said, "The competition is taking place in a few weeks. I recommend working on speed and technique. If you do that, you are guaranteed to win. Lastly, even though this is an exclusive engagement, feel free to invite your family and friends."

When she mentioned the word "friends," I started crying, and it wasn't the silent type. It was one of those loud cries, you know the ones where it sounds like you're hyperventilating, and your nose starts running uncontrollably. Yep, that's what happened right in front of my teacher. It was even more embarrassing that I didn't have a tissue to wipe the snot running from my nose. Don't judge me, but I had to use my shirt; I had no choice.

"Manushka, what happened? Did I say something wrong? Are you OK?" Mrs. Franca asked as she quickly approached me.

"Sorry, I didn't mean to cry. And no, you didn't say anything. It's just that—" Again, I started sobbing before finishing the sentence. She led me into her classroom and encouraged me to get the rest of the tears out. After crying for what seemed like forever, I explained the situation.

As usual, Mrs. Franca had expert advice. She said, "I've heard and seen a lot of drama within friend groups, specifically girls. Based on the interaction I've seen between you and your friends in the past, I wouldn't be surprised if you were to rebuild your friendship soon. In time, things may work out. Right now, the wound is still fresh and all of you are hurting. Until you figure things out, feel free to eat lunch in my classroom as long as I'm here."

After listening to her, I felt a little more at peace, especially since she gave me an open invitation to having lunch in her classroom. Eating in her room would save me the stress of avoiding their stares and figuring out where to sit. "Mrs. Franca, thank you for being such a great teacher. I appreciate everything you've done for me."

I was planning not to eat at all, but after hearing my stomach growl, I knew skipping lunch wasn't an option; I had to eat something. On my way to class, I walked right past Widelene and Janae. They decided to ignore me by avoiding eye contact. Seeing my friends and knowing they continually chose not to see me was painful. Invisible is what I was to them, and alone is how I felt. Was my relationship with Yohane worth it? *But they don't know him like I do. They don't know about his dreams. They don't know about the hardships he experienced, they don't know about his desires, and they don't know how good he treats me. Why can't they just give him a chance, and why can't they just give me another chance?* How could they overlook years of friendship? They were the ones who encouraged me to date, so I'd forget about Devonte. I felt so alone. My social life was nonexistent. No friends to hang out with, not even my sister. Fabienne and Claude's relationship was going strong; he was, in fact, a "changed man," just like he promised. As much as I didn't want to admit it, I was happy for them. Claude attended school more often, even pulling his grades up to Bs and Cs.

Enough about the happy couple. I wanted my best friends back but didn't want to break up with Yohane, at least not yet. He was so good to me: respectful, thoughtful, charming, funny, and, of course, *fine*. No more hanging out at the mall or being friends with knuckleheads; he was mature, grounded, and focused.

Moving on, my new routine over the next couple of months was walking alone or with Fabienne and Claude to the train station at the end of the school day. Yohane offered to meet me after school, but I didn't want him to miss his classes for me, especially since he was trying so hard to stay on track. Once home, I did routine chores, homework, refined my painting skills for the upcoming competition, and occasionally watched the local news with my dad. I looked forward to the weekends because I got to hang out with Yohane and work with Ms. Stephanie in preparation for the wedding. She approved the ideas I proposed and allowed me to begin painting. Seeing the excitement on Ms. Stephanie's face when I showed her the completed artwork was priceless. Her reaction helped me to feel more confident in my skills as an artist.

Chapter 36

Sadly, a life without best friends was the new reality I was forced to accept. Some would say, 'just make new friends,' but it's not as easy as it sounds. It's practically impossible to join new friend groups during senior year. By now, bonds have been made, which practically closes the door to new friendships. The only alternative was walking to school with Fabienne and Claude. The hope of seeing Janae and Widelene waiting for me in the morning continued to dwindle. I ate lunch in Mrs. Franca's classroom every day. I was overall a little more focused on studying and preparing for the art competition. As much as I missed my friends, there was a bright side. My dad and I began bonding more as we watched the evening news together in the evenings. All the reports on the local news always seemed so foreign—until one day.

No, it couldn't be! How could this happen? Nicole, the girl who spoke to us about teen dating violence, was murdered. Her boyfriend killed her. Nicole ended up dating him again despite the history of abuse. What was she thinking?

Based on the news report, the guy shot Nicole several times in what was described as a jealous rage. I wanted to cry while watching the news segment covering the story, but withheld tears to avoid having a full discussion about the situation since my mother has the tendency to automatically generalize the story. Her logic would be to stay away from all boys until you get married. The only people who could truly understand how I was feeling were Janae and Widelene. I wondered if they saw the story. I wanted to call, but chances are, they wouldn't pick up the phone.

That night, I decided to go to bed earlier than usual. The pain of the news was too much to handle. Thinking about the story also reminded me of Devonte. I missed him, but that part of my life was over. At least, that's what I wanted to believe.

I went to school alone the following day since Fabienne left earlier than usual for a field trip. I couldn't get Nicole out of my head. She was so young and beautiful. Why did she go back to that guy? Lost in my thoughts, I couldn't hear anything happening around me until I felt a tap on my shoulder. I turned around, surprised to see both Widelene and Janae standing at our meet-up spot. Speechless, I couldn't find my words. Instead, I stood there and listened to them speak. Of course, Janae spoke first, "Girl, do you know what happened last night? Okay, okay, no time to go back and forth. Nicole, the girl who spoke about teen dating violence, was shot by her boyfriend, a guy named Raphael. He had to be the guy she was in that abusive relationship with because she referred to him as R. As soon as I saw the story, I called Widelene. While on the phone, we both thought about you." Janae looked over at Widelene, who shook her head in agreement.

Widelene then chimed in. "We made a pact the day we heard Nicole speak. Part of the pact was to be best friends forever through good and bad times. Honestly, Manushka, I wasn't a good friend to you. I shouldn't have shut you out of my life so quickly without even talking about the situation. I was wrong. I'm sorry for the way I treated you. I hope you can find a way to forgive me."

Janae said, "Girl, you know I could be just a little crazy sometimes. Being mad at you for so long was way too much work for me. My face was hurting, trying to give you dirty stares all the time. And, you know I was missing your mother's riri Joe-Joe. So, I hope you can forgive me too."

Before I could utter a word, Janae and Widelene were both hugging me. As we embraced, we all began to cry. There were so many mixed emotions between Nicole's death and the issues we had in our friendship.

It was time for me to respond. I took a deep breath. "First of all—" Their eyes widened in response to my tone. " It is not riri Joe-Joe. For the last time, it's diri djondjon. Repeat after me, di-ri djon-djon. Janae, you need to get it right!"

"Girl, like I told you last time, I just eat the rice; I don't make it. I can eat that rice for breakfast, lunch, and dinner. Now, when can I get a plate? It's long overdue." We all laughed as Janae rubbed her stomach.

I continued, "And yes, I forgive the both of you. I missed my best friends. I hope you forgive me for keeping my dating situation a secret."

Right before they responded, my phone rang. It was Yohane calling to keep me company on the walk to school. Conflicted, I didn't know if I should pick up or ignore the call.

"Girl, we know your man is calling you. Just pick up the phone," Janae said.

I took a couple of steps away from the girls to pick up the phone. I quickly told Yohane what was happening before hanging up.

"Manushka, so you know, Yohane tracked us down one day to explain the mall situation," Widelene said. "He sincerely apologized for not trying to help us. Yohane also shared a little about his life. He was willing to break up with you so we could be friends again. So, he's aight, but we still have to keep a close eye on him a bit longer. Enough about Yohane, how do you always manage to find good guys? Tell me your secret."

Jokingly, Janae said, "What about rice-cake-Melvin? The love of your life."

We all laughed on the way to school. Just like that, the crew was back together again. I decided to have lunch in Mrs. Franca's classroom one last time to share the good news and thank her for her support. She reminded me of the upcoming competition. Because of Mrs. Franca's excitement and belief in me, I was determined to win.

On the way home, I told Janae and Widelene about the competition and asked if they wanted to attend. Before I could finish the sentence, Janae said, "Girl, you don't even have to ask. I got you. Just give me the time, and address. Besides, I don't have any plans this weekend. Oh, and I want to witness you winning first place."

"You can count me in, too," Widelene said. "I don't have any plans this weekend either."

It was such a relief to know my best friends would be there to support me on such short notice. I went straight home after school, determined to prepare for the competition, especially since so many people believed in me.

On the morning of the competition, the challenge of shaking off what felt like knots in my stomach intensified with each passing minute. A few trips to the bathroom, along with deep breaths, helped maintain some degree of composure. But was it enough to get through the competition? "Manunu, Manunu, let's go." The sound of my mother's voice snapped me out of what could have been a downward spiral. It was time to leave—no turning back now. I quietly sat in the back of the car, gazing out the window during the drive. Thoughts crossed my mind, but I must admit, most of them were negative. Second place in the last competition wasn't so bad, but suppose I come in last place or worse yet, suppose I get eliminated. Maybe my mother is right; pursuing a career as a nurse, engineer, or lawyer is a more guaranteed path to success. As I continued to sulk, back-to-back texts came from my friends, Yohane, and Mrs. Stephanie. Although brief, the messages arrived at the perfect time with the encouragement I needed to step out of the car.

Mrs. Franca stood at the entrance with a warm smile greeting everyone who walked through the doors. The facility was beautiful and much bigger than expected. I was in awe of the art on the wall and the overall décor. Colors I would have never considered pairing somehow complemented each other. As I walked further into the facility, it was as though I was passing through different eras. *Wow, just wow* is all

I could think of as I experienced a loss for words. Finally reaching the designated area, I was told to wait in a room with the other forty-nine contestants. Apparently, even though I was early, I was still the last person to arrive. Within minutes, the moderators for the event explained the instructions to include time frames, different rounds, and the criteria required to avoid elimination. We were separated into ten different groups. Only one person from each group would move to the next round.

Self-doubt crept in, but I was determined to think positively. I took a few deep breaths. Rather than being in separate rooms, the contestants were all positioned in a circle to allow the judges to have the opportunity to walk around as we painted. My friends and family all looked on, which gave me some comfort. "For this round, the theme for your painting is wilderness. What is your perception of the wilderness? Remember, you are an artist, please use your creative liberty: no need to confine yourself to the norm. The judges are now ready, contestants should be ready, now start," one of the moderators said.

Before painting, I quickly envisioned a wilderness in my head. It took about two minutes to come up with an idea. By that time, everyone else had already started. I began with the first stroke, feeling like my knees were about to buckle under pressure. I quickly looked around the room, making eye contact with my mother, which was reassuring.

"Three more minutes," the moderator said as the judges made their way around the circle, taking notes as we painted. With seconds remaining, the countdown began, "10, 9, 8, 7, 6, 5, 4, 3, 2, and 1. Artist, please drop your paint brushes and stand behind your paintings," the moderator said. Then, he continued, "The judges have made their decision as to who will be moving on to the next round. When I call your name, please step forward. John Benjamin, Phyliss Bragford, Manushka Jean-Pierre—"

After my name was called, I couldn't hear anything else. I was shocked and excited. Moving on to the next round was a much-needed confidence booster. The word for the next round was "dreams." I applied the same technique, thinking about the full concept before painting. With each stroke of the brush, my vision was coming to life. Before I knew it, the round was over. Again, I advanced through the next few rounds. My name was called first a couple of times—that had to be a good sign. The competition was down to five contestants in the final round. For this round, the word was "support." This time, I looked into the crowd for inspiration.

My sea of support inspired me: friends, family, Mrs. Franca, Ms. Stephanie, and Yohane, of course. I wanted this painting to capture my love and appreciation for each one. I attempted to capture everything I was feeling on this canvas. "10, 9, 8, 7, 6, 5, 4, 3, 2 and 1. Contestants, please drop your brushes and stand behind your paintings," the moderator said. The competition was over. It was time for the judges to analyze our paintings to make the final decision. As I waited, I noticed a familiar face. But it couldn't be, no way!

Chapter 37

It was Devonte standing right beside Yohane. He showed up unexpectedly. How did he even know about the competition? I couldn't contain my smile as our eyes met. Seeing him instantly brought so many special memories to mind. Oh no, Yohane was smiling back at me; he thought I was looking at him. My heart and mind were conflicted. I wanted to think about Yohane, but I drifted further into memories of Devonte until someone nudged me on the shoulder.

"Hey! You won first place!" one of the other contestants said.

I snapped out of the daze. "What? I won!"

With a slight attitude, the other contestant nodded yes, then said, "If you don't want first place, I'll gladly take it."

I ran toward the podium, where the judges stood waiting with a trophy.

As the trophy was handed to me, Mrs. Franca emerged from behind the curtain with one of those huge paper checks in hand. First place! It was real; I won the competition. I looked into the crowd and saw my parents, Widelene, Janae, Ms. Stephanie, Yohane, Naomi, and Fabienne clapping. Of course, Claude had to be extra, chanting, "Manushka, Manushka, Manushka!" As I continued to scan the crowd, I didn't see Devonte. Was it my imagination? Was he really there? Or was I just having a flashback of the last competition? Nevertheless, Devonte was nowhere to be found, which was great because I felt kind of guilty thinking about him, considering I was dating Yohane, who was standing there with a big bouquet of flowers.

As I descended the staircase, I saw my mother holding back her tears. Her pride was evident, but my mother avoided being completely vulnerable, especially in public. I hugged her and then told a joke to help in holding back the tears. As much as she wanted to speak, my mother remained quiet as she stared at me with admiration. At that moment, I knew she was thinking about her countless sacrifices to ensure I had the opportunity to get an education.

I hugged my dad, who said, "Good job, Manunu." My dad never showed much emotion, but I knew his way of demonstrating love was to be present, provide, and protect.

As my emotions grew to tears, my friends danced and sang, "Go, Manushka! You did it: first place! You're the winner! You won money, so take us to dinner! Go, Manushka! Go, Manushka!" The lyrics were so catchy that I danced, too. After our little singing and dancing episode, Janae and Widelene hugged me.

Janae decided to hug me a little longer as she whispered, "I have something to tell you later." I figured the whispering was because Yohane and Ms. Stephanie walked toward us.

Ms. Stephanie approached me with open arms, fully prepared to give me a congratulatory hug. "Manushka, words cannot describe how proud I am of you. Between your technique, poise under pressure, and creativity, I was absolutely mesmerized by your performance today. This time around, you had so much more confidence. Like I told you before, there is power in your words. What you think and believe about yourself is what truly matters. 'As a man thinketh in his heart, so he is.' From this moment on, I want you to give yourself permission to dream big." I welcomed both the hug and encouraging words from my amazing mentor.

Mrs. Franca approached us and said, "I'm sure Stephanie mentioned everything I planned to tell you. Let me give you a hug, too."

The way I felt was indescribable because the whole idea of being an artist was feeling like it could happen for me one day, my future reality.

As we walked toward the car, I thought about what Ms. Stephanie said, and part of it was in the Bible somewhere. The condition of my heart had the power to direct my path. The statement was kind of deep, so I had plans to get more clarification from her one day. On the car ride home, my mother expressed how proud she was of me, followed by some tears, which was a little shocking because she seemed more vulnerable than usual, at least for a moment.

My father shared his feelings about my work and his pride in me. This car ride was becoming unexpectedly emotional. As proud as my parents were of my art accomplishments, I still knew that there would never be a perfect moment to share that I wanted to be an artist instead of a nurse or doctor. "Mommy and Papi, I want to do art. I want to be an artist when I grow up. An artist like Ms. Stephanie. I don't want to be a nurse, doctor, engineer, or lawyer." Without much thought, I blurted out my desire for the future.

After a long pause, my mother said, "Manunu, nurse, doctor, engineer, and lawyer make a lot of money. I want you live good." Listening to her response was discouraging. I knew why she felt that way, it came from a place of love but I wanted and needed the support.

As I slipped further into discouragement, my father came to the rescue. "Manunu, don't be a nurse. Be a good artist, OK." My dad was a man of few words, but when he spoke, it was powerful, so everyone listened.

After his statement, my parents got into a little argument as my father defended my dreams of becoming an artist. I want to be an ARTIST! Finally, the secret was out; it was one less thing my parents didn't know about. My art debut outside of competitions would take place at Ms. Stephanie's wedding in just two more weeks. Life was great. I had my best friends back, a fantastic boyfriend, and my parents knew I had no plans of becoming a nurse, lawyer, doctor, or any of those expected professions.

I was looking forward to meeting up with my friends on Monday morning. Yohane planned to meet me in the morning since his school was closed for one of those private school holidays. I was a few minutes late, so everyone was waiting for me. Before hugging Yohane, I quickly asked Janae what she'd been trying to tell me, but for some reason, she whispered that she would tell me later. This whole idea of Janae whispering was strange, but nothing to worry about, I hope.

We walked to school together, laughing at Janae's crazy jokes. When we got to the front of the building, my mouth hit the floor. I couldn't believe it. Devonte was standing right in front of the school.

Janae whispered, "Sorry, girl, that's what I've been meaning to tell you. Devonte is here for a couple of weeks and wants to see you. I told him about the art competition. He mentioned something about missing you and wanting to get back together."

I quickly said, "Janae, this is what you would call an emergency, red alert. You should have told me, girl."

As I looked in his direction, Devonte smiled. As much as I wanted to return the smile, I kept a straight face as Yohane stood beside me.

Rather than waiting for Yohane to leave, Devonte approached us. "Hey, Manushka! I wanted to surprise you this morning," Devonte said.

"Um, yes, this is what I would call a surprise. Um, Devonte, it's great to see you. Um, this is Yohane. He is my, um, boyfriend because we're dating and that makes me his girlfriend." I was having a difficult time speaking during this extremely awkward moment.

Seeing my struggle, Janae and Widelene immediately kicked into action. Widelene began talking to Yohane, and Janae began speaking to Devonte, which gave me enough time to gather my thoughts.

"Um, the bell is about to ring, and I don't want to be late to class today, especially since there's a quiz first period," I said, hoping it would be enough for Yohane and Devonte to leave.

"Manushka, I'll meet you right here after school," Yohane said. As he hugged me, he stared directly at Devonte.

Within seconds of hugging Yohane, Devonte confidently approached. "I'm ready to make our relationship work. I miss my girl and I know you miss me too!" As Devone hugged me, I remained still, my arms limp at my sides, betraying the turmoil within. I desperately wanted to return the hug considering how our relationship ended. The words he uttered sent my thoughts into a whirlwind. Oh, my goodness, this was a complicated situation, yet the familiarity of his arms around me was undeniably comforting. Yohane took a few steps back while he watched Devonte hug me. I then stood between the two in what appeared to be a battle of the male egos.

"Yohane, see you after school. And goodbye, Devonte, seeing you today was quite the surprise." After my final word, I quickly rushed into the school building without looking back.

Thankfully, I didn't have a quiz during the first period. If I did, chances are I would've failed because thoughts of Yohane and Devonte filled my mind. As soon as the bell rang for lunch, I went straight to the cafeteria to meet with my friends. "No time to have lunch today; I need advice from the both of you now. Devonte's back, and he wants us to date again. Can you believe it? What makes him think he can waltz right back into my life after the way he broke up with me."

Widelene spoke first, "Girl, that's straight drama. This is out of my league. Just so you know, I would pick Devonte because he's fine, yeah, and he's nice too. He was your first boyfriend."

Janae chimed in. "The situation this morning was crazy. The only thing missing was popcorn. I mean, your ex-boyfriend and current boyfriend in the same place at the same time, with the same goal of capturing your heart. It felt like I was about to witness a duel for Lady Manuskha." Janae stood up and pretended to poke Widelene with an imaginary sword. Taking the bait, Widlene attacked her with her sword.

"Guys, I'm happy you're having fun, but this is serious. We needed to get back to the situation at hand. I wanted and needed my friends to be focused. It was the only way to get the best advice."

Janae responded, "Sorry girl, just having a little fun. Since you can't date both of them, pick Yohane. You guys have a lot in common, and I can tell he cares about you. But Devonte is fine, though. Seriously, you should go with your gut—at least, that's what my mom says when I have to make tough decisions. Do what feels right." Janae had a good point, but I was so torn with this decision.

I needed to make my mind up before meeting with Yohane after school, just in case he had questions. For the rest of the day, I thought about the decision I'd have to make. The day went by fast, which didn't make any sense because other days in school felt endless—but the day I needed a little extra time, it flew by. After much contemplation, I finally made a decision, hopefully the right one.

Widelene, Janae, and I walked out of the building together. Standing right outside the gate was Yohane. I couldn't read his face. He didn't look upset, but he also didn't look happy. I walked straight toward him. Yohane usually greeted me with a hug, but this time, he said, "We need to talk."

Widelene and Janae took that as a cue to walk a few steps behind us.

"Yes, we do need to talk. I've been thinking about you all day." Technically, I didn't lie. I was thinking about Yohane all day, but I was also thinking about Devonte.

Yohane smiled half-heartedly. "The situation this morning was uncomfortable. I saw the way he looked at you. Let's just get straight to the point. Do you want to continue our relationship?"

Since I didn't want Yohane to doubt my decision, I said quickly, "Yeah, I was uncomfortable, too. Listen, you have nothing to worry about because I still want to be your girlfriend. Right now, I can only think about my future with you." I reached for his hand, you know, to add a little romantic feel to the situation, make it less intense. I must admit, my lines were a little smooth.

Intertwining his fingers with mine, Yohane gently grabbed hold of my hand. As we walked toward the train station, we were unusually quiet for the first time since we started dating. I thought I made the right decision.

Within seconds of him leaving, my phone rang. It was Devonte! Should I pick up on the second ring or just miss the call altogether? I picked up on the fourth ring, you know, I played it cool.

"Hey, Manushka," Devonte said.

I felt butterflies at the sound of his voice, but I was hoping it was a case of gas, especially since I picked Yohane. Nevertheless, memories of our first kiss on the Brooklyn Bridge, our date at the botanical garden, and the countless times we walked down the hallways hand in hand ran through my mind.

"Oh, hey, Devonte. I didn't expect to see you today, especially since we haven't spoken in months, you know, after the way you broke up with me at the mall." That came off a little bitter, but I didn't care.

"Well, I didn't expect to see you with a new boyfriend. I guess I expected you to wait for me."

Did he just say I should have waited for him? Did Florida make Devonte lose his mind? Sharply, I said, "You had more than enough time to call, but you never did, so I moved on."

"I'm sorry for not calling you. Life got a little hectic, but that's the past. I want my girl back 'cause we got history."

Highly annoyed, I said, "Did you expect me to sit by the phone waiting for you to call? Sorry, but never that. You didn't even return my phone calls. Just so you know, I'm dating Yohane now, and I don't plan on breaking up with him for you today or any other day."

After a few moments of silence, Devonte said, "What else do you want me to say? I already apologized. Like I said before, life was hectic. I wasn't gone long enough for you to find another boyfriend. It seems like you're into this Your-heinie dude so—"

Before Devonte could finish, I interjected. "No, his name is Yohane, not Your-heinie, so please get it right."

Devonte continued, "I guess I'll have to apologize for that too. I don't agree, but I respect your decision. If you and Your-heinie, I mean

Yohane, don't work out, call me." Devonte paused for a few seconds. "Manushka, I love you."

When Devonte said he loved me, it was like my heart skipped a beat or my pulse raced. I can't explain it other than my heart did something super strange. Not sure how to respond, I faintly heard Devonte say, "Manushka, are you OK?"

I didn't want him to know that his words affected me. I said, "Yeah, I'm okay. I thought I saw a loose dog; you know how scared I am of dogs. On that note, I have to go now. Have a safe trip back to Florida."

Saying goodbye to Devonte this time around felt different. It felt like the complete end of any possibility of us ever being together again. It truly was a sad moment. My mom says there's a season for everything. Devonte just doesn't fit in this season of my life. Maybe he'll fit in the future, or possibly never.

After a long sigh, I went home and headed straight to bed. I needed a little extra time to fully accept the end of my relationship and friendship with Devonte. As I stared at the ceiling, Yohane called. I quickly sat up and cleared my throat. "Hey, Yohane, I was just thinking about you!" I said, trying to demonstrate as much excitement as possible. Technically, I didn't lie because Yohane crossed my mind while thinking about Devonte again. Thinking about Yohane and Devonte at the same time was happening a little too much for me to keep track.

"I was thinking about you, too! I can't wait to see your beautiful face at the wedding tomorrow. I know a lot of guys will be jealous since I'll have the prettiest girl at the wedding as my date. I know you're a little nervous about your paintings being on display, but don't worry because Aunt Stephanie loves everything you created. I even heard her say that displaying your paintings is one of the highlights of the wedding.

Hearing Yohane share how Ms. Stephanie felt was reassuring. In fact, the words eased my nervousness. "I'm happy she loves everything. I'm not as nervous as before; I'm just excited. This is a huge opportunity. Your aunt knows a lot of influential people in the art world. Who knows what doors this will open for me after the wedding? Aside from seeing how beautiful Ms. Stephanie will look tomorrow, I can't wait to see you dressed up in a suit lookin' all dapper. Hey, remember my mom will be there, so we have to tone things down a little. Lord knows I don't want to lose my beloved phone ever again. Well, I have to go now—time to get my hair done. You know the hair situation is always a process. Bye, Yohane, see you tomorrow."

"Bye, Manushka. I love you," Yohane said right before hanging up. I couldn't respond. The words *I love you* couldn't leave my mouth. Was it because I was thinking about Devonte earlier, or was it guilt? This whole Devonte thing was causing unnecessary stress and drama in my life. He was part of my past, and that's how I intended to keep things. I must admit, knowing that two guys, I mean two fine and intelligent guys wanted to date me, was a confidence booster for sure.

Chapter 38

The day of the wedding finally arrived. My mother decided to wear a matching two-piece suit that included a below the knee length skirt and jacket. The first step was putting on her stockings. Can't forget about her stockings, also known as pantyhose. My mother didn't feel dressed unless she had them on.

"Manunu, get my *jipon*," my mother said. In case you don't know, a *jipon* is called a slip in English. It's usually worn under a skirt. If you ask me, I think slips are useless, but my mother insists on wearing one whenever she wears a skirt or dress. I retrieved the slip from my mother's third drawer. Just like she said, the slip was underneath a pair of black stockings in the third drawer, on the left. My mother is just about the most organized person I've ever met. She can tell you exactly where to find everything. She completed her outfit with the gold jewelry she hid underneath the mattress, right beside important papers like birth certificates, social security cards, and passports. Underneath the mattress is my mother's version of a file cabinet and safe. As I watched her get dressed, I found it quite interesting that she never has one of those dreams that would make her cancel plans and stay home. The way my mother was looking and feeling, I don't think a dream, blizzard, or any natural disaster could stop her from attending this wedding.

After helping my mother, it was time for me to get dressed. I made sure my *mouchwa*—or headscarf—was still in place. Wearing one to bed was so ingrained in my mind that I couldn't sleep without it. In fact,

I had several different *mouchwa*, but of course, I had a favorite one that was red with blue flowers. Although my beloved *mouchwa* was cotton, there was absolutely no way I was planning to give it up. It was faithful and dedicated; it stayed on my head throughout the night and covered my hair and ears. I slipped the dress over my head then sat on the edge of the bed to put on a pair of heels. After my makeup was done; I added accessories and perfume for the final touches.

Between my hair, make-up, and dress, everything looked perfect. Fabienne did a great job with my hair again; she always does a great job. To think I initially didn't want her to move in made me feel just a little guilty. One day, I'll get over the guilt but every once in a while the thought is bothersome, especially when Fabienne comes to my rescue. I'm still amazed by how fast we managed to make our relationship work. She helped me, and I helped her—this is what you would call a mutually beneficial relationship. Fabienne, an early riser, was already done and waiting for Claude to arrive, which he finally did right before we walked out the door. I used to wrestle with the fact that Fabienne was allowed to date but eventually let it go. I mean, she is eighteen. My mother still didn't enforce certain rules on Fabienne. She was careful still about trying not to overstep her boundaries as a stepmother. My dad didn't mind Fabienne having a boyfriend. His only requirement was that Claude always demonstrate respect. That said, in usual Claude fashion, he was flashy, overly confident, and highly annoying.

"Hello, Mommy and Papi," Claude said. "Mommy, you look like a supermodel, very beautiful. I think you're getting younger every day." Haitian parents, specifically mothers, love a little extra attention, and Claude knows that. The look on my mother's face after Claude's list of compliments was confirmation that his little plan worked.

Of course, he continued to talk. "Papi, I'll make sure everyone is safe. Don't worry about anything." My father simply nodded after Claude decided to finally stop talking. Some would say my father isn't friendly, but I would say he's more of an introvert, a friendly introvert, you know, the person who only speaks when they feel the need to.

My father decided to stay home instead of going to the wedding. He planned to drop us off and pick us up later. He was most likely planning to watch soccer or the news while eating the food my mother prepared for him.

And again, Claude continued to speak. "Manushka, you look aight. I'm sure someone will be excited to see you. Fabienne, you look absolutely gorgeous. I've never seen an angel before, but I can't imagine any angel being more beautiful than you. Wow! I think you might even look better than the bride." Yes, Claude was my plus one since my dad decided not to attend. As much as he got on my nerves, I was still grateful that Claude stood up for me when I had the issue with Janae and Widelene.

Moments later, we arrived at the venue.

Both the wedding ceremony and reception were scheduled to take place in the same venue. As I stood outside, I was in absolute awe. The architecture was mesmerizing. Everything was beautiful, from the colors to the intricate details that some would easily overlook. I couldn't wait to see the inside. As we entered, my mother ran back to the car to remind my father where to find the food she prepared for him. I never understood why she did that. Seriously, for the last ten years or more, she always left the food in the same exact spot, covered by a plastic mesh thing.

My mother adjusted her clothing and then had the nerve to say, "Manunu, let's go," as if she'd been waiting on me the entire time.

As soon as we walked in, we were greeted by a gentleman in a suit. He handed us a program and then led us to an elevator to the rooftop. When the door opened, a beautiful circular arch appeared, draped with hundreds of white roses. The white carpet runner between the chairs for the bridal party's entrance was lined by white and blush rose petals. To the left and right of the roof, I could see several bare tree branches adorned with crystal beads that resembled beautifully crafted icicles. The lights shimmering from the crystal beads were timed perfectly to create synchronicity from top to bottom.

"Manushka, Manushka," I could hear a distant voice calling my name. It was Fabienne trying to pull me from my deep thoughts. "Manushka, are you okay?" She asked.

To avoid possible concern, I quickly said, "I'm fine, girl. This place is just so beautiful."

Fabienne learned English quickly, I felt comfortable speaking to her like I spoke to Janae and Widelene. Only occasionally did I talk to her in Creole, when certain concepts were too difficult to understand in English.

As Fabienne and I spoke, a gentleman dressed in a suit led us to our seats. Thankfully, I had a seat right by the aisle, the perfect spot to see the bride make her grand entrance. After about fifteen minutes, the pianist began playing a song. The tone of the song perfectly matched the magical and romantic atmosphere. The door gently opened, allowing Mr. Elijah to make his entrance first. Once positioned by the arch, the bridal party made their entrance. The bridal party was surprisingly smaller than I expected, with six people, including a maid of honor, best man, one bridesmaid, one groomsman, a flower girl, and the cutest ringbearer I had ever seen.

I made eye contact with Yohane as he walked down the aisle. I must say, my man was lookin' finer than ever between the fresh cut and the perfectly tailored suit. Based on how he looked at me, it was clear that Devonte, I mean Yohane, approved of my attire. Wait! Did I just say Devonte? I couldn't let that mistake happen again. Devonte was part of my past, plain and simple, my past. He was the one who'd left without trying to work out our relationship, not me. And now, he thought, for some reason, I would drop everything just because he wanted me back. Absolutely not! Who does he think he is? In the past, Devonte would remain! Okay, enough about him. It was time for the moment all the guests were waiting for.

"Everyone, please rise to your feet as the bride makes her entrance," the gentleman holding the microphone said. The door was closed, and everyone was anticipating Ms. Stephanie's entrance. A woman with an angelic voice sang. Her voice was powerful yet gentle at the same time. As the woman continued singing, Ms. Stephanie appeared along with her father. She looked stunning. Her mermaid-style dress was simple and elegant. Her cathedral-length veil was filled with beads that beautifully complemented her dress. Oh, and Ms. Stephanie's tiara was amazing. She was seriously giving princess vibes. With each approaching step, I could see both the bride and groom holding back their tears. I think Ms. Stephanie was holding back a little more; I'm sure she didn't want her makeup to run yet. As I turned back to watch her walk down the aisle, Mr. Elijah let out a sob that caused everyone to look in his direction. Naturally, tears slid down Ms. Stephanie's face. The love between them was so strong, I'm sure everyone at the wedding could feel it. Finally, she made it to the altar. The pastor made a couple of jokes. It was clear that he had a close relationship with them.

Rather than using the traditional vows, they'd written their own. By the time the vows were read, it seemed like everyone was crying. After the ring exchange, the ceremony ended with sparklers as they made their way down the aisle as husband and wife.

All wedding guests were escorted to a designated area for cocktail hour. I was impressed by all the food and thought everything was delicious. Once cocktail hour ended, we went to the reception room. It was the moment of truth. I took a deep breath and closed my eyes briefly before walking in. I opened my eyes and was speechless. She used my paintings as centerpieces for each table. The floral arrangements at the tables perfectly complemented the unique paintings. I nervously walked around to inspect each table. I wanted to run, jump, cry, and laugh. With so many emotions running through my mind, I just didn't know how to feel. We finally sat down at our assigned table with another family who happened to be nice. I could overhear them saying how beautiful my work was, but they had no idea I created it. Of course, my mother chimed in. "My daughter Manushka make the art. She do very good job."

The woman seated across from her said, "I'm sure you're proud of your daughter." She turned to me. "It is quite clear you'll have a bright future as an artist. You are talented indeed, young lady."

After thanking the woman for her kind words, I smiled from ear to ear.

From the moment we arrived at the wedding, Claude had started acting weirder than usual. I figured his flashy suit was causing some discomfort, but out of concern and obligation, I asked, "Are you okay?"

In usual Claude fashion, he said, "Yep, why wouldn't I be? I'm sitting beside the most beautiful person at this wedding." Fabienne looked at Claude and smiled as he attempted to reach for her hand under the table discreetly. Claude said he was fine, so there was no reason to be concerned.

"Attention, everyone, it's time to get this reception started," the emcee said. The bridal party entered the reception room first, with each group doing a semi-choreographed dance to get the guests hyped. The emcee continued, "Okay, everyone, it's now the moment we've all been waiting for. Please rise to your feet as we introduce Mr. and Mrs. Middleton for the very first time." We all cheered as the newlyweds entered the reception room to start their first dance. As smoke engulfed the dance floor, Mrs. Stephanie and Mr. Elijah looked at each other as if they were the only two people in the room. The moment seemed magical.

After the first dance, a few speeches and toasts took place before the party got started. The DJ had everyone up and dancing, even my mother, when the Konpa hits began to play. The room was filled with smiles, laughter, positivity, and energy from the people on the dance floor to the onlookers who remained seated. After dancing for what seemed like an hour, it was time for food to be served. As we ate, Ms. Stephanie, I mean Mrs. Stephanie, made her way around the room, stopping at each table for a brief conversation. Once at our table, she spoke to everyone but asked me to follow. Unsure of her plan, I still followed willingly.

"Manushka, there are a few people I would like you to meet." Mrs. Stephanie introduced me to a table occupied by artists and designers. Her fellow artist friends wanted to know who created the paintings at each table. They all gave me compliments, words of encouragement, and business cards. This wasn't my wedding, but Mrs. Stephanie sure was making me feel extra special. The fact that she took time during her special day to introduce me to a few people meant a lot. With a few business cards in hand, I rushed back to the table to share the news with my mother and Fabienne.

After dinner, it was time to do the traditional garter and bouquet toss. As usual, the men didn't rush to catch the garter. In fact, some of them needed encouragement in the form of a push but not too forceful though. Now, when it came to the women, it seemed like almost half the room wanted to catch the bouquet. Mrs. Stephanie took her place in front of the large group of women and began a countdown before throwing the bouquet. Five, four, three, two—

Chapter 39

To everyone's surprise, the bouquet lands on a table directly in front of Fabienne instead of the dance floor where all the single women congregated. At that moment, Claude whispers, "That's the sign, that's the sign I've been praying about!" Out of nowhere, a barefoot woman lunges forward and grabs the bouquet right out of Fabienne's hand. Fully amused, I can't contain my laughter while witnessing this older woman aggressively snatching a bouquet out of the hands of a teenager as if it's her last hope at marriage. "Manushka, I said that's the sign! Don't you get it?' Not understanding what Claude is yapping about, I continue to laugh but eventually have to acknowledge him.

"I have no clue what you're talking about. You're speaking in code as if I'm some mind reader."

His tone is dismissive. "Just get Yohane and meet me outside now."

Confused, I comply by calling Yohane over to the table. In a sense, Claude is predictable: he usually says or does something ridiculous. Whatever he does, I hope it's funny because laughter is good for the heart, at least that's what I read in an article.

"All right, Claude. We're here. What do you want? And make it fast because the DJ is playing some hits, so I need to get my dance on. That's my song!" As I waited for his response, I couldn't help but dance as the rhythm of the music drew my attention.

"Manushka, I need you to be serious for a moment," Claude says. "Can you do that? Can you pretend to be mature for just a few minutes? This moment right here is special to me."

Oh, I know he didn't just check me. Let me take a couple of deep breaths and listen to this fool. The air conditioner is blasting, so why in the world is Claude sweating like he just ran a half-marathon? Wait, no way, he can't possibly be—

"Fabienne, my days of entertaining the ladies ended the moment I looked into your beautiful eyes. When the bouquet landed on your lap, I knew it was time. I wasn't planning to do this today, but I can't wait any longer. Will you marry me? I mean, not this week, next month, or even this year, but one day in the distant future." A few people in the lobby look on as Claude remains on his knee, waiting for an answer.

Fabienne covers her mouth with both hands. Then says, "Yes, Claude, I want to marry you one day." She still appears in disbelief as Claude slips an imaginary ring onto her finger. How is she even impressed by an imaginary ring? This is just about the oddest marriage proposal I've ever seen or heard of.

After they hug, I pull Claude aside for a quick conversation. "Hey, what are you thinking, proposing to my sister now? Both of you are still in high school, and even though my parents let you date, they're definitely going to flip out about this situation. And who proposes with an imaginary ring anyway?"

Claude places a hand on my shoulder. "Chill out! I saw something in a movie about a promise ring. I'm just promising to marry Fabienne one day. You did hear what I said, right? Not this week, next month, or even this year, but one day in the distant future. And I do plan to get her a real promise ring as soon as I find a job. If I don't find one, I'll just use my Christmas money."

I step back and take a look at him. "Claude, you're seriously giving me a headache right now."

"If you're lucky, someone may give you a promise ring one day. Just be patient. I'll say a prayer or two for you. Dear God, please let

Manushka find someone almost like me who will be willing to marry her one day. God, I know finding someone just like me may be hard, but you can make the impossible possible. Amen!" He pats my back after saying the most ridiculous prayer. In response, all I could do was shake my head. Unfortunately, he continued speaking. "Don't worry, Manushka. Dreams do come true, even for people like you. Keep praying and have unwavering faith. Remember, he may not be as handsome as me, but who is? As your future brother-in-law, I don't want you to be discouraged."

I stare at Claude in disbelief. He really thinks what he's said makes sense. I say a quick prayer, hoping my mother is not in the lobby to witness this foolishness. God, please keep my mother out of the lobby or cover her ears before word gets around. Surely, if my mother hears this, I'll be locked in the house forever, only to leave the day I get married. I look to the left and right, relieved she isn't beside me. But the coast isn't completely clear. I have to look from all angles. I turn around slowly, and yes, you've guessed it, my mother is standing behind me.

Oh no, she's standing behind me with a fierce stare. Wait, why in the world am I getting this stare, especially when Fabienne is the one who got kind of engaged? My parents allowed her to date; they're the ones who bent the rules or, should I say, didn't apply the rules. My mother slowly walks toward me and whispers, "*Manushka, na pale pita.*" Why does she want to have a conversation with me about this later? Fabienne and Claude's decision has nothing to do with me. They're the ones she needs to talk to. My mother glances in Fabienne's direction and then returns to the reception without saying a word. Lord knows somehow-someway I'll be implicated in this whole engagement fiasco later.

Claude, Fabienne, Yohane, and I quietly reenter the reception, not wanting to take attention away from the bride. Yohane, of course, runs to the middle of the dance floor. He's cute but has no rhythm. It's as though he can't hear the beat. Uncoordinated and all, Yohane is having a great time. As I stare at him, I can't help but think about my decision again. Interrupting my thoughts, Yohane calls me to the dance floor. I slip away while my mother is talking to the women at our table. As usual, we're having a great time together. He looked into my eyes and said, "Manushka, I think I love you. I said it to you before on the phone, but you didn't hear me. "

Taken by surprise, I quickly glance at my mother to make sure she isn't looking in my direction. Thankfully, she's fully engaged in a conversation that includes some laughter. Great, I don't have to worry about her for a few minutes, but I'm worried about my response. I can feel the moisture building up in my palms and armpits. This is the second time Yohane has professed his love for me. I really do like him, but is it love? Enough stalling—it's time to respond. After a deep breath, I look into his eyes and then say, "I love you too, Devonte."

Did I just call him Devonte? I meant Yohane, Oh. My. Goodness. There's no way to cover this up. By the look on his face, I know he heard me. He freezes, then takes a few steps backward.

"Wait!" I need to explain myself before he leaves. I consider running after him, but the last thing I want is for my mother to take this whole Claude and Fabienne proposal thing out on me. So, instead of chasing after Yohane, I frantically call his phone several times, but he doesn't answer. Is this the end of our beautiful relationship? No, it can't be, not now and not this way.

"Yohane, please pick up the phone. I need to talk to you. Please, please. Pick up? We need to talk. I made a mistake." Voicemail after voicemail, but still no response. I know Yohane is still in the building; there's no way he left his aunt's wedding, especially since Mrs. Stephanie means so much to him. I have to get to Yohane somehow.

"Mommy, I'll be back. I need to use the bathroom." That's the only excuse I can think of. Thankfully, she's too distracted by her conversation to object or join me. With no time to waste, I'm on a quest to find Yohane. Shoes in hand, I search the entire facility, including the rooftop, but still can't find him.

As I stand in the middle of the lobby, thinking of where he could've possibly gone, an older woman stops by to speak to me. "Young lady, do you need help?" In an effort to provide some comfort, she places a hand on my shoulder while waiting for me to respond.

Her question causes an unexpected reaction. All of a sudden, my eyes fill up with tears. "I'm okay, just looking for a friend."

"Well, I saw a tall handsome teenage boy in a suit standing in this very spot not too long ago. If that's the friend you're talking about, he left before I could speak to him. Seems like the young man had a lot on his mind."

"Thanks for letting me know." Sadly, I've missed Yohane by a few minutes. I guess he's trying to avoid a conversation.

"Young love. I don't know what you are going through. Just know that things will work out the way they're supposed to. So, don't trouble yourself too much." She winks before walking away.

Defeated and in a slump, I sit down to put on my shoes. It's time to stop the search for Yohane. I stand up, adjust my dress then wipe my face. This time around, walking back to the reception room seems longer. Hearing laughter and seeing smiles on the faces of couples, young and old, is kind of hard. I really did mess up this time.

Steps away from reentering the room, I feel a tap on my shoulder. Hoping and believing it's Yohane, I turn around with a smile. It isn't him! It's a man from the reception, one of the guys Mrs. Stephanie introduced me to.

"I had the opportunity to look at the paintings on the tables. Everything is outstanding." As the man speaks, out of the counter of my eye I can see Yohane walking by. Not wanting to be rude, I try my best to listen to what he is saying while being laser focused on Yohane's every move. I can't lose track of him now.

"Thank you for the kind words, sir. Bye!"

Quickly walking toward Yohane, I analyze his face to determine what to say.

Before I can say a word, he begins to speak. "Hey, I got your messages. I just needed some time alone to think." Yohane, clearly hurt, is keeping his distance from me.

Wanting him to see the sincerity on my face, I approach him. "I'm so sorry about what happened. I made my decision already, and I chose you."

"I'm not convinced," Yohane says. "You called me Devonte. Listen, if you want to be with him, I understand. Just do what you need to do."

I reach for his hand. "The truth is, everything between us happened too fast. I want to be with you, but we need to slow things down a little. Just so you know, I told Devonte that I want to be with you." I have feelings for Yohane, but it isn't love yet—at least, I don't think it is.

"I get it. Everything between us happened quickly. Within a couple of months, we went from practically hating each other to holding hands. I agree that we should slow things down a little, like you said. But the next time you call me Devonte, I'm out. Besides, he got nothin' on me." Yohane repositions his body in a playful stance while flexing his muscles.

"Don't worry, I won't ever make that mistake again, scout's honor." I hold my right hand up in the air as though making an oath. "Gotta get back to my mom, especially since I've been searching for you for a while. Last thing I want is for her to find us standing here alone. Call me when you get home later."

My heart is at peace knowing we resolved what could have been the end of our relationship. I give him a high five before returning to the reception. Like a skilled ninja, with carefully measured steps, I manage to slip into the seat beside my mother without causing any embarrassing disturbance like spilling a glass of water all over the table or interrupting her conversation. I watch a few couples dance slowly, with what seems like perfectly coordinated steps. As the servers clear the tables, I scan the room, but Fabienne and Claude are nowhere to be found. Did they run off into the sunset, like in the movies? I mean, where can they be especially since Claude doesn't have a car? This scenario is getting worse and more complicated with each passing moment. At this point, I'm preparing to get in trouble for something I had nothing to do with, unnecessary drama compliments of Claude. Yeah, Mr. Unnecessary Drama sounds like the perfect name for him.

Why Claude, why? is all I can think. Still confused by the situation, my hands are tied. Since Fabienne left, there's now way to strategies before getting home. I want to help my sister, but self-preservation is definitely one of my goals. I don't want to sound selfish, but the rules in our house don't apply to Fabienne. Sadly, the anger and disappointment will be directed toward me in some way. What new rules will my mother impose? Will I be bound to the house only to leave for school and church? Or will she take my beloved phone every night as a new routine? Claude is single-handedly ruining my social life during senior year, the supposed pinnacle of my high school journey.

The sound of my mother's voice interrupts a flood of thoughts running through my mind. "*Leve, leve, leve, ann ale. Papa w ap tann nou anba. M bezwen di l de Fabienne ak Claude. Epi m ap oblije rele Sè Françoise aswè a. Li dwe konnen sa k ap pase ak pitit gason l lan.*" The sense of urgency to leave is evident in her voice. As I follow my mother towards the exit, I can feel the tension in each step she takes— no slowing down or avoiding the inevitable. She wants to give my dad a detailed report about Fabienne and Claude's engagement debacle, and call Sè Françoise, the gossip, out of obligation.

Before the car door closes, my mother begins speaking at a rate faster than I've ever heard but still clear and deliberate. Her description of the situation is extra dramatic, each word carefully chosen to paint a vivid picture, with the goal of getting a big reaction from my father. Listening intently he drives about a block or two before pulling the car over to fully grasp the situation. Silence fills the car as he begins to rub the back of his neck and shoulders, which is what my father typically does when feeling tense or stressed.

He finally speaks. "*Ki sa ou di? Mwen pa gen bouch pou m pale. Kisa mwen ka fè? Repete sa ou sot di a.*" Now with both hands on his head in the state of shock, his words come out slowly, searching for understanding. He wants my mother to retell the entire story. Without hesitation, she retells the story with the same level of intensity as before.

"*Manushka, kijan ou fè kite sa rive? Kote w te ye?*" Just like that, I get pulled into the situation—not at all unexpected. With reproach in his voice, my father wants to know how I let the engagement happen and where I was. As I listen to him speak, I have to be conscious of my facial expressions to avoid showing any signs of anger that will be misinterpreted as an act of disrespect.

When did I become Fabienne's keeper, especially since they've allowed her to date? Confused by his question, I really don't know what he expects me to say as I search for the right words. "Papi, I didn't even know this was going to happen."

My mother chimes in to add to the conflict by saying I was standing right beside Claude and Fabienne.

Feeling defensive and somewhat cornered, I know it's time to fight back—with words alone, as I'm not trying to risk my life. "I was only standing there because Claude asked me to come outside. This whole thing was a surprise for everyone. I didn't do anything." At this point, it feels as though I'm desperately pleading for my freedom.

My parents continue to speak but my mother dominates the conversation with authority.

As soon as the car is parked, my movements are quick, yet my mind is racing even faster. I run upstairs eagerly, hoping to speak to Fabienne first. I open the door to find her sitting on the couch, nonchalantly eating vanilla ice cream from a bowl.

"Fabienne, girl, what happened? Where did you go? You know this is going to be a big problem for me– I mean *for you*, right?" I speak as fast as possible hoping to have enough time for a conversation and to get some clarity.

Before she can respond to the questions, my parents walk in. My mother begins grunting and making all sorts of other sounds out of frustration.

The bell rings, redirecting everyone's attention. Talk about terrible timing. Who could be ringing the bell now? Especially since I'm trying to listen to this conversation.

"Manushka, *ale ouvri pòt la*."

Reluctantly, I open the door at my mother's request. It's Sè Françoise wearing a white hat, a blue shirt that's been partially tucked into a floral ankle-length skirt, with black running sneakers—her outfit looks more like a rush job than something planned, yet distinctly her style. Claude emerges from behind his mother and walks right past me toward Fabienne with determination.

He begins professing his love for Fabienne as my father calmly and quietly listens and analyzes the situation. Sè Françoise interrupts Claude's proclamation mid-sentence: any young lady is lucky to have a smart and talented young man like Claude in their life, she says in full confidence.

Knowing she fully believes in her statement about Claude, I can't contain my laughter. Everyone glares at me.

"Sorry, I wasn't laughing at Sè Françoise, I was thinking about something the teacher said in class." That's the only thing I can think of to stop the angry stares and avoid my mother's infamous pinch with a spin.

According to Sè Françoise, Fabienne is a bad influence on Claude, and the whole engagement idea wasn't her son's. Sensing my father's anger about Sè Françoise's accusation, my mother takes the liberty of speaking on his behalf to defend Fabienne, to my surprise. Both women begin speaking over each other as their voices progressively escalate in volume and intensity.

For the first time ever, Claude is quiet. Not a peep for a whole ten minutes as our mothers shout at each other, creating a dramatic sense. Then, all of a sudden, Claude grabs Fabienne's hand. Together, they walk out the door despite demands from the adults to return.

I stare at the door, dumbfounded. My sister just left without saying a word, not even to me. Hurt and still shocked, I take a few steps forward, hoping to catch up with her. As I reach for the doorknob the words *"Manushka, ale nan chanm ou, ou pa pral okenn kote,"* echoes throughout the house.

How can I go to my room at a time like this? I need to support my sister the same way she supports me. The thought of leaving her to face everything alone is unsettling. "But mommy, I need to….."

She doesn't wait for me to finish. "Manushka Jean-Pierre, go to your room—right now! *Pa fè bouch mwen long.*" The word-for-word translation of *pa fè bouch mwen long* is don't make my mouth long. This is one of those Haitian sayings that lose meaning when translated, but it basically means, don't make me talk too much. My mother's stance left no room for negotiation.

Momentarily shaken by the tone of her voice, I have no choice but to follow my mother's command. Head down with rounded shoulders, I walk to my room. The conversation between the adults continues as I sit in on the bed, hoping and praying Fabienne will soon return.

After Sè Françoise has left, the house is silent but only for a couple of minutes. "Manushka, Manushka!" With full authority, I'm being summoned to the living room by my mother. My steps slow as I brace for what's to come. While standing in front of her, my phone rings: Yohane. Talk about bad timing. I decline, but he calls right back.

"Who call you at this time?" my mother asks.

There is no denying the truth especially since his contact picture appeared on the screen. Is this a trick question? Did she not see the photo? In full panic mode, I have no idea what to do or say. "Um, that was Yohane. You know, Mrs. Stephanie's nephew."

What was she thinking? The suspense is almost unbearable. I look over to my father who's sitting with his head in his hands. He has way too much on his mind to save me from this conversation.

"Hmm, ok!" That was her way of saying she would be watching me. Her words, though few, carry a warning as clear as day. *"Chita la, m bezwen pale avè w."* It's time to have one of those serious chats.

My mother uses Fabienne and Claude's situation as an example of why I should stay away from boys until I get married. She says a few other things that I really can't pay attention to. All I care about right now is my sister and when she might return home.

After the long speech, I go straight to my room, no questions, small talk or detours. I call Fabienne twice but her phone goes straight to voicemail. Desperate to speak to her and feeling a mix of frustration and concern, I have no choice but to call Claude who picks up on the third ring.

"Where's my sister?"

"I know you're upset, but it's still no way to call my phone. I'll give you a pass this time," Claude says.

No time for pleasantries. As far as I'm concerned, he's caused all of this unnecessary drama. I wait as he passes the phone to her.

"Hello…," Fabienne says.

Without giving her an opportunity to speak, I begin with questions. "Where are you? Why did you leave? *Ou konnen papa nou fache? Tanpri tounen lakay aswè a.* I spoke to her in both English and Creole to make sure to get answers and fully convey my concerns..

"*Mwen konnen li fache. Men mwen pa pral marye ak Claude kounye a. Nou twò jèn. Petèt nan kèk ane lè nou pi gran.*" Fabienne knows my parents are upset. She also understood that she is too young to get married—the marriage, she says, will take place when she's older.

"Please come home now. The longer you stay out, the worse the situation will be," I plead.

"*Pa enkyete w. Mwen nan wout kounye a. Mwen pa t pran telefòn nan paske batri a mouri. Se pa paske mwen pat vle pale avè w.*" Thankfully, Fabienne is on her way home. Her phone actually died, which is why it went straight to voicemail earlier. Listening to her words has brought me some relief and hope about the situation.

I patiently wait in my room avoiding contact with my parents until she arrives. As soon as the bell rings, I race down the stairs, heart pounding, eager to see her. I open the door and give my sister a much-needed hug. Claude leaves right away to avoid causing even more damage. That is actually the best idea he had all night.

Fabienne speaks to my parents, assuring them that she has no plans of getting married any time soon. She also apologizes profusely about the entire situation. From the looks on my parents' face along with their body language, they are now at ease. As Fabienne continues speaking, I slip away into my room and close the door with only a few minutes to call Yohane.

In a whisper, I say, "The whole wedding proposal thing got a little crazy today. And my mom saw your contact photo when you called."

"Oh, sorry. I hope you didn't get in trouble." The calmness of his voice makes me smile.

"She's a little suspicious so it'll be a couple of days before I call you again."

"I get it. Hey, despite the craziness, I had fun dancing with you today. I see you couldn't keep up with my dance moves."

"You right, I was trying to protect my toes from your two left feet." Uncoordinated and all, I imagine the two of us dancing again. But this time, it's prom night.

"No need to be jealous, I can teach you my dance moves for free."

" Um, no thank you sir. I'll pass any and every dance lesson you offer." We both laugh momentarily. "You know I can talk to you all night but I gotta go. Good night, Yohane."

"Good night, Manushka."

After we hang up, I think about prom again with Yohane as my date and my heart skips a beat. I quickly take a look at a few pictures of us at the wedding before rejoining my family in the living room.

My mom looks at me suspiciously. She can sense I've been on the phone, and I know that after tonight, she'll watch me like a hawk. Something is going to change but who knows what's in store for me next?

I get it, this unpredictable journey is a part of growing up. But nothing, and I mean *nothing*, is getting in the way of prom. Over the years I've heard stories and looked at countless pictures of prom dresses, and it'll soon finally be my turn to experience the lavishness of it all. Floor length, fitted, ruffles, beading, slit—just a few ideas in mind for the perfect dress. It'll be high fashion for sure. My date has to match, but will he pick me up? I mean, can he pick me up considering my mother's views on dating? Going to prom with someone doesn't mean you're dating, I'll need to craft the perfect argument to convince her. I'm sure Janae and Widelene will help me come up with something.

Imagine if I win prom queen? The spotlight on my dress, cheers from the crowd, a beautiful crown, anything is possible. Manushka Jean-Pierre, prom queen of Paul Millerson....

So much to think about.

But for now—a sigh of relief.

9 7 9 8 2 1 8 2 6 8 5 8 9